Select praise for Linda Lael Miller

"This second-chance romance is set in the perfect setting of Painted Pony Creek. Curl up in your favorite reading chair and get lost in the pages of this book."
—Debbie Macomber,
#1 *New York Times* bestselling author, on *Country Strong*

"Miller enthralls, once again, in...an engrossing, contemporary western romance."
—*Publishers Weekly* on *McKettrick's Pride*

"*Always a Cowboy* is a western romance with a very valuable story line and crazy good characters... Simply another gem from Linda Lael Miller."
—*Fresh Fiction*

"Likable protagonists, a wealth of memorable secondary characters, and [a] heart-touching plot make this warm, family-centered, information-rich 1910 prequel a good choice for series fans and new readers as well."
—*Library Journal* on *A Creed Country Christmas*

"Miller's name is synonymous with the finest in Western romance."
—*RT Book Reviews*

"A passionate love too long denied drives the action in this multifaceted, emotionally rich reunion story that overflows with breathtaking sexual chemistry."
—*Library Journal* on *McKettricks of Texas: Tate*

"Miller's down-home, easy-to-read style keeps the plot moving, and she includes...likable characters, picturesque descriptions and some very sweet pets."
—*Publishers Weekly* on *Big Sky Country*

"Miller tugs at the heartstrings as few authors can."
—*Publishers Weekly*

LINDA LAEL
MILLER

A LAWMAN'S
CHRISTMAS

Recycling programs
for this product may
not exist in your area.

HQN®

ISBN-13: 978-1-335-44990-0

A Lawman's Christmas
First published in 2011. This edition published in 2022.
Copyright © 2011 by Linda Lael Miller

Coming Home
Copyright © 2022 by Hometown Girl Makes Good, Inc.

For questions and comments about the quality of this book,
please contact us at CustomerService@Harlequin.com.

HQN
22 Adelaide St. West, 41st Floor
Toronto, Ontario M5H 4E3, Canada
www.Harlequin.com

Printed in U.S.A.

CONTENTS

A LAWMAN'S CHRISTMAS   7

COMING HOME   217

1

A LAWMAN'S
CHRISTMAS

CHAPTER ONE

Early December, 1914

IF THE SPARK-THROWING screech of iron-on-iron hadn't wrenched Clay McKettrick out of his uneasy sleep, the train's lurching stop—which nearly pitched him onto the facing seat—would surely have done the trick.

Grumbling, Clay sat up straight and glowered out the window, shoving splayed fingers through his dark hair.

Blue River, Texas. His new home. And more, for as the new marshal, he'd be responsible for protecting the town and its residents.

Not that he could see much of it just then, with all that steam from the smokestack billowing between the train and the depot.

The view didn't particularly matter to him, anyhow, since he'd paid a brief visit to the town a few months back and seen what there was to see—which hadn't been much, even in the sun-spangled, blue-sky days of summer. Now that winter was coming on—Clay's granddad, Angus, claimed it snowed dust and chiggers in that part of Texas—the rutted roads and weathered facades of the ramshackle buildings would no doubt be of bleak appearance.

With an inward sigh, Clay stood to retrieve his black, round-brimmed hat and worn duster from the wooden rack overhead. In the process, he allowed himself to ponder, yet again, all he'd left behind to come to this place at the hind end of beyond and carve out a life of his own making.

He'd left plenty.

A woman, to start with. And then there was his family, the sprawling McKettrick clan, including his ma and pa, Chloe and Jeb, his two older sisters and the thriving Triple M Ranch, with its plentitude of space and water and good grass.

A fragment of a Bible verse strayed across his brain. *The cattle on a thousand hills...*

There were considerably fewer than a thousand hills on the Triple M, big as it was, but the cattle were legion.

To his granddad's way of thinking, those hills and the land they anchored might have been on loan from the Almighty, but everything else—cows, cousins, mineral deposits and timber included—belonged to Angus McKettrick, his four sons and his daughter, Katie.

Clay shrugged into the long coat and put on his hat. His holster and pistol were stowed in his trunk in the baggage compartment, and his paint gelding, Outlaw, rode all alone in the car reserved for livestock.

The only other passenger on board, an angular woman with severe features and no noticeable inclination toward small talk, remained seated, with the biggest Bible Clay had ever seen resting open on her lap. She seemed poised to leap right into the pages at the first hint of sin and disappear into all those apocalyptic threats and grand promises. According to the conductor, a fitful little fellow bearing the pitted scars of a long-ago case of smallpox, the lady had come all the way from Cincinnati with the express purpose of saving the heathen.

Clay—bone-tired, homesick for the ranch and for his kinfolks, and wryly amused, all of a piece—nodded a respectful farewell to the woman as he passed her seat, resisting the temptation to stop and inquire about the apparent shortage of heathens in Cincinnati.

Most likely, he decided, reaching the door, she'd already converted the bunch of them, and now she was out to wrestle the devil for the whole state of Texas. He wouldn't have given two cents for old Scratch's chances.

A chill wind, laced with tiny flakes of snow, buffeted Clay as he stepped down onto the small platform, where all three members of the town council, each one stuffed into his Sunday best and half-strangled by a celluloid collar, waited to greet the new marshal.

Mayor Wilson Ponder spoke for the group. "Welcome to Blue River, Mr. McKettrick," the fat man boomed, a blustery old cuss with white muttonchop whiskers and piano-key teeth that seemed to operate independently of his gums.

Clay, still in his late twenties and among the youngest of the McKettrick cousins, wasn't accustomed to being addressed as "mister"—around home, he answered to "hey, you"—and he sort of liked the novelty of it. "Call me Clay," he said.

There were handshakes all around.

The conductor lugged Clay's trunk out of the baggage car and plunked it down on the platform, then busily consulted his pocket watch.

"Better unload that horse of yours," he told Clay, in the officious tone so often adopted by short men who didn't weigh a hundred pounds sopping wet, "if you don't want him going right on to Fort Worth. This train pulls out in five minutes."

Clay nodded, figuring Outlaw would be ready by now for fresh air and a chance to stretch his legs, since he'd been cooped up in a rolling box ever since Flagstaff.

Taking his leave from the welcoming committee with a touch to the brim of his hat and a promise to meet them later at the marshal's office, he crossed the small platform, descended the rough-hewn steps and walked through cinders and lingering wisps of steam to the open door of the livestock car. He lowered the heavy ramp himself and climbed into the dim, horse-scented enclosure.

Outlaw nickered a greeting, and Clay smiled and patted the horse's long neck before picking up his saddle and other gear and tossing the lot of it to the ground beside the tracks.

That done, he loosed the knot in Outlaw's halter rope and led the animal toward the ramp.

Some horses balked at the unfamiliar, but not Outlaw. He and Clay had been sidekicks for more than a decade, and they trusted each other in all circumstances.

Outside, in the brisk, snow-dappled wind, having traversed the slanted iron plate with no difficulty, Outlaw blinked, adjusting his unusual blue eyes to the light of midafternoon. Clay meant to let the gelding stand untethered while he put the ramp back in place, but before he could turn around, a little girl hurried around the corner of the brick depot and took a competent hold on the lead rope.

She couldn't have been older than seven, and she was small even for that tender age. She wore a threadbare calico dress, a brown bonnet and a coat that, although clean, had seen many a better day. A blond sausage curl tumbled from inside the bonnet to gleam against her forehead, and she smiled with the confidence of a seasoned wrangler.

"My name is Miss Edrina Nolan," she announced importantly. "Are you the new marshal?"

Amused, Clay tugged at his hat brim to acknowledge her properly and replied, "I am. Name's Clay McKettrick."

Edrina put out her free hand. "How do you do, Mr. McKettrick?" she asked.

"I do just fine," he said, with a little smile. Growing up on the Triple M, he and all his cousins had been around horses all their lives, so the child's remarkable ease with a critter many times her size did not surprise him.

It was impressive, though.

"I'll hold your horse," she said. "You'd better help the railroad man with that ramp. He's liable to hurt himself if you don't."

Clay looked back over one shoulder and, sure enough, there was the banty rooster of a conductor, struggling to hoist that heavy slab of rust-speckled iron off the ground so the train could get under way again. He lent his assistance, figuring he'd just spared the man a hernia, if not a heart attack, and got a glare for his trouble, rather than thanks.

Since the fellow's opinion made no real never-mind to Clay either way, he simply turned back to the little girl, ready to reclaim his horse.

She was up on the horse's back, her faded skirts billowing around her, and with the snow-strained sunlight framing her, she looked like one of those cherub-children gracing the pages of calendars, Valentines and boxes of ready-made cookies.

"Whoa, now," he said, automatically taking hold of the lead rope. Given that he hadn't saddled Outlaw yet, he was somewhat mystified as to how she'd managed to mount up the way she had. Maybe she really was a cherub, with little stubby wings hidden under that thin black coat.

Up ahead, the engineer blew the whistle to signal imminent departure, and Outlaw started at the sound, though he didn't buck, thank the good Lord.

"Whoa," Clay repeated, very calmly but with a note of sternness. It was then that he spotted the stump on the other side of the horse and realized that Edrina must have scrambled up on that to reach Outlaw's back.

They all waited—man, horse and cherub—until the train pulled out and the racket subsided somewhat.

Edrina smiled serenely down at him. "Mama says we'll all have to go to the poorhouse, now that you're here," she announced.

"Is that so?" Clay asked mildly, as he reached up, took the child by the waist and lifted her off the horse, setting her gently on her feet. Then he commenced to collecting Outlaw's blanket, saddle and bridle from where they'd landed when he tossed them out of the railroad car, and tacking up. Out of the corner of his eye, he saw the town-council contingent straggling off the platform.

Edrina nodded in reply to his rhetorical question, still smiling, and the curl resting on her forehead bobbed with the motion of her head. "My papa was the marshal a while back," she informed Clay matter-of-factly, "but then he died in the arms of a misguided woman in a room above the Bitter Gulch Saloon and left us high and dry."

Clay blinked, wondering if he'd mistaken Edrina Nolan for a child when she was actually a lot older. Say, forty.

"I see," he said, after clearing his throat. "That's unfortunate. That your papa passed on, I mean." Clay had known the details of his predecessor's death, having been regaled with the story the first time he set foot in Blue River, but it took him aback that Edrina knew it, too.

She folded her arms and watched critically as he threw on Outlaw's beat-up saddle and put the cinch through the buckle. "Can you shoot a gun and everything?" she wanted to know.

Clay spared her a sidelong glance and a nod. Why wasn't this child in school? Did her mother know she was running loose like a wild thing and leaping onto the backs of other people's horses when they weren't looking?

And where the heck had a kid her age learned to ride like that?

"Good," Edrina said, with a relieved sigh, her little arms still folded. "Because Papa couldn't be trusted with a firearm. Once, when he was cleaning a pistol, meaning to go out and hunt rabbits for stew, it went off by accident and made a big hole in the floor. Mama put a chair over it—she said it was so my sister, Harriet, and I wouldn't fall in and wind up under the house, with all the cobwebs and the mice, but I know it was really because she was embarrassed for anybody to see what Papa had done. Even Harriet has more sense than to fall in a hole, for heaven's sake, and she's only five."

Clay suppressed a smile, tugged at the saddle to make sure it would hold his weight, put a foot into the stirrup and swung up. Adjusted his hat in a gesture of farewell. "I'll be seeing you, chatterbox," he said kindly.

"What about your trunk?" Edrina wanted to know. "Are you just going to leave it behind, on the platform?"

"I mean to come back for it later in the day," Clay explained, wondering why he felt compelled to clarify the matter at all. "This horse and I, we've been on that train for a goodly while, and right now, we need to stretch our muscles a bit."

"I could show you where our house is," Edrina persisted, scampering along beside Outlaw when Clay urged the horse into a walk. "Well, I guess it's *your* house now."

"Maybe you ought to run along home," Clay said. "Your mama's probably worried about you."

"No," Edrina said. "Mama has no call to worry. She thinks I'm in school."

Clay bit back another grin.

They'd climbed the grassy embankment leading to the street curving past the depot and on into Blue River by then. The members of the town's governing body waddled just ahead, single file, along a plank sidewalk like a trio of black ducks wearing top hats.

"And why *aren't* you in school?" Clay inquired affably, adjusting his hat again, and squaring his shoulders against the nippy breeze and the swirling specks of snow, each one sharp-edged as a razor.

She shivered slightly, but that was the only sign that she'd paid any notice at all to the state of the weather. While Miss Edrina Nolan pondered her reply, Clay maneuvered the horse to her other side, hoping to block the bitter wind at least a little.

"I already know everything they have to teach at that school," Edrina said at last, in a tone of unshakable conviction. "And then some."

Clay chuckled under his breath, though he refrained from comment. It wasn't as if anybody were asking his opinion.

The first ragtag shreds of Blue River were no more impressive than he recalled them to be—a livery on one side of the road, and an abandoned saloon on the other. Waist-high grass, most of it dead, surrounded the latter; craggy shards of filthy glass edged its one narrow window, and the sign above the door dangled by a lone, rusty nail.

Last Hope: Saloon and Games of Chance, it read in painted letters nearly worn away by time and weather.

"You shouldn't be out in this weather," Clay told Edrina, who was still hiking along beside him and Outlaw, eschewing the broken plank sidewalk for the road. "Too cold."

"I like it," she said. "The cold is very bracing, don't you think? Makes a body feel wide-awake."

The town's buildings, though unpainted, began to look a little better as they progressed. Smoke curled from twisted chimneys and doors were closed up tight.

There were few people on the streets, Clay noticed, though he glimpsed curious faces at various windows as they went by.

He raised his collar against the rising wind, figuring he'd had all the "bracing" he needed, thank you very much, and he was sure enough "wide-awake" now that he was off the train and back in the saddle.

He was hungry, too, and he wanted a bath and barbering.

And ten to twelve hours of sleep, lying prone instead of sitting upright in a hard seat.

"I reckon maybe you ought to show me where you live, after all," he said, at some length. At least that way, he could steer the child homeward, where she belonged, make sure she got there, and rest easy thereafter, where her welfare was concerned.

Edrina pointed past a general store, a telegraph and telephone office, the humble jailhouse where he would soon be officiating and a tiny white church surrounded by a rickety picket fence, much in need of whitewash. "It's one street over," she said, already veering off a little, as though she meant to duck between buildings and take off. "Our place, that is. It's the one with an apple tree in the yard and a chicken house out back."

Clay drew up his horse with a nearly imperceptible tug of the reins. "Hold it right there," he said, with quiet authority, when Edrina started to turn away.

She froze. Turned slowly to look at him with huge china-blue eyes. "You're going to tell Mama I haven't been at school, aren't you?" she asked, sounding sadly resigned to whatever fate awaited her.

"I reckon it's *your* place to tell her that, not mine."

Edrina blinked, and a series of emotions flashed across her face—confusion, hope and, finally, despair. "She'll be sorely vexed when she finds out," the girl said. "Mama places great store in learning."

"Most sensible people do," Clay observed, biting the inside of his lower lip so he wouldn't laugh out loud. Edrina might have been little more than a baby, but she sat a horse like a Comanche brave—he'd seen that for himself back at the depot—and carried herself with a dignity out of all proportion to her size, situation and hand-me-down clothes. "Maybe from now on, you ought to pay better heed to what your mama says. She has your best interests at heart, you know."

Edrina gave a great, theatrical sigh, one that seemed to involve her entire small personage. "I suppose Miss Krenshaw will tell Mama I've been absent since recess, anyway," she said. "Even if *you* don't."

Miss Krenshaw, Clay figured, was probably the schoolmarm.

Outlaw's well-shod hooves made a lonely, *clompety-clip* kind of sound on the hard dirt of the road. The horse turned a little, to go around a trough with a lacy green scum floating atop the water.

"Word's sure to get out," Clay agreed reasonably, thinking of all those faces, at all those windows, "one way or another."

"Thunderation and spit!" Edrina exclaimed, with the vigor of total sincerity. "I don't know why folks can't just tend to their own affairs and leave me to do as I please."

Clay made a choking sound, disguised it as a cough, as best he could, anyway. "How old are you?" he asked, genuinely interested in the answer.

"Six," Edrina replied.

He'd have bet she was a short ten, maybe even eleven. "So you're in the first grade at school?"

"I'm in the second," Edrina said, trudging along beside his horse. "I already knew how to read when I started in September, and I can cipher, too, so Miss Krenshaw let me skip a grade. Actually, she suggested I enter *third* grade, but Mama said no, that wouldn't do at all, because I needed time to be a child. As if I could *help* being a child."

She sounded wholly exasperated.

Clay hid yet another grin by tilting his head, in hopes that his hat brim would cast a shadow over his face. "You'll be all grown up sooner than you think," he allowed. "I reckon if asked, I'd be inclined to take your mama's part in the matter."

"You weren't asked, though," Edrina pointed out thoughtfully, and with an utter lack of guile or rancor.

"True enough," Clay agreed moderately.

They were quiet, passing by the little white church,

then the adjoining graveyard, where, Clay speculated, the last marshal, Parnell Nolan, must be buried. Edrina hurried ahead when they reached the corner, and Clay and Outlaw followed at an easy pace.

Clay hadn't bothered to visit the house that came with the marshal's job on his previous stopover in Blue River. At the time, he'd just signed the deed for two thousand acres of raw ranch land, and his thoughts had been on the house and barn he meant to build there, the cattle and horses he would buy, the wells he would dig and the fences he would put up. He could have waited, of course, bided on the Triple M until spring, living the life he'd always lived, but he'd been too impatient and too proud to do that.

Besides, it was his nature to be restless, and so, in order to keep himself occupied until spring, he'd accepted the town's offer of a laughable salary and a star-shaped badge to pin on his coat until they could rustle up some damn fool to take up the occupation for good.

"There it is," Edrina said, with a note of sadness in her voice that caught and pulled at Clay's heart like a fishhook snagging on something underwater.

Clay barely had time to take in the ramshackle place—the council referred to it as a "cottage," though he would have called it a shack—before one of the prettiest women he'd ever laid eyes on shot out through the front door like a bullet and stormed down the path toward them.

Chickens scattered, clucking and squawking, as she passed.

Her hair was the color of pale cider, pinned up in back

and fluffing out around her flushed face, as was the fashion among his sisters and female cousins back home in Arizona. Her eyes might have been blue, but they might have been green, too, and right now, they were shooting fire hot enough to brand the toughest hide.

Reaching the rusty-hinged gate in the falling-down fence, she stopped suddenly, fixed those changeable eyes on him and glared.

Clay felt a jolt inside, as though Zeus had flung a lightning bolt his way and he'd caught it with both hands instead of sidestepping it, like a wiser man would have done.

The woman's gaze sliced to the little girl.

"Edrina Louise Nolan," she said, through a fine set of straight white teeth, "what am I going to do with you?" Her skin was good, too, Clay observed, with that part of his brain that usually stood back and assessed things. Smooth, with a peachy glow underneath.

"Let me go to third grade?" Edrina ventured bravely.

Clay gave an appreciative chuckle, quickly quelled by a glare from the lady. He didn't wither easily, though he knew that was the result she'd intended, and he did take some pleasure in thwarting her.

At that, the woman gave a huffy little sigh and turned her attention back to her daughter. She threw out one arm—like Edrina, she wore calico—and pointed toward the gaping door of the shack. "That will be quite enough of your nonsense, young lady," she said, with a reassuring combination of affection and anger, thrusting open the creaky gate. "Get yourself into the house *now* and prepare to contemplate the error of your ways!"

Before obeying her mother's command, Edrina paused just long enough to look up at Clay, who was still in the saddle, as though hoping he'd intercede.

That was a thing he had no right to do, of course, but he felt a pang on the little girl's behalf just the same. And against his own better judgment he dismounted, took off his hat, holding it in one hand and shoving the other through his hair, fingers splayed.

"You go on and do what your mama tells you," he said to Edrina, though his words had the tone of a suggestion, rather than a command.

Edrina's very fetching mother looked him over again, this time with something that might have been chagrin. Then she bristled again, like a little bird ruffling up faded feathers. "You're *him*, aren't you?" she accused. "The new marshal?"

"Yes, ma'am," Clay said, confounded by the strange mixture of terror and jubilation rising up within him. "I am the new marshal. And you are...?"

"Dara Rose Nolan. You may address me as *Mrs.* Nolan, if you have any further *reason* to address me, which I do not anticipate."

With that, she turned on one shabby-heeled shoe and pointed herself toward the "cottage," with its sagging roof, leaking rain barrel and sparkling-clean windows.

Edrina and another little girl—the aforementioned Harriet, no doubt—darted out of the doorway as their mother approached, vanishing into the interior of the house.

Clay watched appreciatively as the widow Nolan retreated hurriedly up the walk, with nary a backward glance.

Chickens, pecking peacefully at the ground, squawked and flapped their wings as they fled.

The door slammed behind her.

Clay smiled, resettled his hat and got back on his horse.

Before, he'd dreaded the long and probably idle months ahead, expecting the season to be a lonesome one, and boring, to boot, since he knew nothing much ever happened in Blue River, when it came to crime. That was the main reason the town fathers hadn't been in any big rush to replace Parnell Nolan.

Now, reining Outlaw away toward the edge of town, and the open country beyond, meaning to ride up onto a ridge he knew of, where the view extended for miles in every direction, Clay figured the coming winter might not be so dull, after all.

INSIDE THE HOUSE, Dara Rose drew a deep breath and sighed it out hard.

Heaven knew, she hadn't been looking forward to the new marshal's arrival, given the problems that were sure to result, but she hadn't planned on losing her composure and behaving rudely, either. Poor as she was, Dara Rose still had high standards, and she believed in setting a good example for her children, prided herself on her good manners and even temperament.

Imagining how she must have looked to Clay Mc-Kettrick, rushing out of the house, scaring the chickens half to death in the process, she closed her eyes for a moment, then sighed again.

Edrina and Harriet watched her from the big rocking chair over by the wood-burning stove, Edrina wisely holding her tongue, Harriet perched close beside her, her rag doll, Molly, resting in the curve of one small arm.

The regulator clock ticked ponderously on the wall, lending a solemn rhythm to the silence, and snow swirled past the windows, as if trying to find a way in.

Dara Rose shivered.

"What are we going to do, Mama?" Edrina asked reasonably, and at some length. She was a good child, normally, helpful and even tempered, but her restlessness and curiosity often led her straight into mischief.

Dara Rose looked up at the oval-framed image of her late husband, Parnell Nolan, and her throat thickened as fresh despair swept over her. Despite the scandalous way he died, she missed him, missed the steadiness of his presence, missed his quiet ways and his wit.

"I don't rightly know," Dara Rose admitted, after swallowing hard and blinking back the scalding tears that were always so close to the surface these days. "But never you mind—I'll think of something."

Edrina slipped a reassuring arm around Harriet, who was sucking her thumb.

Dara Rose didn't comment on the thumb-sucking, though it was worrisome to her. Harriet had left that habit behind when she was three, but after Parnell's death, nearly a year ago now, she'd taken it up again. It wasn't hard to figure out why—the poor little thing was frightened and confused.

So was Dara Rose, for that matter, though of course she didn't let on. With heavy-handed generosity, Mayor Ponder and the town council had allowed her and the children to remain in the cottage on the stipulation that they'd have to vacate when a marshal was hired to take Parnell's place.

"Don't worry," Edrina told her sister, tightening her little arm around the child, just briefly. "Mama *always* thinks of something."

It was true that Dara Rose had managed to put food on the table by raising vegetables in her garden patch, taking in sewing and the occasional bundle of laundry and sometimes sweeping floors in the shops and businesses along Main Street. As industrious as she was, however, the pickings were already slim; without the house, the situation would go from worrisome to destitute.

Oh, she had choices—there were always choices, weren't there?—but they were wretched ones.

She could become a lady of the evening over at the Bitter Gulch Saloon and maybe—*maybe*—earn enough to board her children somewhere nearby, where she could see them now and then. How long would it be before they realized how she was earning their living and came to despise her? A year, two years? Three?

Her second option was only slightly more palatable; Ezra Maddox had offered her a job as his cook and housekeeper, on his remote ranch, but he'd plainly stipulated that she couldn't bring her little girls along. In fact, he'd come right out and said she ought to just put Edrina and Harriet in an orphans' home or farm them out to work for their keep. It would be good for their character, he'd claimed.

In fact, the last time he'd come to call, the previous Sunday after church, he'd stood in this very room, beaming at his own generosity, and announced that if Dara Rose measured up, he might even marry her.

The mere thought made her shudder.

And the *audacity* of the man. He expected her to turn her daughters over to strangers and spend the rest of her days darning his socks and cooking his food, and in return, he offered room, board and a pittance in wages. If she "measured up," as he put it, she'd be required to share his bed and give up the salary he'd been paying her, too.

Dara Rose's final prospect was to take her paltry savings—she kept them in a fruit jar, hidden behind the cookstove in the tiny kitchen—purchase train tickets for herself and her children and travel to San Antonio or Dallas or Houston, where she might find honest work and decent lodgings.

But suppose she *didn't* find work? Times were hard. The little bit of money she had would soon be eaten up by living expenses, and *then* what?

Dara Rose knew she'd be paralyzed by these various scenarios if she didn't put them out of her head and get busy doing something constructive, so she headed for the kitchen, meaning to start supper.

Last fall, someone had given her the hindquarter of a deer, and she'd cut the meat into strips and carefully preserved it in jars. There were green beans and corn and stubby orange carrots from the garden, too, along with apples and pears from the fruit trees growing behind the church, and berries she and the girls had gathered during the summer and brought home in lard tins and baskets. Thanks to the chickens, there were plenty of eggs, some of which she sold, and some she traded over at the mercantile for small amounts of sugar and flour and other staples. Once in a great while, she bought tea, but that was a luxury.

She straightened her spine when she realized Edrina had followed her into the little lean-to of a kitchen.

"I like Mr. McKettrick," the child said conversationally. "Don't you?"

Keeping her back to the child, Dara Rose donned her apron and tied it in back with brisk motions of her hands. "My opinion of the new marshal is neither here nor there," she replied. "And don't think for one moment, Edrina Louise Nolan, that I've forgotten that you ran away from school again. You are in serious trouble."

Edrina gave a philosophical little sigh. "How serious?" she wanted to know.

"*Very* serious," Dara Rose answered, adding wood to the fire in the cookstove and jabbing at it with a poker.

"I think we're *all* in serious trouble," Edrina observed sagely.

Out of the mouths of babes, Dara Rose thought.

"Do we have to be orphans now, Mama?" Harriet asked. As usual, she'd followed Edrina.

Dara Rose put the poker back in its stand beside the stove and turned to look at her daughters. Harriet clung to her big sister's hand, looking up at her mother with enormous, worried eyes.

"We are a family," she said, kneeling and wrapping an arm around each of them, pulling them close, drawing in the sweet scent of their hair and skin, "and we are going to stay together. I promise."

Now to find a way to *keep* that promise.

CHAPTER TWO

THE SNOW WAS coming down harder and faster when Clay returned to Blue River from the high ridge, where he'd breathed in the sight of his land, the wide expanse of it and the sheer potential, Outlaw strong and steady beneath him.

Dusk was fast approaching now, and lamps glowed in some of the windows on Main Street, along with the occasional stark dazzle of a lightbulb. Clay had yet to decide whether or not he'd have his place wired for electricity when the time came; like the telephone, it was still a newfangled invention as far as he was concerned, and he wasn't entirely sure it would last.

At the livery stable, Clay made arrangements for Outlaw and then headed in the direction of the Bitter Gulch Saloon, where he figured the mayor and the town council were most likely to be waiting for him.

Most of the businesses were sealed up tight against the weather, but the saloon's swinging doors were all that stood between the crowded interior and the sidewalk. A piano tinkled a merry if discordant tune somewhere in all that roiling blue cigar smoke, and bottles rattled against the rims of glasses.

The floor was covered in sawdust; the bar was long

and ornately carved with various bare-breasted women pouring water into urns decorated with all sorts of flowers and mythical animals and assorted other decorations.

Clay removed his hat, thumped the underside of the brim with one forefinger to knock off the light coating of snow and caught a glimpse of his own reflection in the chipped and murky glass of the mirror in back of the bar.

He didn't commonly frequent saloons, not being much of a drinker, but he knew he'd be dropping in at the Bitter Gulch on a regular basis, once he'd been sworn in as marshal and taken up his duties. Douse the seeds of trouble with enough whiskey and they were bound to take root, break ground and sprout foliage faster than the green beans his ma liked to plant in her garden every spring.

One glance told him he'd been right to look for Mayor Ponder and his cronies here—they'd gathered around a table over in the corner, near the potbellied stove, each with his own glass and his own bottle.

Inwardly, Clay sighed, but he managed a smile as he approached the table, snow melting on the shoulders of his duster.

"Good to see you, Clay," Mayor Ponder said cordially, as one of the others in the party dragged a chair over from a nearby table. "Sent a boy to fetch your trunk from the depot," the older man went on, as Clay joined them, taking the offered seat without removing his coat. He didn't plan on staying long. "You didn't say where you wanted your gear sent, so I told Billy to haul it over to the jailhouse for the time being."

"Thanks," Clay said mildly, setting his hat on the table. At home, the McKettrick women enforced their own private ordinance against such liberties, on the grounds that it was not only unmannerly, but bad luck and a mite on the slovenly side, too.

"Have a drink with us?" Ponder asked, studying Clay thoughtfully through the shifting haze of smoke. The smell of unwashed bodies and poor dental hygiene was so thick it was nearly visible, and he felt a strong and sudden yearning to be outside again, in the fresh air.

Clay shook his head. "Not now," he said. "It's been a long day, and I'm ready for a meal, a hot bath and a bed."

Ponder cleared his throat. "Speaking of, well, beds, I'm afraid the house we offered you is still occupied. We've been telling Dara Rose that she'd have to move when we found a replacement for Parnell, but so far, she's stayed put."

Dara Rose. Clay smiled slightly at the reminder of the fiery little woman who'd burst through the door of that shack a couple of hours before when he showed up with Edrina, stormed through a flock of cacophonous chickens and let him know, in no uncertain terms, that she wasn't at all glad to see him.

There had been no shortage of women in Clay McKettrick's life—he'd even fallen in love with one, to his eventual sorrow—but none of them had affected him quite the way the widow Nolan did.

"No hurry," Clay said easily, resting his hands on

his thighs. "I can get a room at the hotel, or bunk in at the jailhouse."

"The town of Blue River cannot stand good for the cost of lodgings," Ponder said, looking worried. "Having that power line strung all the way out here from Austin depleted our treasury."

One of the other men huffed at that, and poured himself another shot of whiskey. "Hell," he said, with a hiccup, "we're flat busted and up to our hind ends in debt."

Ponder flushed, and his big whiskers quivered along with those heavy jowls of his. "We *can* pay the agreed-upon salary," he stated, after glaring over at his colleague for a long moment. "Seventy-five dollars a month and living quarters, as agreed." He paused, flushed. "I'll speak to Mrs. Nolan in the morning," he clarified. "Tell her she needs to make other arrangements immediately."

"Don't do that," Clay said, quietly but quickly, too. He took a breath, slowed himself down on the inside. "I don't mind paying for a hotel room or sleeping at the jail, for the time being."

The little group exchanged looks.

Snow spun at the few high windows the Bitter Gulch Saloon boasted, like millions of tiny ghosts in search of someplace to haunt.

"A deal," Ponder finally blustered, "is a deal. We offered you a place to live as part of your salary, and we intend to keep our word."

Clay rubbed his chin thoughtfully. His beard was coming in again, even though he'd shaved that morning, on board the train. Nearly cut his own throat in the process, as it happened, because of the way the car jostled along the tracks. "Where are Mrs. Nolan and her little girls likely to wind up?" he asked, hoping he didn't sound too concerned. "Once they've moved out of that house, I mean."

"Ezra Maddox offered for her," said another member of the council. "He's a hard man, old Ezra, but he's got a farm and a herd of dairy cows and money in the bank, and she could do a lot worse when it comes to husbands."

Clay felt a strange stab at the news, deep inside, but he was careful not to let his reaction show. He felt *something* for Dara Rose Nolan, but what that something was exactly was a matter that would require some sorting out.

"Ezra ain't willing to take the girls along with their mama, though," imparted the first man, pouring himself yet another dose of whiskey and throwing it back without so much as a shudder or a wince. The stuff might have been creek water, for all the effect it seemed to have going down the fellow's gullet. "And he didn't actually offer to marry up with Dara Rose right there at the beginning, either. He means to try her out as a housekeeper before he makes her his wife. Ezra likes to know what he's getting."

Someplace in the middle of Clay's chest, one emotion broke away from the tangle and filled all the space he occupied.

It was pure anger, cold and urgent and prickly around the edges.

What kind of man expects a woman to part with her

own children? he wondered, silently furious. His neck turned hot, and he had to release his jaw muscles by force of will.

"Dara Rose is a bit shy on choices at the moment, if you ask me," Ponder put in, taking a defensive tone suggesting he was a friend of Ezra Maddox's and meant to take the man's part if a controversy arose. With a wave of one hand, he indicated their surroundings, including the half dozen saloon girls, waiting tables in their moth-eaten finery. "If she turns Ezra down, she'll wind up right here." He paused to indulge in a slight smile, and Clay underwent another internal struggle just to keep from backhanding the mayor of Blue Creek hard enough to send him sprawling in the dirty sawdust. "Can't say as I'd mind that, really."

Clay seethed, but his expression was schooled to quiet amusement. He'd grown up playing poker with his granddad, his pa and uncles, his many rambunctious cousins, male and female. He knew how to keep his emotions to himself.

Mostly.

"And you a married man," scolded one of the other council members, but his tone was indulgent. "For shame."

Clay pushed his chair back, slowly, and stood. Stretched before retrieving his hat from its place on the table. "I will leave you gentlemen to your discussion," he said, with a slight but ironic emphasis on the word *gentlemen.*

"But we meant to swear you in," Ponder protested. "Make it official."

"Morning will be here soon enough," Clay said, putting his hat on. "I'll meet you at the jailhouse at eight o'clock. Bring a badge and a Bible."

Ponder did not look pleased; he was used to piping the tune, it was obvious, and most folks probably danced to it.

Most folks weren't McKettricks, though.

Clay smiled an idle smile, tugged at the brim of his hat in a gesture of farewell and turned to leave the saloon. Just beyond the swinging doors, he paused on the sidewalk to draw in some fresh air and look up at the sky.

It was snow-shrouded and dark, that sky, and Clay wished for a glimpse, however brief, of the stars.

He'd come to Blue River to start a ranch of his own, marry some good woman and raise a bunch of kids with her, build a legacy comparable to the one his granddad had established on the Triple M. Figuring he'd never love anybody but Annabel Carson, who had made up her mind to wed his cousin Sawyer, come hell or high water, he hadn't been especially stringent with his requirements for a bride.

He wanted a wife and a partner, somebody loyal who'd stand shoulder to shoulder with him in good times and bad. She had to be smart and have a sense of humor—ranching was too hard a life for folks lacking in those characteristics, in his opinion—but she didn't necessarily have to be pretty.

Annabel was mighty easy on the eyes, after all, and look where *that* got him. Up shit creek without a paddle, that was where. She'd claimed to love Clay with her whole heart, but at the first disagreement, she'd thrown his promise ring in his face and gone chasing after Sawyer.

Even now, all these months later, the recollection carried a powerful sting, racing through Clay's veins like snake venom.

Crossing the street to the town's only hotel, its electric lights glowing a dull gold at the downstairs windows, Clay rode out the sensation, the way he'd trained himself to do, but a remarkable thing happened at the point when Annabel's face usually loomed up in his mind's eye.

He saw Dara Rose Nolan there instead.

BY THE TIME Dara Rose got up the next morning, washed and dressed and built up the fires, then headed out to feed and water the chickens and gather the eggs, the snow had stopped, the ground was bare and the sky was a soft blue.

She hadn't slept well, but the crisp bite of approaching winter cleared some of the cobwebs from her beleaguered brain, and she smiled as she worked. Her situation was as dire as ever, of course, but daylight invariably raised her hopes and quieted her fears.

When the sun was up, she could believe things would work out in the long run if she did her best and maintained her faith.

She *would* find a way to earn an honest living and keep her family together. She had to believe that to keep putting one foot in front of the other.

This very day, as soon as the children had had their breakfast and Edrina had gone off to school, Dara Rose decided, flinging out ground corn for the chickens, now clucking and flapping around her skirts and pecking at the ground, she and her youngest daughter would set out to knock on every respectable door in town if they had to.

Someone in Blue River surely needed a cook, a housekeeper, a nurse or some combination thereof. She'd work for room and board, for herself and the girls, and they wouldn't take up much space, the three of them. What little cash they needed, she could earn by taking in sewing.

The idea wasn't new, and it wasn't likely to come to fruition, either, given that most people in town were only a little better off than she was and therefore not in the market for household help, but it heartened Dara Rose a little, just the same, as she finished feeding the chickens, dusted her hands together and went to retrieve the egg basket, hanging by its handle from a nail near the back door.

Holding her skirts up with one hand, Dara Rose ducked into the tumbledown chicken coop and began gathering eggs from the straw where the hens roosted.

That morning, there were more than a dozen—fifteen, by her count—which meant she and Edrina and Harriet could each have one for breakfast. The remainder could be traded at the mercantile for salt—she was running a little low on that—and perhaps some lard and a small scoop of white sugar.

Thinking these thoughts, Dara Rose was humming under her breath as she left the chicken coop, carrying the egg basket.

She nearly dropped the whole bunch of them right

to the ground when she caught sight of the new marshal, riding his fancy spotted horse, reining in just the other side of the fence, a shiny nickel star gleaming on his worn coat.

It made him look like a gunslinger, that long coat, and the round-brimmed hat only added to the rakish impression.

Already bristling, Dara Rose drew a deep breath and rustled up a smile. It wasn't as if the man existed merely to irritate and inconvenience *her*, after all.

The marshal, swinging down out of the saddle and approaching the rickety side gate to stroll, bold as anything, into her yard, did not smile back.

Dara Rose's high hopes shriveled instantly as the obvious finally struck her: Clay McKettrick had come to send her and the children packing. He'd want to move himself—and possibly a family—in, and soon. The fact that he had a fair claim to the house did nothing whatsoever to make her feel better.

"Mornin'," he said, standing directly in front of her now, and pulling politely at the brim of his hat before taking it off.

"Good morning," Dara Rose replied cautiously, still mindful of her rudeness the day before and the regret it had caused her. Her gaze moved to the polished star pinned to his coat, and she felt an achy twinge of loss, remembering Parnell.

Poor, well-meaning, chivalrous Parnell.

Greetings exchanged, both of them just stood there looking at each other, for what seemed like a long time.

Finally, Marshal McKettrick cleared his throat, holding his hat in both hands now, and the wintry sun caught in his dark hair. He looked as clean as could be, standing there, his clothes fresh, except for the coat, and his boots brushed to a shine.

Dara Rose felt a small, peculiar shift in a place behind her heart.

"I just wanted to say," the man began awkwardly, inclining his head toward the house, "that there's no need for you and the kids to clear out right away. I spent last night at the hotel, but there's a cot and a stove at the jailhouse, and that will suit me fine for now."

Dara Rose's throat tightened, and the backs of her eyes burned. She didn't quite dare to believe her own ears. "But you're entitled to live here," she reminded him, and then could have nipped off her tongue. "And surely your wife wouldn't want to set up housekeeping in a—"

In that instant, the awkwardness was gone. The marshal's mouth slanted in a grin, and mischief sparkled in his eyes. They were the color of new denim, those eyes.

"I don't have a wife," he said simply. "Not yet, anyhow."

That grin. It did something unnerving to Dara Rose's insides.

Her heartbeat quickened inexplicably, nearly racing, then fairly lurched to a stop. Did Clay McKettrick expect something in return for his kindness? If he was looking for favors, he was going to be disappointed, because she wasn't that kind of woman.

Not anymore.

"It's almost Christmas," Clay said, assessing the sky briefly before meeting her gaze again.

Confused, Dara Rose squinted up at him. Christmas was important to Edrina and Harriet, as it was to most children, but it was the least of her own concerns.

"Do you need spectacles?" Clay asked.

Taken aback by the question, Dara Rose opened her mouth to speak, found herself at a complete loss for words and pressed her lips together. Then she shook her head.

Clay McKettrick chuckled and reached for the egg basket.

It wasn't heavy, and the contents were precious, but Dara Rose offered no resistance. She let him take it.

"Where did Edrina learn to ride a horse?" he asked.

They were moving now, heading slowly toward the house, as though it were the least bit proper for the two of them to be behind closed doors together.

Dara Rose blinked, feeling as muddled as if he'd spoken to her in a foreign language instead of plain English. "I beg your pardon?"

They stepped into the small kitchen, with its slanted wall and iron cookstove, Dara Rose in the lead, and the marshal set the basket of eggs on the table, which was comprised of two barrels with a board nailed across their tops.

"Edrina was there to meet Outlaw and me when we got off the train yesterday," Clay explained quietly, keeping his distance and folding his arms loosely across his chest. "The child has a way with horses."

Dara Rose heard the girls stirring in the tiny room

the three of them shared, just off the kitchen, and such a rush of love for her babies came over her that she almost teared up. "Yes," she said. "Parnell—my husband—kept a strawberry roan named Gawain. Edrina's been quite at home in the saddle since she was a tiny thing."

"What happened to him?" Clay asked.

"Parnell?" Dara Rose asked stupidly, feeling her cheeks go crimson.

"I know what happened to your husband, ma'am," Clay said quietly. "I was asking about the horse."

Dara Rose felt dazed, but she straightened her spine and looked Clay McKettrick in the eye. "We had to sell Gawain after my husband died," she said. It was the simple truth, and almost as much of a sore spot as Parnell's death. They'd all loved the gelding, but Ezra Maddox had offered a good price for him, and Dara Rose had needed the money for food and firewood and kerosene for the lamps.

Edrina, already mourning the man she'd believed to be her father, had cried for days.

"I see," Clay said gravely, a bright smile breaking over his handsome face like a sunrise as Edrina and Harriet hopped into the room and hurried to stand by the stove, wearing their calico dresses but no shoes or stockings.

"Do we have to go live in the poorhouse now?" Harriet asked, groping for Edrina's hand, finding it and evidently forgetting that the floor was cold enough to sting her bare feet. In the dead of winter, the planks sometimes frosted over.

To Dara Rose's surprise, Clay crouched, putting himself nearly at eye level with both children. He kept his balance easily, still holding his hat, and when his coat opened a ways, she caught an ominous glimpse of the gun belt buckled around his lean hips.

"You don't have to go anywhere," he said, very solemnly.

Edrina's eyes widened. Her unbrushed curls rioted around her face, like gold in motion, and her bow-shaped lips formed a smile. "Really and truly?" she asked. "We can stay here?"

Clay nodded.

"But where will *you* live?" Harriet wanted to know. Like her sister, she was astute and well-spoken. Dara Rose had never used baby talk with her girls, and she'd been reading aloud to them since before they were born.

"I'll be fine over at the jailhouse, at least until spring," Clay replied, rising once again to his full height. He was tall, this man from Arizona, broad through the shoulders and thick in the chest, but the impression he gave was of leanness and agility. He was probably fast with that pistol he carried, Dara Rose thought, and was disturbed by the knowledge.

It was the twentieth century, after all, and the West was no longer wild. Hardly anyone, save sheriffs and marshals, carried a firearm.

"I'm going to school today," Edrina announced happily, "and I plan on staying until Miss Krenshaw rings the bell at three o'clock, too."

Clay crooked a smile, but his gaze, Dara Rose discovered, had found its way back to her. "That's good," he said.

"Why don't you stay for breakfast?" Edrina asked the man wearing her father's badge pinned to his coat.

"Edrina," Dara Rose almost whispered, embarrassed.

"I've already eaten," Clay replied. "Had the ham and egg special in the hotel dining room before Mayor Ponder swore me in."

"Oh," Edrina said, clearly disappointed.

"That's a fine horse, mister," Harriet chimed in, her head tipped way back so she could look up into Clay's recently shaven face.

Dara Rose was still trying to bring the newest blush in her cheeks under control, and she could only manage that by avoiding Clay McKettrick's eyes.

"Yes, indeed," Clay answered the child. "His name's Outlaw, but you can't go by that. He's a good old cayuse."

"I got to ride him yesterday, down by the railroad tracks," Edrina boasted. Then her face fell a little. "Sort of."

"If it's all right with your mother," Clay offered, "and you go to school like you ought to, you can ride Outlaw again."

"Me, too?" Harriet asked, breathless with excitement at the prospect.

Clay caught Dara Rose's gaze again. "That's your mother's decision to make, not mine," he said, so at home in his own skin that she wondered what kind of life he'd led, before his arrival in Blue River. An easy one, most likely.

But something in his eyes refuted that.

"We'll see," Dara Rose said.

Both girls groaned, wanting a "yes" instead of a "maybe."

"I'd best be getting on with my day," Clay said, with another slow, crooked grin.

And then he was at the door, ducking his head so he wouldn't bump it, putting on his hat and walking away.

Dara Rose watched through the little window over the sink until he'd gone through the side gate and mounted his horse.

"We don't have to go to the orphanage!" Harriet crowed, clapping her plump little hands in celebration.

"There will be no more talk of orphanages," Dara Rose decreed briskly, pumping water at the rusty sink to wash her hands.

"Does Mr. McKettrick have a wife?" Edrina piped up. "Because if he doesn't, you could marry him. I don't think he'd send Harriet and me away, like Mr. Maddox wants to do."

Dara Rose kept her back to her daughters as she began breakfast preparations, using all her considerable willpower to keep her voice calm and even. "That's none of your business," she said firmly. "Nor mine, either. And don't you *dare* pry into Mr. McKettrick's private affairs by asking, either one of you."

Both girls sighed at this.

"Go get your shoes and stockings on," Dara Rose ordered, setting the cast-iron skillet on the stove, plopping in the last smidgeon of bacon grease to keep the eggs from sticking.

"I need to go to the outhouse," Harriet said.

"Put your shoes on first," Dara Rose countered. "It's a nice day out, but the ground is cold."

The children obeyed readily, which threw her a little. She was raising her daughters to have minds of their own, but that meant they were often obstinate and sometimes even defiant.

Parnell had accused her of spoiling them, though he'd indulged the girls plenty himself, buying them hair ribbons and peppermint sticks and letting them ride his horse. Edrina, rough and tumble as any boy but at the same time all girl, was virtually fearless as well as outspoken, and trying as the child sometimes was, Dara Rose wouldn't have changed anything about her. Except, of course, for her tendency to play hooky from school.

Harriet, just a year younger than her sister, was more tentative, less likely to take risks than Edrina was. Too small to really understand death, Harriet very probably expected her papa to come home one day, riding Gawain, his saddlebags bulging with presents.

Dara Rose's eyes smarted again and, inwardly, she brought herself up short.

She and the girls had been given a reprieve, that was all. They could go on living in the marshal's house for a while, but other arrangements would have to be made eventually, just the same.

Which was why, when she and the girls had eaten, and the dishes had been washed and the fires banked, Dara Rose followed through with her original plan.

She and Harriet walked Edrina to the one-room schoolhouse at the edge of town, and then took the eggs to the mercantile, to be traded for staples.

It was warm inside the general store, and Harriet became so captivated by the lovely doll on display in the tinsel-draped front window that Dara Rose feared the child would refuse to leave the place at all.

"Look, Mama," she breathed, without taking her eyes from the beautiful toy when Dara Rose approached and took her hand. "Isn't she pretty? She's almost as tall as *I am*."

"She's pretty," Dara Rose conceded, trying to keep the sadness out of her voice. "But not nearly as pretty as you are."

Harriet looked up at her, enchanted. "Edrina says there's no such person as St. Nicholas," she said. "She says it was you and Papa who filled our stockings last Christmas Eve."

Dara Rose's throat ached. She had to swallow before she replied, "Edrina is right, sweetheart," she said hoarsely. Other people could afford to pretend that magical things happened, at least while their children were young, but she did not have that luxury.

"I guess the doll probably costs a lot," Harriet said, her voice small and wistful.

Dara Rose checked the price tag dangling from the doll's delicate wrist, though she already knew it would be far out of her reach.

Two dollars and fifty cents.

What was the world coming to?

"She comes with a trunk full of clothes," the storekeeper put in helpfully. Philo Bickham meant well, to be sure, but he wasn't the most thoughtful man on earth. "That's real human hair on her head, too, and she came all the way from Germany."

Harriet's eyes widened with something that might have been alarm. "But didn't the hair *belong* to someone?" she asked, no doubt picturing a bald child wandering sadly through the Black Forest.

"People sometimes sell their hair," Dara Rose explained, giving Mr. Bickham a less than friendly glance as she drew her daughter toward the door. "And then it grows back."

Harriet immediately brightened. "Could we sell *my* hair? For two dollars and fifty cents?"

"No," Dara Rose said, and instantly regretted speaking so abruptly. She dropped to her haunches, tucked stray golden curls into Harriet's tattered bonnet. "Your hair is much too beautiful to sell, sweetheart."

"But I could grow more," Harriet reasoned. "You said so yourself, Mama."

Dara Rose smiled, mainly to keep from crying, and stood very straight, juggling the egg basket, now containing a small tin of lard, roughly three-quarters of a cup of sugar scooped into a paper sack and a box of table salt, from one wrist to the other.

"We'll be on our way now, Harriet," she said. "We have things to do."

CHAPTER THREE

As HE RODE slowly along every street in Blue River that morning, touching his hat brim to all he encountered so the town folks would know they had a marshal again, one who meant to live up to the accompanying responsibilities, Clay found himself thinking about Parnell Nolan. Blessed with a beautiful wife and two fine daughters, and well-liked from what little Clay had learned about him, Nolan had still managed to be in a whorehouse when he drew his last breath.

Yes, plenty of men indulged themselves in brothels—bachelors and husbands, sons and fathers alike—but they usually exercised some degree of discretion, in Clay's experience.

Always inclined to give somebody the benefit of the doubt, at least until they'd proven themselves unworthy of the courtesy, Clay figured Parnell might have done his sinning in secret, with the notion that he was therefore protecting his wife and children from scandal. But Blue River was a small place, like Clay's hometown of Indian Rock, and stories that were too good not to tell had a way of getting around. Fast.

Of course, Nolan surely hadn't planned on dying

that particular night, in the midst of awkward circumstances.

Reaching the end of the last street in town, near the schoolhouse, Clay stopped to watch, leaning on the pommel of his saddle and letting Outlaw nibble at the patchy grass, as children spilled out the door of the little red building, shouting to one another, eager to make the most of recess.

He spotted Edrina right away—her bonnet hung down her back by its laces, revealing that unmistakable head of spun-gold hair, and her cheeks glowed with exuberance and good health and the nippy coolness of the weather.

As Clay watched, she found a stick, etched the squares for a game of hopscotch in the bare dirt and jumped right in. Within moments, the other little girls were clamoring to join her, while the boys played kick-the-can at an artfully disdainful distance, making as much racket as they could muster up.

The schoolmarm—a plain woman, spare and tall, and probably younger than she looked—surveyed the melee from the steps of the building, but she was quick to notice the horse and rider looking on from the road.

Clay tugged at his hat brim and nodded a silent greeting. His ma, Chloe, had been a schoolteacher when she was younger, and he had an ingrained respect for the profession. It was invariably a hard row to hoe.

The teacher nodded back, descended the schoolhouse steps with care, lest she trip over the hem of her brown woolen dress. Instead of a coat or a cloak, she wore a dark blue shawl to keep warm.

Clay waited as she approached, then dismounted to meet her at the gate, though he kept to his own side and she kept to hers, as was proper.

The lady introduced herself. "Miss Alvira Krenshaw," she said, putting out a bony hand. She hadn't missed the star pinned to his coat, of course; her eyes had gone right to it. "You must be our new town marshal."

Clay shook her hand and acknowledged her supposition with another nod and, "Clay McKettrick."

"How do you do?" she said, not expecting an answer.

Clay gave her one, anyway. "So far, so good," he replied, with a slight grin. Miss Alvira Krenshaw looked like a sturdy, no-nonsense soul, and although she wasn't pretty, she wasn't homely, either. She'd probably make some man a good wife, given half a chance, and though thin, she looked capable of carrying healthy babies to full-term, delivering them without a lot of fuss and raising them to competent adulthood.

Wanting a wife to carry over the threshold of his new house, come spring, and impregnate as soon as possible, Clay might have set right to courting Miss Alvira, provided she was receptive to such attentions, if not for one problem. He'd gone and met Dara Rose Nolan.

Stepping off the train the day before, he'd been sure of almost everything that concerned him. What he wanted, what sort of man he was, all of it. Now, after just two brief encounters with his predecessor's widow, he wasn't sure of much of *anything.*

Considerable figuring out would be called for before he undertook to win himself a bride, and that was for certain.

Over Alvira's shoulder, he saw a boy run over to where the girls were playing hopscotch, grab at Edrina's dangling bonnet and yank on it hard enough to knock her down.

The bonnet laces held, though, and the boy ran, laughing, his friends shouting a mingling of mockery and encouragement, while a disgruntled, flaming-faced Edrina got back to her feet, dusting off her coat as she glared at the transgressor.

"Looks like trouble," Clay observed dryly, causing Miss Alvira to flare out her long, narrow nostrils and then spin around to see for herself.

Edrina, still flushed with fury, marched right into the middle of that cluster of small but earnest rascals, stood face-to-face with the primary mischief-maker and landed a solid punch to his middle. Knocked the wind right out of him.

Miss Alvira was on the run by then, blowing shrill toots through the whistle every schoolmarm seemed to come equipped with, but the damage, such as it was, was done.

The thwarted bonnet thief was on his knees now, clutching his belly and gasping for breath, and though his dignity had certainly suffered, he didn't look seriously hurt.

Clay suppressed a smile and lingered there by the gate, watching.

Edrina looked a mite calmer by then, but she was still pink in the face and her fists remained clenched. She stood her ground, spotted Clay when she turned her head toward Miss Alvira and that earsplitting whistle of hers.

"What is going on here?" Alvira demanded, her voice carrying, almost as shrill as the whistle. She reached down, caught the gasping boy from behind, where his suspenders crossed, and wrenched him unceremoniously to his feet.

Clay felt a flash of sympathy for the little fellow. Like as not, he'd taken a shine to Edrina and, boys being what boys have always been, hoped to gain her notice by snatching her bonnet and running off with it—the equivalent of tugging at a girl's pigtail or surprising her with a close-up look at a bullfrog or a squirmy garter snake, and glory be and hallelujah if she squealed.

Miss Alvira, still gripping the boy's suspenders, turned to frown at Edrina.

"Edrina Nolan," she said, "young ladies do not strike others with their fists."

Edrina, who had been looking in Clay's direction until that moment, faced her accuser, folded her arms and staunchly replied, "He had it coming."

"Go inside this instant," Alvira ordered both children, indicating the open door of the schoolhouse with a pointing of her index finger. "Thomas, you will stand in the corner behind my desk, by the bookcase. Edrina, you will occupy the one next to the cloakroom."

"For how long?" Edrina wanted to know.

Clay had to admire the child's spirit.

"Until I tell you that you may take your seats," Miss Alvira answered firmly, shooing the rest of her brood toward the hallowed halls of learning with a waving motion of her free arm. "Inside," she called. "All of you. Recess is over."

The command elicited groans of protest, but the children obeyed.

Thomas, clearly humiliated because he'd been publicly bested by a girl, slunk, head down, toward the schoolhouse, and Edrina followed in her own time, literally dragging her feet by scuffing the toe of first one shoe and then the other in the dirt as she walked. Finally, she looked back over one shoulder, caught Clay's eye and gave an eloquent little shrug of resignation.

He hoped the distance and the shadow cast by the brim of his hat would hide his smile.

That kid should have been born a McKettrick.

DARA ROSE MADE the rounds that morning just as she'd planned, swallowing her pride and knocking on each door to ask for work, with little Harriet trudging along, uncomplaining, at her side.

There were only half a dozen real *houses* in Blue River; the rest were mostly hovels and shanties, shacks like the one she lived in. The folks there were no better off than she was and, in many cases, things were worse for them. Thin smoke wafted from crooked chimneys and scrawny chickens pecked at the small expanses of bare dirt that passed for yards.

Mrs. O'Reilly, whose husband had run off with a dance hall girl six months ago and left her with three children to look after, all of them under five years old, was outside. The woman was probably in her early twenties, but she looked a generation older; there were already streaks of gray at her temples and she'd lost one of her eye teeth.

She had a bonfire going, with a big tin washtub teetering atop the works, full of other people's laundry. Steam boiled up into the crisp air as she stirred the soapy soup, and Peg O'Reilly managed a semblance of a smile when she caught sight of Dara Rose and Harriet.

Two of the O'Reilly children, both boys, ran whooping around their mother like Sioux braves on the warpath, both of them barefoot and coatless. Their older sister, Addie, must have been inside, where it was, Dara Rose devoutly hoped, comparatively warm.

"Mornin', Miz Nolan," Peg called, though she didn't smile. She was probably self-conscious about that missing tooth, Dara Rose figured, with a stab of well-hidden pity.

Dara Rose smiled, offered a wave and paused at the edge of the road, even though she'd meant to keep going. Lord knew, she had reason enough to be discouraged herself, after being turned away from all those doors, but she just couldn't bring herself to pass on by.

Harriet, no doubt weary from keeping up with Dara Rose all morning, tugged reluctantly at her mother's hand, wanting to go on.

"How's Addie?" Dara Rose asked.

"She's poorly," Peg replied. "Been abed since yesterday, so she's not much help with these little yahoos." Still tending to the wash, which was just coming to a simmer, she indicated the boys with a nod of her head.

They had both stopped their chasing game to stare at Harriet in abject wonder. Even in her poor clothes and the shoes she would outgrow all too soon, she probably looked as pretty to them as that doll over at the mercantile did to her.

"Mama," Harriet whispered, looking up at Dara Rose from beneath the drooping brim of her bonnet, "what's that smell?"

"Hush," Dara Rose whispered back, hoping Peg hadn't heard the little girl's voice over the crackling of the fire and the barking of a neighbor's dog.

Peg let go of the old broomstick she used to stir the shirts and trousers and small clothes as they soaked, and wiped a forearm across her brow. The sleeves of her calico dress were rolled up to her elbows, and her apron was little more than a rag.

"Could you use some eggs?" Dara Rose asked, in the manner of one asking a favor. "I've got plenty put by."

A flicker of yearning showed in Peg O'Reilly's care-worn face before she squared her shoulders and raised her chin a notch. "I'd say no, on grounds that I've got my pride and I know you're having a hard time of it, too, but for the young'uns," she replied. "The last of the oatmeal is used up, and we're almost out of pinto beans, but a nice fried egg might put some color in Addie's cheeks and that's for sure."

"I'll send Edrina over with a basket right after she gets home from school," Dara Rose said.

"You understand that I can't pay you nothin'," Peg warned, stiffening her backbone.

"I understand," Dara Rose confirmed lightly, though every egg her hens laid was precious, since it could be sold for cash money or traded for things she couldn't raise, like flour. "I've got too many, and I don't want them to go to waste."

"Mama," Harriet interjected, "we don't—"

This time, Dara Rose didn't hush her daughter out loud, but simply squeezed the child's hand a little more tightly than she might otherwise have done.

"Obliged, then," Peg said, and went back to her stirring.

Dara Rose nodded and started off toward home again, poor Harriet scrambling to keep up.

"Mama," the child insisted, half-breathless, "you already traded away all the eggs, remember? Over at the mercantile? And the hens probably haven't laid any new ones yet."

"There are nearly two dozen in the crock on the pantry shelf," Dara Rose reminded her daughter. Like the potatoes, carrots, turnips and onions she'd squirreled away down in the root cellar, along with a few bushels of apples from the tree in her yard, the eggs suspended in water glass were part of her skimpy reserves, something she and the girls could eat if the hens stopped laying or the hawks got them.

"Yes," Harriet reasoned, intrepidly logical, "but what if there's a hard winter and *we* need to eat them?"

"Harriet," Dara Rose replied, walking a little faster because it was almost time for Edrina to come home for the midday meal, "there are times when a person simply has to help somebody who needs a hand and hope the good Lord pays heed and makes recompense." Parting with a few eggs didn't trouble her nearly as much as the realization that her five-year-old daughter had obviously been worrying about whether or not there would be enough food to get them through.

"What's 'recompense'?" Harriet asked.

"Never mind," Dara Rose answered.

They reached the house, removed their bonnets and their wraps—Dara Rose's cloak and Harriet's coat—and Dara Rose ladled warm water out of the stove reservoir for the washing of hands.

In her mind, she heard Peg O'Reilly's words of brave despair. *The last of the oatmeal is used up, and we're almost out of pinto beans...*

Peg earned a pittance taking in laundry as it was, and what little money she earned probably went to pay for starvation rations and to meet the rent on that converted chicken coop of a house they all lived in.

As she reheated the canned venison leftover from last night's supper, then sliced and thinly buttered the last of the bread she'd made a few days before, Dara Rose silently reminded herself of something Parnell had often told her. "No matter how tough things get," he used to say, "you won't have to look far to find somebody else who'd be glad to trade places with you."

Her children were healthy, unlike Peg's eldest, and the three of them had a roof over their heads. And Parnell, at least, hadn't left them willingly, the way Jack O'Reilly had done.

Harriet, her mother's busy little helper, set three places at the table and then dragged a chair over to the side window so she could stand on the seat and keep a lookout for her sister. Although they had their scuffles and tiffs, like all children, Harriet's admiration for Edrina knew no bounds.

"There she is!" Harriet shouted gleefully, after a few moments of peering through the glass. "There's Edrina!"

Dara Rose smiled and began ladling warm venison and broth into enamel-coated bowls. She'd just set the bread plate in the middle of the improvised table when Edrina dragged in, looking despondent.

"You might as well know straightaway that I'm in trouble again," she immediately confessed. "Thomas Phillips tried to steal my bonnet at recess, and near strangled me with the ties while he was at it, and I socked him in the stomach. Miss Krenshaw made me stand in the corner for a whole hour, and I have to stay after school to wash the blackboard every day this week."

Dara Rose sighed, shook her head in feigned dismay and placed her hands on her hips. "Edrina," she said, on a long breath, and shook her head again.

"Did Thomas have to stand in the corner, too?" Harriet inquired, already a great believer in fair play.

"Yes," Edrina answered, with precious little satisfaction. "He has to carry in the drinking water for the whole school."

"Wash your hands," Dara Rose said mildly, when her elder daughter would have sat down to her meal instead.

Edrina obeyed, with a sigh of her own, and pulled the stool out from under the sink to climb up and plunge her small hands into the basin of warm water Dara Rose had set there.

"Mr. McKettrick came by the schoolhouse today," the child announced. "That sure is a fine horse he rides."

Dara Rose felt an odd little catch at the mention of the new marshal and, to her shame, caught herself wondering if he'd found Alvira Krenshaw at all fetching. She was certainly eligible, Miss Krenshaw was, and while she wouldn't win any prizes for looks, most people agreed that she was a handsome woman with a good head on her shoulders.

"Was there some kind of trouble? Besides your disagreement with Thomas?"

Edrina had finished washing up, and she climbed deftly back down off the stool, drying her hands on her skirts as she approached the table. "No," she replied, "but he talked to Miss Krenshaw at the gate for a long time."

Dara Rose, who had long since learned to choose her battles, decided to let the hand-drying incident pass. She hoisted Harriet onto the stool, helped her lather to her elbows and then rinse and lifted her down again.

The three of them gathered at the table.

It was Harriet's turn to say grace. "Thank you for the venison and the bread," she said, in her direct way, her bright head bowed and her eyes squeezed shut. "And if there's any way I could get that pretty doll in the window of the mercantile for my very own, I would appreciate the kindness. Amen."

Dara Rose suppressed a smile even as she endured another pang to her heart. Much as she'd have loved to give her daughters toys for Christmas, she couldn't afford to do it. And even if she'd had any spare money at all, Edrina and Harriet needed shoes and warm clothes and nourishing food, like milk.

"What do you want St. Nicholas to bring you for Christmas?" Harriet asked Edrina, with companionable interest, as they all began to eat.

Edrina answered without hesitation, a note of gentle tolerance in her voice. "You know there isn't any St. Nicholas, Harriet," she reminded her sister. "He's just a story person, made up by that Mr. Moore."

"Couldn't we just *pretend* he's real?" Harriet wanted to know. "Just 'til lunch is over?" She sounded more like an adult than a little girl and Dara Rose, though proud of her bright daughters, hoped they weren't growing up too fast.

"It wouldn't hurt to pretend," she put in quietly.

Harriet's face lit up. "What do *you* want for Christmas, Mama?" she asked eagerly, forgetting all about her food.

Dara Rose pretended to think very hard for a few moments. "A cow, I think," she finally decided. "Then we'd have milk and butter of our own. Maybe even cheese."

Harriet looked nonplussed. "A cow?" she repeated.

Edrina glanced at Dara Rose, her expression almost conspiratorial, and considered the question under discussion. "I know what *I'd* want," she said presently. "Books. Exciting ones, with bears and outlaws and spooks in them."

Again, Dara Rose's heart pinched. She'd be lucky to afford peppermint sticks to drop into the girls' Christmas stockings this year, never mind dolls and books.

She cleared her throat. "Harriet and I stopped by the

O'Reilly place today," she said. "Little Addie's under the weather again, and those boys looked hungry enough to dip spoons into the laundry kettle."

"And something smells bad there," Harriet added.

Dara Rose didn't scold her, but went right on. "I think they'd be grateful to have firewood and enough to eat, like we do," she said, hoping she'd made her point and wouldn't have to follow up with a sermon on Christian charity.

"Mama's giving them some of our eggs," Harriet said matter-of-factly. "She says sometimes a person just has to help somebody else and hope the good Lord pays heed and makes competition."

Edrina didn't say anything, since she had a mouthful of bread.

Dara Rose wondered if Harriet even knew what it meant to pay heed. "The two of you can take a basket over to the O'Reillys', as soon as school's out for the day," she said. "And furthermore, Harriet Nolan, you will *not* remark on the bad smell."

"It's probably the outhouse that stinks," Edrina said. "Ours might get that way, too, without Papa around to shovel lye into it once in a while."

"Edrina," Dara Rose said, "we are at the table."

A long pause ensued.

"I have to stay after to wash the blackboard," Edrina reminded her mother.

"Fine," Dara Rose answered, pushing back her chair and carrying her bowl and spoon to the sink. "I'll wash the eggs and put them in the basket and you can drop them off at the O'Reilly place on your way back to school."

"There will be hell to pay if I'm late for class," Edrina said frankly. "Don't forget, I'm already in trouble for slugging Thomas Phillips in the stomach."

Dara Rose bit the inside of her lower lip to keep from smiling. "I won't forget," she said, heading for the single shelf that served as a pantry, bowl in hand, and fishing eight perfect brown ovals out of the crock filled to the brim with water glass. "If you hurry, you can deliver the eggs and still get back to school before Miss Krenshaw rings the bell. *And* I will thank you not to swear, Edrina Nolan."

Harriet, who staunchly maintained that she was too old to take naps, was already getting heavy-lidded, chin drooping, and yawning a little.

Dara Rose washed the eggs and put them into the basket, covering them with a flour-sack dish towel. She handed them to Edrina, who was already buttoning her coat. "Wear your bonnet," she instructed. "The sky may be blue as summer, but the wind has a bite to it."

Edrina nodded, resigned, and let herself out, taking the egg basket with her.

"Bring that basket home," Dara Rose called after her. "And the dish towel, too."

Edrina replied, but Dara Rose didn't hear what she said. She was already scooping up her sleepy child and carrying her to bed.

CLAY CHECKED THE Bitter Gulch Saloon and looked in at the bank, but there was no malfeasance afoot in either place.

Figuring it was indeed going to be a long winter, he

walked back to the jailhouse, where he had a tiny office, a potbellied stove and a cot, and helped himself to a cup of the passable coffee he'd made earlier.

The stuff was stale and lukewarm, but stout enough to rouse a dead man from his eternal rest.

That, he supposed, was what this coming winter was going to feel like. Eternal rest.

He sighed, crossed to the single cell and peered through the bars, almost wishing he had a prisoner. That way, there would have been somebody to talk to, at least.

Alas, lawbreakers seemed to be pretty thin on the ground around those parts at the moment, a fact he supposed he should have been grateful to note.

Clay sat down in the creaky wooden chair behind the scarred wooden table that served as a desk and reached for the dusty stack of wanted posters and old mail piled on one corner.

If anybody stopped by, he'd like to give the impression that he was working, even if he wasn't. It made him smile to imagine what his granddad would think if he could see him now, collecting seventy-five dollars a month for doing not much of anything except drinking bad coffee and flipping through somebody else's correspondence.

He set aside the older wanted posters and read the few missives that looked even remotely official—none of them were, it turned out—and he was thinking maybe he ought to meander over to the livery stable and brush old Outlaw down, when he came to the last two letters and realized they were addressed to Mrs. Parnell B. Nolan.

The first, from an outfit called the Wildflower Salve Company, was most likely a sales pitch of some kind, but the second looked personal and smelled faintly of lemon verbena. The envelope was fat, made of good vellum, and the handwriting on the front was flowing cursive, with all kinds of loops and swirls.

Clay looked at the postmark, but couldn't make out where the letter had been mailed, or when, and there wasn't any return address.

Not that any of this was his concern in the first place.

Clay frowned, wondering how long the letters had been moldering in that pile, and then he smiled, holding the envelopes in one hand and lightly slapping them against the opposite palm.

Maybe it wasn't his sworn duty to make sure the mail got delivered, but it was as good an excuse as any for calling on Dara Rose Nolan.

Clay rose from his chair, fetched his coat and hat and set out on foot.

THERE HE STOOD, on her front doorstep this time, looking affably handsome.

For the briefest fraction of a moment, Dara Rose feared that Clay McKettrick had changed his mind, decided he wanted the house, after all. Her stomach quivered in a peculiar way that didn't seem to have much to do with the fear of eviction.

"I found these letters over at the office," he said, and produced two envelopes from an inside pocket of his duster. "They're addressed to you."

Dara Rose's eyes rounded. Getting a letter was a

rare thing indeed. Getting two at once was virtually unheard-of.

She opened the door a little wider, extended a hand for the envelopes and spoke very quietly because Harriet was napping. "Thank you," she said.

He let her take the envelopes, but he held on to them for a second longer than necessary, too.

Although her curiosity was great, Dara Rose wanted to savor the prospect of those letters for a little while. She'd read them later, by lamplight, when the girls were both down for the night and the house was quiet.

She tucked them into the pocket of her apron, blushing a little.

"Come in," she heard her own voice say, much to her surprise.

It simply wasn't proper for a widow to invite a man into her home, even in broad daylight, but she'd done just that and already stepped back so he could pass, and the marshal didn't hesitate to step over the threshold.

He stood in the middle of the front room, seeming to fill it to capacity with the width of his shoulders and the sheer unwieldy substance of his presence. His gaze went straight to the oversize daguerreotype of Parnell on one wall.

He seemed to consider her late husband's visage for a few moments, before turning to meet her eyes.

"He doesn't look like the kind of man who'd die in a brothel," he remarked.

Dara Rose was jangled, but not offended. Everyone knew what had happened to Parnell, and the scandal, though still alive, had long since died down to an occasional whisper, especially since Jack O'Reilly had left his wife and children for a sloe-eyed girl from the Bitter Gulch Saloon.

"He wasn't," she said, very softly, and then colored up again. "That kind of man, I mean. Not really."

Dara Rose had never confided the truth about her marriage to Parnell Nolan to a single living soul west of the Mississippi River, and she was confounded by a sudden urge to tell Marshal McKettrick everything.

Not a chance, she thought, running her hands down the front of her apron as if they'd been wet.

"It must have been hard for you and the children," Clay said quietly. His eyes, blue as cornflowers in high summer, took on a solemn expression. "Not just his dying, but being left on your own and all."

"We manage," Dara Rose said.

"I reckon you do," he agreed, and he looked more puzzled than solemn now.

She knew he was wondering why she hadn't found another husband, but she wasn't about to volunteer an explanation. Maybe she hadn't actually loved Parnell Nolan, but she'd liked him. Depended on him. Even respected him.

Parnell had been kind to her, cherished the girls like they were his daughters instead of his nieces, and married her.

She would have felt disloyal, discussing Parnell with a relative stranger; though, oddly enough, in some ways she felt as if she'd always known Clay McKettrick, and known him well. He stirred vague memories in her, like dreams that left only an echo behind when the sun rose.

The silence was awkward.

Dara Rose didn't ask the marshal to sit down, and she couldn't offer him coffee because she didn't have any.

So the two of them just stood there, each one waiting for the other to speak.

Finally, Clay grinned ever so slightly and turned his hat decisively in his hands. He went to the door and opened it, pausing to look back at Dara Rose, his impressive form rimmed in wintry light.

"Good day to you, Mrs. Nolan," he said.

Dara Rose swallowed. "Good day, Mr. McKettrick," she replied formally. "And, once again, thank you."

"Anytime," he said, and then he left the house, closed the door behind him.

Dara Rose resisted the temptation to rush to the window and watch him heading down the walk.

Harriet appeared in the doorway to the bedroom, hair rumpled, rubbing her eyes with the backs of her hands. "I thought I heard Papa's voice," she said.

Dara Rose's heart cracked and then split down the middle. "Sweetheart," she said, bending her knees so she could look directly into the child's sleep-flushed face, "Papa's gone to heaven, remember?"

Harriet's lower lip wobbled, which further bruised Dara Rose's already injured heart. How could such a small child be expected to understand the permanence of death?

"Is heaven a real place?" Harriet asked. "Or is it just pretend, like St. Nicholas?"

"I believe it's a real place," Dara Rose said.

Harriet frowned, obviously puzzled. "Is it like here? Are there trees and kittens and trains to ride?"

Dara Rose blinked rapidly and rose back to her full height. "I don't know, sweetheart. One day, a long, long time from now, we'll find out for sure, but right now, we have to live in *this* world, and we might as well make the best of it."

"I think I would like this world better," Harriet told her, "if there was a St. Nicholas in it."

Dara Rose gave a small, strangled chuckle at that, and pulled her daughter close for a hug. "We don't need St. Nicholas, you and Edrina and me," she said. "We have one another."

CHAPTER FOUR

AFTER THE CHICKENS were fed and had retreated into their coop to roost for the night, Dara Rose made a simple supper of baked potatoes and last summer's string beans, boiled with bits of salt pork and onion, for herself and the girls, and the three of them sat at the table in the kitchen, eating by the light of a kerosene lantern and chatting quietly.

The subject of St. Nicholas did not come up again, thankfully. In Dara Rose's humble opinion, Clement C. Moore had a lot to answer for. By writing that lengthy and admittedly charming poem, "'Twas the Night Before Christmas," he'd created expectations in children that many parents couldn't hope to meet.

Instead, Edrina recounted her visit to the O'Reillys' after lunch, and fretted that it wasn't fair that she had to wash the blackboard every single day for a week when all she'd done was defend herself against that wretched Thomas. Large flakes of snow drifted, like benevolent ghosts, past the darkened window next to the back door, and brought a sigh to hover in the back of Dara Rose's throat.

Winter. As a privileged only child, back in Massachusetts, she'd loved everything about that season, even the cold. It was a time to skate and sled and build castles out of snow and then drink hot chocolate by the fire while Nanny told stories or recited long, exciting poems about shipwrecks and ghosts and Paul Revere's ride.

Had she ever really lived such a life? Dara Rose wondered now, as she did whenever her childhood came to mind.

"Mama?" Edrina said, breaking the sudden spell the sight of snowflakes had cast over Dara Rose. "Did you hear what I said about Addie O'Reilly?"

Dara Rose gave herself an inward shake and sat up a little straighter in her chair. "I'm sorry," she said, because she was always truthful with the children. "I'm afraid I was woolgathering."

Edrina's perfect little face glowed, heart-shaped, in the light of love and a kerosene lantern. "She's really sick," she informed her mother, in a tone of good-natured patience, as though she were the parent and Dara Rose the child. "Mrs. O'Reilly told me she has romantic fever."

Dara Rose did not correct Edrina. She was too stricken by the tragedy of it, the patent unfairness. *Rheumatic fever.* Was there no end to the sorrows and hardships visited on that poor family?

"That's dreadful," she said.

"And Addie gets lonely, staying inside all the time," Edrina went on. "So I said Harriet and I would come to visit on Saturday morning. We can, can't we, Mama? Because I promised."

Dara Rose's heart swelled with affection for her daughter, and then sank a little. It was like her spirited

Edrina to make such an offer, and follow through on it, too, whether or not she had her mother's permission. When Edrina made a promise, she kept it, which meant she was really asking if Harriet could go with her.

As far as Dara Rose knew, rheumatic fever wasn't contagious, but heaven only knew what other diseases her children might contract during a visit to the O'Reilly house—diphtheria, the dreaded influenza, perhaps even typhoid or cholera.

"You mustn't promise such things, in the future, without speaking to me first," Dara Rose told Edrina, hedging. "I feel as sorry for the O'Reillys as you do, Edrina, but there are other considerations."

"And it stinks over there," Harriet interjected solemnly, her nose twitching a little at the memory.

Dara Rose had lost her appetite, which was fine, because she'd had enough to eat, anyway. "Harriet," she said. "That will be enough of that sort of talk. It is not suitable for the supper table."

Harriet sighed. "It's *never* suitable," she lamented.

"Hush," Dara Rose told her, her attention focused, for the moment, on her elder daughter. "You may visit the O'Reillys on Saturday morning," she stated, rising to begin clearing the table. "But only because you gave your word and I would not ask you to break it."

"If I hadn't promised, you wouldn't let me go?" Edrina pressed. She'd never been one to quit while the quitting was good, a trait she came by honestly, Dara Rose had to admit. She had the same shortcoming herself.

"That's right," she replied, at some length. "I have to think about your safety, Edrina, and that of your sister."

"My safety? The O'Reillys wouldn't hurt us."

"Not deliberately," Dara Rose allowed, "but it isn't the most sanitary place in the world, and you might catch something."

Although she didn't mention it, she was thinking of the diphtheria outbreak two years before, during which four children had perished, all of them from one family.

"Is that suitable talk for the supper table?" Harriet asked sincerely.

"Never mind," Dara Rose said. "It's time you both got ready for bed. Shall I walk with you to the outhouse, or are you brave enough to go on your own?"

Edrina scraped back her chair, rose to fetch her coat and Harriet's from the pegs near the back door. Her expression said she was brave enough to do anything, and protect her little sister in the bargain.

"Maybe that's why Addie's so lonesome," Edrina said, opening the door to the chilly night, with its flurries of snow. "Because everybody is afraid of catching something if they visit."

Chagrin swept over Dara Rose—*out of the mouths of babes*—but she assumed a stern countenance. "Don't stand there with the door open," she said.

Later, when the children were in bed, and she'd read them a story from their one dog-eared book of fairy tales and heard their prayers—Harriet put in another request for the doll from the mercantile—kissed them good-night and tucked them in, Dara Rose returned to the kitchen.

There, she took the two letters Mr. McKettrick had delivered earlier from her apron pocket, and sat down.

The kerosene in the lamp was getting low, and the wick was smoking a little, but Dara Rose did not hurry.

She knew the plump missive was from her cousin, Piper, who taught school in a small town in Maine. She meant to save that one for last, and she took the time to weigh it in her hand, run her fingers over the vellum and examine the stamp before setting it carefully aside.

She opened the letter from the Wildflower Salve Company first, even though she knew it was an advertisement and nothing more, and carefully smoothed the single page on the tabletop.

Her eyes widened a little as she read, and her heart fluttered up into her throat as her excitement grew.

Bold print declared that Dara Rose was holding the key to financial security right there in her hand. She could win prizes, it fairly shouted. She could earn money. And all she had to do was introduce her friends and neighbors to the wonders of Wildflower Salve. Each colorfully decorated round tin—an elegant keepsake in its own right, according to the Wildflower Salve people—sold for a mere fifty cents. And she would get to keep a whopping twenty-five cents for her commission.

Dara Rose sat back, thinking.

Twenty-five cents was a lot of money.

And there were prizes. All sorts of prizes—toys, household goods, luxuries of all sorts—could be had in lieu of commissions, if the "independent business person" preferred.

Out of the goodness of their hearts, the folks at the Wildflower Salve Company, of Racine, Wisconsin, would be happy to send her a full twenty tins of this "medicinal miracle" in good faith. If for some incomprehensible reason her "friends and relations" didn't snap up the whole shipment practically as soon as she opened the parcel, she could return the merchandise and owe nothing.

Five dollars, Dara Rose thought. If she sold twenty tins of Wildflower Salve, she would earn *five dollars*— a virtual fortune.

The kerosene lamp flickered, reminding her that she'd soon be sitting in the dark, and Dara Rose set aside "the opportunity of a lifetime" to open the letter from Piper.

A crisp ten-dollar bill fell out, nearly stopping Dara Rose's heart.

She set it carefully aside, and her hands trembled as she unfolded the clump of pages covered in Piper's lovely cursive. The date was nearly eight months in the past.

"Dearest Cousin," the missive began. "News of your tragic misfortune reached me yesterday, via the telegraph..."

Piper's letter, misplaced all this time, went on to say that she hoped Dara Rose could put the money enclosed to good use—that the weather was fine in Maine, with the spring coming, but she already dreaded the winter. How were the girls faring? Did Dara Rose intend to stay on in "that little Texas town," or would she and the children consider coming to live with her? The teacher's quarters were small, she wrote, bringing tears to Dara Rose's eyes, but they could make do, the four of them, couldn't they? There were crocuses and tulips and daffodils shooting up in people's flower beds, Piper went on to relate, and the days were distinctly longer. For all that, alas, she was lonesome when she wasn't teaching. She'd been briefly engaged, but the fellow had turned out to be a rascal and a rounder, and there didn't seem to be any likely prospects on the horizon.

Dara Rose read the whole letter and then immediately read it again. Besides Edrina and Harriet, Piper was the only blood relation she had left in all the world, and Dara Rose missed her sorely. Holding the letter, seeing the familiar handwriting spanning the pages, was the next best thing to having her cousin right there, in the flesh, sitting across the table from her.

But what must Piper think of her? Dara Rose fretted, after a third reading. She'd written this letter so long ago, and sent such a generous gift of money, only to receive silence in return.

The lantern guttered out.

Dara Rose sighed, folded the letter carefully and tucked it back into its envelope. She took the ten-dollar bill with her to the bedroom, where the girls were sound asleep, and placed it carefully between the pages in her Bible for safekeeping.

She undressed quickly, since the little room was cold, and donned her flannel nightgown, returned to the kitchen carrying a lighted candle stuck to a jar lid and dipped water from the stove reservoir to wash her face. When that was done, she brushed her teeth at the sink and steeled herself to make the trek to the outhouse, through the snowy cold.

When she got back, she locked the door, used the

candle to light her way back to the bedroom, blew out the flame and climbed into bed with her daughters.

She was tired, but too excited to fall asleep right away.

She had ten precious dollars.

The Wildflower Salve Company had offered her honest work.

She'd as good as—well, *almost* as good as—spent an evening with her cousin and dearest friend, Piper.

And Marshal Clay McKettrick had the bluest eyes she'd ever seen.

THE JAILHOUSE, Clay soon discovered, was a lonely place at night.

He'd already had supper over at the hotel dining room— chicken and dumplings almost as good as his ma's—and he'd paid a visit to Outlaw, over at the livery stable, too. He'd even sent a telegram north to Indian Rock, to let his family know he'd arrived and was settling in nicely.

That done, Clay had filled the water bucket and set up the coffeepot for morning, then filled the wood box next to the potbellied stove. There being no place to hang up his clothes, he left them folded in his travel trunk, there in the back room, where the bed was. Most of his books hadn't arrived yet—he had a passel of them and they had to be shipped down from Indian Rock in crates—and he couldn't seem to settle down to read the one favorite he'd brought along on the train, Jules Verne's *Around the World in Eighty Days*. He must have read that book a dozen times over the years, and he never got tired of it, but that night, it failed to hold his interest.

He kept thinking about Dara Rose Nolan, the gold of her hair and the fiery blue spirit in her eyes. He thought about her shapely breasts and small waist and smooth skin and that flash of pride that was so easy to arouse in her.

And the same old question plagued him: Why in the devil would a man with a wife like that squander his time in a whorehouse, the way her husband had done?

Nobody could help dying, of course, but they had at least some choice about *where* they died, didn't they? It was simple common sense—folks didn't turn up their toes in places they hadn't ventured into in the first place.

Knowing he wouldn't sleep, anyhow, Clay strapped on his gun belt, shrugged into his duster and reached for his hat.

He was the marshal, after all.

He'd just take a little stroll up and down Main Street and make sure any visiting cowpokes or drifters were minding their manners. If anybody needed arresting, he'd throw them in the hoosegow and start up a conversation.

What he really needed, he supposed, stepping out onto the dark sidewalk, was a woman. Someone like Dara Rose Nolan.

Maybe he'd get himself a dog—that would provide some companionship. He'd have to do all the talking, of course, but he liked critters. He'd grown up with all manner of them on the ranch.

Yes, sir, he needed a dog.

He hadn't even reached the corner when he heard the first yelp.

He frowned, stopped to pinpoint the direction.

"Dutch, you kick that dog again," he heard a male voice say, "and I'll shoot *you*, 'stead of him!"

Clay, having located the disturbance, pushed his coat back to uncover the handle of his .45 and stepped into the alley.

It was dark, and the snow veiled the moon, but light struggled through the filthy windows of the buildings on either side, and he could make out two men, one holding a pistol, standing over a shivering form huddled close to the ground.

"Hold it right there," Clay said, in deadly earnest, when the man with the pistol raised it to shoot. "What's going on here?"

The dog whimpered.

"Nothin', Marshal," one of the men answered, in a drunken whine. "The poor mutt's half-starved, just a bag of bones. We figured on putting it out of its misery, that's all. Meant it as a kindness."

"Get the hell out of here," Clay said. He could not abide a bully.

The two men responded by turning on their heels and running in the other direction.

Clay waited until they were out of sight before he put the .45 back in its holster and approached the dog. "You in a bad way there, fella?" he asked, crouching to offer a hand.

The animal sniffed cautiously at his fingers and whimpered again.

"Where'd you come from?" Clay asked, gently examining the critter for broken bones or open wounds. He seemed to be all right, though his ribs protruded and his belly was concave and he stunk like all get-out.

The dog whined, though this time there was less sorrow in the sound.

"You know," Clay told the animal companionably, "I was just thinking to myself that what I need is a dog to keep me company. Now, here you are. How'd you like to help me keep the peace in this sorry excuse for a town?"

The dog seemed amenable to the idea, and raised himself slowly, teetering a little, to his four fur-covered feet. He had burrs stuck in his coat, that poor cuss, and there was no telling what color he was, or if he leaned toward any particular breed.

"You come on with me, if you can walk," Clay said. "I brought home what was left of my supper, and it seems to me you could use a decent meal."

With that, he turned to head back toward the sidewalk. The dog limped after him, pausing every few moments, as though afraid he'd committed some transgression without knowing about it.

Back at the jailhouse, Clay got a better look at the dog, after lighting a lantern to see by, but seeing didn't help much. The creature was neither big nor little, and he had floppy ears, but that was the extent of what Clay could make out.

Glad to have something to do, not to mention some companionship, Clay poured the remains of his chicken and dumplings onto the one tin plate he possessed and set it on the floor, near the stove.

The dog sniffed at the food, looked up at Clay with the kind of uncertainty that breaks a decent person's heart and waited.

"You go ahead and have supper," Clay said gently. "I imagine you could use some water, too."

Slowly, cautiously, the dog lowered his muzzle and began to eat.

Clay walked softly, approaching the water bucket, and ladled up a dipperful.

The dog lapped thirstily from the well of the dipper, then returned to his supper, clearly ravenous, licking the plate clean as a whistle.

Clay carried in more water from the pump out back, heated it bucket by bucket on the potbellied stove and finally filled the washtub he'd found in one of the cells. He eased the dog into the warm water and sluiced him down before lathering his hide with his own bar of soap.

The animal didn't raise any fuss, he simply stood there, shivering and looking like nothing so much as a half-drowned rat. Gradually, it became clear that his coat was brown and white, speckled like a pinto horse.

Clay dried him off with one of the two towels he'd purchased earlier, over at the mercantile, hefted him out of the tub and set him gently on his feet, near the stove.

The dog looked up at him curiously, head tilted to one side.

Clay chuckled. "Now, then," he said. "You look a lot more presentable than you did before."

The dog gave a single, tentative *woof*, obviously unsure how the remark would be received in present company.

Clay leaned to pat the animal's damp head. "What you are," he said, "is a coincidence. Like I told you, I was thinking about how much I'd like to have a dog, and then you and I made our acquaintance. But since 'coincidence' would be too much trouble for a name, I figure I'll call you Chester."

"Woof," said Chester, with more confidence than before.

Clay laughed. "Chester it is, then," he agreed.

Using a rough blanket from the cot in the jail cell, Clay fashioned a bed for the dog, close to the stove. Chester sniffed the cloth, stepped gingerly onto it, made a circle and settled down with a sigh.

"Night," Clay said.

Chester closed his eyes, sighed again and slept.

THE HENS HAD only laid three eggs between the lot of them, Dara Rose discovered the next morning, when she visited the chicken coop, but she wasn't as disappointed by this as she normally would have been.

She had ten dollars tucked between the leaves of her Bible—a fortune.

And she had a future, a bright one, as Blue River, Texas's sole distributor of Wildflower Salve. All she had to do was fill out the coupon and mail it in, and before the New Year, she'd be in business.

Granted, there weren't a lot of people in Blue River, but there were plenty of surrounding farms and ranches, and those isolated women would be thrilled to purchase salve in a pretty tin, especially after she explained the benefits of regular use.

Not that she knew exactly what those benefits *were*, but the Wildflower Salve people had promised to send a training guide along with her first shipment.

As soon as she'd gotten Edrina off to school, she intended to write a long letter to Piper, explaining that *her* letter had been accidentally misplaced all this time, and she'd only received it the day before, and that was why her answer was so late in coming. Of course she'd thank her cousin profusely for the generous gift of ten dollars, and bring Piper up-to-date where she and the girls were concerned.

Her mind bumbled back and forth between the planned letter and her impending career in merchandising like a bee trapped inside a jar while she prepared oatmeal for breakfast, toasted bread in the oven and officiated over a debate between Edrina and Harriet, concerning whose turn it was to sleep in the middle of the bed that night.

Neither one wanted to, and Dara Rose finally said *she'd* take the middle, for heaven's sake, and what had she done to deserve two such argumentative daughters?

After breakfast, Dara Rose and Harriet bundled up to walk Edrina to school. Normally, Edrina managed the distance on her own, but today, Dara Rose wanted a word with Miss Krenshaw.

"I'm *already* being punished," Edrina fussed, as the three of them hurried along a road hoary with frost and hardened snow. "I *told you* I have to stay after and wash the blackboard. So why do you need to talk to Miss Krenshaw, when you know all that?"

Dara Rose hid a smile. She was holding Harriet's hand, and trying to pace herself to the child's much shorter strides. "I merely want to inquire about the Christmas pageant," she replied. There was always some sort of program at the schoolhouse, whether it was carol singing, a Nativity play or an evening of recitals, and everyone attended.

"Oh," said Edrina, still sounding not only mystified, but apparently a little nervous, too.

Dara Rose wondered if there was something her daughter should have told her, but hadn't.

"Do you think it will snow again, Mama?" Harriet asked, tilting her head way back to look up at the glowering sky. "Christmas is less than two weeks away, and St. Nicholas will need a lot of snow, since he travels in a sleigh."

"Goose," Edrina said, nudging her sister with one elbow. "There *isn't* any St. Nicholas, remember?"

"Edrina," Dara Rose interceded gently.

"I'm *pretending*, that's all," Harriet said, with a toss of her head. "You can't *stop* me, either."

"Pretending is *stupid*," Edrina said. "It's for babies."

Dara Rose stopped, and both her children had to stop, too, since she was holding Harriet's hand at the time and it was easy to catch Edrina by the shoulder and halt her progress.

"Enough," Dara Rose said firmly.

They began to walk again.

THE SKY WAS heavy and gray that morning when Clay left Chester to digest the leftovers from his hotel dining room breakfast within the warm radius of the jailhouse stove and headed over to the livery stable to fetch Outlaw.

It was cold and getting colder, so Clay raised the collar of his duster as he led the saddled gelding out into the road. There had been snow during the night, leaving a hard crust on the ground, and there would be more, judging by the weighted clouds brooding overhead, but the ride was a short one and he'd be back in Blue River before any serious weather had a chance to set in.

Raised in the high country, where a soft, slow, feathery snowfall could turn into a raging blizzard within a span of ten minutes, he had a sense of what signs he ought to look out for, as well as those he could safely ignore.

Today, all the indications—the direction of wind, the foul promise of the darkening sky, the way the cold bit through the heavy canvas of his duster—inclined a man toward caution.

He let Outlaw have his head once they were out of town, let the horse run for the sheer joy of it, and they soon reached their destination, the flat acres where Clay intended to erect a house and a barn.

There, he dismounted and left Outlaw to catch his breath and graze on the scant remains of last summer's grass, paced off the perimeters of the house and marked the corners with piles of small rocks. He did the same for the barn, then stood a while, the wind slicing clear to his marrow, and imagined the place, finished.

The house, a kit he'd sent away to Sears, Roebuck and Company for, amounted to a sensible rectangle, the kind he could easily add on to as the years went by, with windows on all sides, white clapboard walls and a shingled roof. He'd have to hire some help to put the thing together, of course, but he planned to do a lot of the work with his own hands, and that included everything from laying floorboards to gathering rock for the fireplace and then mortaring the stones together.

With the McKettrick family expanding the way it had been for some years, Clay had helped build several houses, and put up additions, too. The kit wouldn't arrive until late April, but he'd need to have the foundation ready, and the well dug, too.

Of course, a lot depended on what kind of winter they were in for—Blue River was in the Hill Country, and therefore the climate wasn't as temperate as it was in some parts of Texas—but he could already feel the heft of a shovel in his hands, the steady strain in his muscles, and he was heartened.

Next year at this time, he promised himself, he'd be ranching, right here on this land. He'd have a wife and, if possible, a baby on the way. Christmas would be getting close, and he'd go out and cut a tree and bring it into the house to be hung with ornaments and paper garlands, and there would be a fire crackling on the hearth—

But that was next year, and this was now, Clay reminded himself, with a sigh. He assessed the sky again, then whistled, low, for Outlaw.

The horse trotted over, reins dangling, and Clay gathered them and swung up into the saddle.

"We've got our work cut out for us," he told the animal.

The snow began coming down, slowly at first and then in earnest, when they were still about a mile outside of town, and by the time he and Outlaw reached the livery, it was hard to see farther than a dozen feet in any direction.

Zeb Dooley, the old man who ran the stable and adjoining blacksmith's shop, came out to meet him. Taking Outlaw's reins as soon as Clay had stepped down from the saddle, Zeb shouted to be heard over the rising screech of the wind. "Best head on over to the jailhouse or the Bitter Gulch, Marshal, because this blow is bound to get worse before it gets better!"

Clay took the reins back. "I want to look in over at the schoolhouse," he called in reply. "Make sure the children are all right."

Zeb, clad for the cold in dungarees and a heavy coat, shook his balding head. "Miss Krenshaw will keep them there 'til it's safe to leave. The town makes sure there's always a stash of firewood and grub, in case they need it."

Clay's worries were only partially allayed by Zeb's reassurance. A storm like this sure as hell meant trouble for *somebody*, and he didn't feel right about heading for the jailhouse to hunker down with Chester and wait it out, not just yet, anyway.

Clay turned away, mounted up again, bent low over Outlaw's neck to speak to him and started for the far edge of town.

He rode slowly, Outlaw stalwartly shouldering his way through the thickening snow, up one street and down another, until he'd covered all of them. Nobody called out to him as he passed, and lantern light glowed in most of the windows so, after half an hour, he and the horse felt their way back to the livery.

There was no sign of Zeb, and the big double doors of the stables were latched and rattling under the assault of the wind.

Clay opened them, led Outlaw inside and into his stall, gave him hay and made sure his water trough was full. Then he retraced his steps, latched the doors again and walked, wind-battered, toward the jailhouse.

CHAPTER FIVE

DARA ROSE RUBBED the glass in the door of the mercantile with one gloved hand, clearing a circle to look through and seeing nothing but dizzying flurries of angry white. She'd come here to mail her letter to Piper and send off the coupon to the Wildflower Salve Company, and now she wished she hadn't been in such a hurry to leave home.

Mr. Bickham doubled as Blue River's postmaster. Being in a position to know who wrote to whom, and who received letters from whom, he tended to mind everybody's business but his own.

"You might just as well sit down here by the stove as try to see any farther than the end of your nose in weather like this," Philo counseled, from behind his long counter. "That's about the tenth time you wiped off that window, and it just keeps fogging up again."

Dara Rose bit her lower lip, still fretful. She and Harriet were safe and warm, but what about Edrina? Suppose she tried to walk home from school in this storm? Miss Krenshaw could be depended upon to keep her students inside, of course, but Edrina was, as recent history proved, well able to get past her teacher when she chose.

Harriet, who considered the whole thing a marvelous lark, sat on top of a pickle barrel and gazed raptly at the exquisite doll in the display window. Dara Rose, noting this, felt another pinch to the heart.

She had the ten dollars Piper had sent; she could buy the doll for Harriet and several books for Edrina, set it all out for them after they went to bed on Christmas Eve, to find in the morning and rejoice over. But both children still needed warm coats, and sturdy shoes that fit properly, and for all the vegetables she'd stored in the root cellar and the chickens producing fresh eggs right along—until this morning, that was—there was barely enough food to see them through the winter.

This year, with Parnell gone and even the roof over their heads a precarious blessing, there would be no store-bought presents, no brightly decorated tree, no goose or turkey for Christmas dinner.

"I could let you have that doll for two dollars even," Philo whispered, suddenly standing beside Dara Rose and startling her half out of her skin. Because of the thick layers of sawdust covering the floor, she hadn't heard him approach. "Put a dollar down, and you can pay the rest over time, out of the egg money."

Dara Rose looked at him sharply, momentarily distracted from her worry over Edrina, who might at any moment take it into her head to strike out for home, blizzard or no blizzard, perhaps concerned about her mother and sister and the chickens.

That would be like Edrina.

"No, Mr. Bickham," Dara Rose whispered back,

while Harriet paid neither one of them a whit of notice, "I will not be purchasing the doll, and that's final."

"But look at your little girl," the storekeeper cajoled. "She wants that pretty thing in the worst way."

Dara Rose's cheeks throbbed, and her throat thickened. It was only by the sternest exercise of self-control that she did not burst into tears. "I can barely afford to give my children what they *need*," she told him pointedly, though in a very quiet voice. "What they *want* is out of the question just now. Please do not press the matter further."

Philo gave a deep sigh and, at the same moment, the door Dara Rose had been standing next to only moments before burst open on a gust of wind.

Snow blew in, along with a swift and bitter chill, and then Clay McKettrick stepped over the threshold, accompanied by a medium-size dog, coated in white. Even for a strong man like he was, shutting that door again was an effort.

Dara Rose stood looking at the marshal and the dog, feeling oddly stricken, a state this man seemed to inflict upon her at every encounter. *She* might have been the one braving the frigid weather outside, instead of Clay, the way her breath stalled in the back of her throat.

With a smile, Clay took off his hat, dusting off the snow with his other hand, and nodded. "Afternoon, Mrs. Nolan," he said.

His voice was deep and quiet, his manner unhurried.

Dara Rose didn't answer, merely inclined her head briefly in response.

Harriet, meanwhile, forgot the doll she'd been so fascinated by until now, leaped nimbly off the pickle barrel and slowly approached the newcomers.

"Does that dog bite?" she asked forthrightly, studying the animal closely before tilting her head back to look up at Clay.

"I can't rightly say, one way or the other," Clay replied honestly. "He and I just took up with each other last night, so we're not all that well acquainted yet. Offhand, though, I'd say you oughtn't to pet old Chester until we know a little more about his nature."

Harriet smiled, enchanted. "Hullo, Chester," she said.

Chester looked her over, but stayed close to Clay's side.

"I don't normally allow dogs in my store," Philo said. Then, with a smile and a genial spreading of his hands, "But I'll make an exception for you, Marshal."

"I'm obliged," Clay said. "It's a fair hike back to the jailhouse and I'd rather not leave him alone there, anyhow."

Dara Rose opened her mouth, closed it again. When it came to Clay McKettrick, she was as bad as Harriet with the doll, prone to ogle and be struck dumb with awe.

As if to prove himself a gentleman, Chester ambled away from Clay to nestle down in the warm sawdust in front of the stove. With a sigh of grateful contentment, the dog closed his eyes and went to sleep.

Harriet giggled. "He must be tired," she said.

"I reckon he is at that," Clay agreed. "I think old Chester traveled a hard road before he found his way to me."

Dara Rose had never envied a dog before, but she did in that moment. She'd traveled a hard road, too, she and the girls, but it hadn't led to a handsome, steady-minded man who was probably able to handle just about anything.

She cleared her throat, fixing to make another attempt at speaking, but before a word came to her, Harriet had reached out and taken Clay's hand, tugging him in the direction of the display window.

"Look," she said reverently, pointing at the doll.

Dara Rose finally found her voice, but it didn't hold up for long. "Harriet—"

Clay lifted the child easily, holding her in one arm, so she was at eye level with the splendid toy.

"Isn't she pretty?" Harriet murmured, wonderstruck again.

"Not as pretty as you are," Clay told her. His gaze sought Dara Rose, found her, and brought yet another embarrassing blush to her cheeks. His expression was solemn, as if he wanted to ask some question but knew it would be improper to do so.

"If I sold my hair for two dollars and fifty cents," Harriet prattled on, wide-eyed, seemingly as at home in Clay's arms as she would have been in Parnell's, "I could take her home with me for good. Do you know of a place where folks buy hair?"

Dara Rose closed her eyes briefly, mortified.

"Can't say as I do," Clay replied affably. He was still looking at Dara Rose, though; she could feel it.

She opened her eyes, watched, tongue-tied with misery, as he gently set Harriet back on her feet.

"I'd name her Florence," Harriet continued. "Don't you think that's a pretty name? Florence?"

Clay allowed as how it was a very nice name.

Dara Rose realized she was staring and looked quickly away, only to have her gaze collide with Mr. Bickham's. A benevolent smirk wreathed the storekeeper's round face.

"Looks like the snow's letting up a little," Bickham said, with a glance at the window. "Maybe the marshal and his dog here could see you and little Harriet home safe while there's a lull."

Dara Rose needed to get back to her place, in case Edrina was there or on her way, but it wouldn't be wise for her and Harriet to attempt the journey, however short, on their own. So she swallowed her pride and turned back to Clay. "Would you mind?" she asked.

Clay cleared his throat before answering, but his words still came out sounding husky. "No, ma'am," he said, almost shyly. "I wouldn't mind."

So Dara Rose bundled Harriet up as warmly as she could, and then herself, and Clay lifted Harriet up again, simultaneously whistling for the dog.

Chester got up immediately, ready to go.

"You give some thought to what I said, Miz Nolan," Philo shouted after her, as she followed Clay out into the waning snowstorm. "Ain't no shame in buying on credit!"

Dara Rose ignored him.

The snow, having fallen hard and fast all morning, was nearly knee-deep and powdery. Clay and the dog seemed to navigate it with relative ease, Chester moving in a hopping way that might have been comical under more ordinary circumstances, and Dara Rose picked her way along in the tracks of the marshal's boots.

Harriet, snug against Clay's chest, with the front of his coat around her, looked back over his shoulder at Dara Rose, her eyes merry with adventure. The child was clearly reveling in *Mr. McKettrick's* attention—it was imprudent to think of him as "Clay," Dara Rose had decided—and no doubt pretending she had a papa again.

The thought made Dara Rose's throat ache like one big bruise, and her eyes scalded. She was glad Mr. McKettrick couldn't see her face.

They trooped on, Clay forging a way for all of them when the dog grew tired, and the snow was thickening again by the time they reached the house. The respite, it seemed, was nearly over.

The air was shiver-cold, and Chester needed to rest. Even though Dara Rose was mildly alarmed by the thought of the new marshal filling her house with his purely masculine presence, she had no choice but to ask him in.

There was no sign of Edrina, which was both a relief and a worry to Dara Rose. Once she had her elder daughter at home, safe and sound, she'd move on to the other concerns—how the chickens were faring, for a start, and the state of the woodpile stacked against the back of the house. Thanks to the town council, there was a good supply of firewood, but some of it would need drying out before it could be burned.

Clay—*Mr. McKettrick* suddenly seemed too unwieldy even in her thoughts—walked straight through to the kitchen, set Harriet on her feet and went about building up the dwindling fire in the cookstove.

Chester practically collapsed on the rug in front of the sink.

"I'll go on to the schoolhouse," Clay told Dara Rose, when he'd finished at the stove, "and see about bringing Edrina home. It would be a favor to me, Mrs. Nolan, if you'd let my dog stay here while I'm gone, since he's probably too tuckered out to go much farther."

This time, Dara Rose welcomed the heat that surged through her, pulsing in her face. They weren't without their blessings, she and the children. "Of course," she said awkwardly. "Harriet and I will look after Chester. And I don't mind admitting I'm worried that Edrina might try to make her way home on her own."

Clay nodded, grinned a little. "She might, at that," he said.

That grin *did* something to Dara Rose. She told herself it was simple thankfulness. She needed help, and someone was there to give it and that was that.

"What about the other children?" she asked, as Clay started for the back door.

"If any of them are stranded at the schoolhouse," he answered, his hand on the knob, "I'll make sure they get where they're supposed to go—after I bring your girl home, that is." He turned toward Harriet, who was now on her knees next to Chester, all concern for his temperament evidently past, drying off his coat with a flour-sack dish towel, and tugged at the brim of his hat. "Thank you for minding my friend, there," he told the child. "Looks as though he likes you."

Harriet beamed. "I *knew* he wouldn't bite me," she said.

Clay smiled briefly then, opened the door, leaned into the wind that rushed to meet him and stepped outside. The door closed behind him.

CLAY FOUND HIS way to the schoolhouse more from memory than by use of his eyesight, and Miss Krenshaw met him at the door, took him firmly by the arm and pulled him inside, out of the cold and the wind and the blinding assault of the snow.

Except for Edrina, who was huddled close to the stove and bundled inside a faded quilt, the schoolmarm was alone. Evidently, the other kids had already been collected by kinfolks and taken home.

Edrina smiled at him. "I knew you'd come to fetch me, if Mama didn't," she said, with a certainty that warmed his heart.

"Sit down, Marshal," Miss Krenshaw all but commanded, indicating her desk chair, which was the only one in the schoolroom big enough for an adult. "I've got some coffee brewing in back."

Clay didn't plan to tarry long, since the storm was more likely to get worse than it was to get better, and he wanted to get Edrina back to her mother and sister while the getting was good. But hot coffee sounded mighty nice to him just then, and he wouldn't mind sitting for a few minutes, either. He was still a young man, and fit, but that cold made his bones ache.

"Thank you," he said, and took the offered chair.

Miss Krenshaw disappeared into the back, where she

probably had private quarters, and returned promptly
with the promised coffee.

"Thanks," Clay repeated, taking the steaming mug
from her hand.

Not one to be idle, it would seem, Miss Alvira got
busy erasing the day's lessons off the blackboard.

"You'll be all right here, on your own?" Clay asked
presently, restored by the tasty brew. Miss Alvira had
laced it with whiskey, which raised her a notch in his
already high estimation. Too bad he couldn't work up
an interest in courting the lady.

"I'll be just fine," Miss Alvira said, still busy. She
sounded a mite affronted by the question, in fact. "I
have everything I need, right here."

Edrina, still seated by the stove, took in the conversation, but offered no comment. She did look somewhat
pensive, though, and Clay wondered briefly what was
going through that busy little brain of hers.

He finished the coffee, got to his feet, glanced at one
of the windows.

There was no letup to the snow, as far as he could tell.

Miss Alvira marched into the cloakroom, came out
with Edrina's coat and bonnet and briskly prepared
the child for the journey home. For good measure, she
wrapped the quilt around Edrina again, too.

"There," she said, with a slight smile.

Clay put his hat back on—he'd left it on a peg next
to the door, coming in—and hoisted Edrina, quilt and
all, into his arms. As he'd done with Harriet, leaving the
mercantile, he tried to cover her with his coat, as well.

"You're sure there's nowhere you'd like to go?" he asked Miss Alvira, before opening the door. "To the hotel, maybe? There're bound to be some folks around, and I could walk you over—"

The schoolmarm gave a little sniff and hiked up her chin again. "Marshal," she said, putting a point on the word, "as I've already told you, I am quite capable of looking after myself, and besides, I wouldn't think of spending good money on a hotel room."

"All right, then," Clay said, with a slight smile and a nod of farewell.

He followed his own quickly disappearing boot prints back to Dara Rose's front door, shoulders braced against the wind, his arms tight around the little girl tucked in the folds of that old quilt.

A lamp burned in the center of Dara Rose's kitchen table, and the house was not only blessedly warm, but there was something savory simmering on the stove.

Her face lit up at their return, and even though Clay knew most of that joy was for Edrina, he basked in the welcome, anyway. And Chester was just about beside himself, he was so happy to see Clay.

"You'll stay for supper," Dara Rose informed Clay briskly, once he'd set Edrina down, and then she commenced to unwinding that now-damp quilt from around the little girl.

Clay just stood there for a long moment, in his snowy duster and his wet hat, waiting for his bones and sinews to thaw and just enjoying the sight of her. Dara Rose's aquamarine eyes were bright and her cheeks flushed, probably from the heat of the stove and happiness because Edrina was home.

"All right," he said, finally realizing that her statement called for some kind of response, however mundane. "Whatever you're cooking, it smells good."

She smiled at him, briefly, distractedly, and all but set him back on his heels by the doing of it.

"Edrina, you go in and change into dry clothes," she told the child.

Edrina hesitated, then left the room. Harriet, after trying in vain to get Chester to come along on the jaunt, followed her sister, chattering about the walk home from the mercantile.

It was a heady thing, being alone with Dara Rose in that steamy little room.

And Clay, a quiet man but not a shy one, couldn't come up with a single thing to say.

Dara Rose tightened the bands on her apron, a reach-back motion that made her shapely bosom rise and jut out a little. "If the chickens survive this," she said, with an anxious glance toward the room's one opaque window, "it will be a miracle, and I sure hope some of the men in town give a thought to the O'Reillys, like they generally do at times like this…"

Her voice fell away, and she gnawed fretfully at her lower lip, likely pondering the fate of the poultry, the family she'd just mentioned, or both.

"The O'Reillys?" Clay croaked out, grabbing hold of the rapidly sinking conversational lifeline with the first thing that jumped off his tongue.

Dara Rose sighed again, turned away from him to

stir whatever was cooking in that pot. The scent of it made his stomach rumble, and it came to him that, except for Miss Krenshaw's whiskeyed-up coffee, he hadn't had anything since breakfast.

"Peg O'Reilly's no-good excuse for a husband," she said quietly, after a glance in the direction of the doorway the little girls had hurried through earlier, "ran off with some…some…*woman* he met at the Bitter Gulch Saloon, and left a wife and three children behind to fend for themselves!"

For a moment, Clay was taken aback—not by the story, which unfortunately was not an uncommon one, especially with the war in Europe picking up momentum—but by Dara Rose's apparent failure to draw any correlation between Mrs. O'Reilly's situation and her own. Except for one obvious variable—Parnell had had the bad fortune to die, while the long-gone Mr. O'Reilly was presumably still alive--the two women had essentially been dealt the same bad hand of cards.

Dara Rose seemed to sense that he was looking at her, and she turned to meet his gaze, colored up again and looked quickly away. The girls returned to the kitchen just then, before anything more could be said, Harriet going on about that doll she meant to name Florence, and Edrina replying in lofty, big-sister fashion that Harriet ought to wish in one hand and spit in the other and see which one got full faster.

Clay went to the sink, rolled up his shirtsleeves and commenced to washing his hands with the harsh yellow soap Dara Rose kept in an old saucer wedged behind the pump handle.

He felt a combination of things while he was at it, but mainly, he realized, he was glad. Glad just to be where he was, right there in that kitchen, out of the cold wind, with a lovely woman, two kids and a dog for company.

For the first time since he'd left Arizona, Clay didn't have to fight down a hankering for home, didn't second-guess his decision to strike out on his own instead of making a life on the ever-expanding Triple M with the rest of the family.

Be sure you're leaving because it's what you really want to do, Clay, his pa had counseled him, *and not because Annabel Carson broke your heart.*

It made Clay smile a little to remember that conversation, and others like it, with various members of the home outfit, and he reckoned now that Annabel hadn't broken his heart at all—she'd just sprained it a little.

The stuff in the pot on the stove turned out to be some kind of mixture of canned venison and leftover vegetable preserves, and it was better, in Clay's opinion, than a big steak at Delmonico's.

"Miss Krenshaw keeps a picture of a soldier in her top desk drawer," Edrina chimed, in the middle of the meal, pretty much out of nowhere.

Snow rasped at the windows and the small cookstove seemed to strain to put out more heat.

"And how would you know a thing like that, Edrina Nolan?" Dara Rose asked, arching one eyebrow, her spoon poised halfway between her mouth and the bowl of soup sitting in front of her.

"She takes it out and looks at it, when she thinks nobody's looking," Edrina explained nonchalantly. "Sometimes, she gets tears in her eyes, and her lips move like she's talking to somebody."

Clay's gaze connected with Dara Rose's.

"Are you going to fight in the war, Mr. McKettrick?" Edrina asked, without missing a beat.

"No," Clay answered. The armed forces would need beef, and plenty of it, and like his granddad said, somebody had to raise the critters. "But my cousin Gabriel thinks he might join up, if things don't simmer down some over the next year or two."

A sad expression flickered across Dara Rose's expressive face; he figured the war was a subject she tried not to think about, since there was nothing she could do to change it.

After supper, Edrina and Harriet cleared the table and set the dishes in the sink, without being told.

Dara Rose crossed the room to take her cloak and bonnet down from their peg near the door. She clearly dreaded whatever she was about to do, and Clay found himself beside her before he'd made a conscious decision to move, reaching for his hat and duster.

Dara Rose looked up at him, and he caught the briefest glimpse into the shimmering vastness of her heart and mind and spirit. There was so much more to her than just her flesh-and-blood person, he realized, with a start akin to waking up suddenly after a long, deep sleep.

"The chickens—" she began, and then went silent.

"I'll see to them," Clay said, very quietly. "You stay here, with the girls."

She considered the idea briefly, then shook her head no. She meant to go out to that chicken coop and that was that. He'd be wasting his breath to argue.

"I'll heat water to wash the dishes when I get back," she told the children. "Don't get too close to the stove, and no scuffling."

"Oh, Mama," Edrina said, with a roll of her eyes. "You've told us that a *thousand times* already."

A smile quirked at one corner of Dara Rose's mouth. Like the rest of her, visible and invisible, that mouth fascinated Clay out of all good sense and reason. "Well," she said, "now it's a thousand and *one*."

After a glance at Clay's face, she opened the door and stepped right out into that blizzard.

Clay followed, and the wind was so strong that it buffeted her back a step, so they collided, her back to his torso. He put his arms out to steady her, and a powerful jolt of...*something*...shot through him.

Since it was too cold to dally, they recovered quickly and advanced toward the rickety coop.

The chickens had taken refuge inside and, with the exception of the rooster, who squawked indignantly as he paced the floor of that shed, as though fussing over the pure injustice of a snowstorm, the birds huddled close to one another on the length of wood that served as a roost.

There was a visible easing in Dara Rose as she looked around. "At least none of them have frozen to death," she said, and she might have been addressing herself, not him, trundling over to lift the lid off a wooden bend and lean inside to scoop out feed. Judging by how *far* she had to lean—Lordy, she had a shapely backside—the supply was starting to run low.

Like a lot of other things in her life, probably.

Clay watched, offering no comment, as Dara Rose filled a shallow pan with feed and set it out for the hens to peck at. That done, she picked up a second pan, went to the doorway and shoveled up some snow. The stuff was already melting around the edges, cold as that chicken coop was, when Dara Rose waded back into the center of the noisy flock to set the second pan down beside the first.

They fought their way back to the house, side by side, heads down, shoulders braced. Clay wanted to put an arm around Dara Rose's waist, so she wouldn't fall or blow away, but every instinct warned against it.

The woman had a right to her pride, probably needed it just to press on from one day to the next.

By the time they got back inside the house, the girls had left the kitchen for the front room.

Their voices carried, a happy sound, like the chiming of bells somewhere off in the muffled distance.

Dara Rose moved to untie her bonnet laces, but Clay closed his hands over hers. "You've done a fine job raising those girls of yours," he said, though he hadn't actually planned the words ahead of time.

Those wonderful eyes of hers searched his face, almost warily. Then she smiled and went on to take off her bonnet, Clay's hands falling away from hers and back to his sides.

"Thank you, Mr. McKettrick," she said, stepping back to shed her snow-speckled cloak.

"Clay," he said, knowing she wanted him to step aside so she could get on with whatever it was she planned to do next but stubbornly holding his ground. "I don't generally answer to 'Mr. McKettrick,' as it happens. Usually, when folks use that moniker, they're talking to my granddad."

She blushed, but her eyes flashed. "When I say it," she told him, "I'm addressing *you*. We haven't known each other long enough to use first names."

He chuckled at that. Curved his finger sideways under her chin and lifted. "Have it your way... Dara Rose," he said, partly to get under her hide and partly because he just liked saying her name.

Still wearing his coat and hat, he summoned the dog with a soft whistle.

Edrina and Harriet immediately appeared in the inside doorway, squashed together as though there was barely enough room in the gap to contain both of them. Their eyes were wide with curiosity and something else—maybe worry.

"You're going?" Edrina asked.

"And taking Chester?" Harriet added.

Clay touched the brim of his hat, momentarily ignoring Dara Rose, who was probably still prickly over his impertinent use of her Christian name. "Yep," he said. "Chester and I ought to be getting over to the jailhouse, in case somebody comes looking for us."

"But it's getting dark," Edrina protested.

"And it's still snowing *really hard*," Harriet said. "What if you and Chester get lost?"

"We'll find our way," Clay promised, his voice a little huskier than normal. "Don't you worry about us."

Dara Rose surprised him by laying a hand on his arm. "Take the lantern," she said.

Clay was moved by the offer, but he didn't let it show, of course. He just shook his head and smiled a little. "It wouldn't do much good, hard as the wind's blowing," he said. "But I thank you kindly, just the same. And thanks for supper, too, and a right pleasant evening."

Dara Rose opened her mouth, closed it again and then sighed. "Be careful," she said.

"I will certainly do that, ma'am," he answered.

The winter night bit into him like teeth when he moved out into it, Chester struggling along at his side.

Before they got as far as the gate, the dog was practically sinking out of sight with every cautious step, so Clay picked him up, carrying him in the curve of his right arm.

With his free hand, Clay pulled his hat brim down low over his eyes and blinked a couple of times, until he could see. If it weren't for thin snatches of lamplight, spilling from various windows along the way, he and Chester might have been in some trouble.

As it was, Clay was half-frozen by the time he fumbled with the latch on his office door, stepped over the threshold and set the dog down to feel along the wall for the metal box that held the matches for the stove and the lanterns.

Chester gave a low growl as Clay struck the match. There was a shuffling clatter over by the desk, followed by the sound of boot soles striking the plank floor and a grumbled curse.

"Damn it, Clay," growled his cousin Sawyer, "you oughtn't to sneak up on a man like that, especially when he's sleeping."

CHAPTER SIX

"I THOUGHT IT didn't snow in Texas," Sawyer said, after stretching and letting go with a lusty yawn.

Clay patted the dog, reassured him with a few quiet words and lit one of the two lanterns he had on hand. "What are you doing here, Sawyer?" he countered gruffly.

"I *was* catching up on my shut-eye," Sawyer replied affably, grinning that cocky grin that sometimes made Clay want to backhand his cousin, "until you came banging through the door and disturbed me."

Clay lit the other lantern, the one that stood on the bookcase, and then went to the stove to build up the fire. The last time he'd seen his cousin and one-time best friend, they'd had words, not just about Annabel, but about a few other things, too.

"You're a long way from home, cousin," Clay finally remarked.

"So are you," Sawyer answered, perching on the edge of Clay's desk now, with his arms folded. The youngest son of Clay's uncle Kade and aunt Mandy, Sawyer had the fair hair and dark blue eyes that ran in intergenerational streaks through the McKettrick bloodline.

Clay shut the stove door with a clang and rustled up some leftovers for Chester, who seemed to have decided that the surprise visitor made acceptable company.

Which just went to show what a dog knew about anything, Clay thought glumly. Most of them liked everybody, and Chester was no exception.

"I'm going to ask you once more," Clay said evenly, "*just once*, what you're doing here, and if I don't get a clear answer, I swear I'll toss you behind bars on a trespassing charge."

Sawyer chuckled. "I'm just passing through," he said. "Since I was in your neck of the woods, I decided to board my horse in San Antonio and take the train to Blue River, see how you're faring and all."

"I'm faring just fine," Clay responded, "so you can get on tomorrow's train, if it makes it through, and go right back to San Antonio."

Sawyer strolled to the window, in no evident hurry to get there. He had the born horseman's rolling, easy stride. "Good thing I didn't bring the horse," he said, as though Clay hadn't as good as told him, straight out, that he wasn't welcome. "We'd probably be out there in the blizzard someplace, freezing to death." A visible shudder moved through his lean, agile form, but he didn't turn around. "Like I said, nothing anybody ever told me about Texas prepared me for ass-deep snow."

Clay ladled water into the coffeepot, a dented metal receptacle coated with blue enamel, and set it on top of the potbellied stove. Then he commenced to spoon ground coffee beans into it, along with a pinch of salt to makc the grounds settle after the stuff brewed. "That's the thing about weather," he said, at considerable length. "It's unpredictable."

Sawyer finally turned around, but he lingered at the window, frost-coated and all but opaque behind him. "Annabel Carson got married soon after you left," he said, gruffly and with care.

"Not to you, it appears," Clay said, turning his back to the stove and absorbing the heat.

Sawyer made a sound that might have been a chuckle, though it contained no noticeable amusement. "Not to me," he confirmed. "She got hitched to Whit Taggard, over near Stone Creek. You know, that banker in his fifties, with more money than one man ever ought to have? She swears it's a love match."

"You came all the way to Blue River to tell me that?" Clay asked, strangely unmoved by news that probably would have devastated him not so long ago. Chester had finished his meal of leftovers from the hotel dining room and gone to curl up on his blanket. The wind howled and hissed under the eaves, as if it were fixing to raise the roof right off that old jailhouse and carry it next door, if not farther.

"No," Sawyer said. "I came all the way to Blue River because your mama's been worried about you, and I love my aunt Chloe."

Clay sighed. "I already sent Ma and Pa a wire," he said, mildly exasperated. "They know I'm fine."

"Your saying it and their knowing it for sure are two different things, Clay," Sawyer went on, his tone reasonable and quiet, as if he were calming a jittery horse or a cow mired in deep mud and struggling against the ropes meant to pull it onto dry ground. "It's not every day a man picks up and leaves the place and the people he's known all his life."

Clay had no answer for that, had already done all the explaining he ever intended to do, where the decision to put home behind him for good—at least as far as living there—was concerned, anyhow. Much as he loved his granddad and his pa and his uncles, he didn't want to spend the rest of his life taking orders from them. He wanted to build and run his own outfit, marry and have sons and daughters, grandchildren and great-grandchildren.

"You hungry?" Clay asked, hoping to get the conversation going in another direction.

"I had fried chicken over at the hotel, soon as I'd checked in and stowed my gear," Sawyer answered, with a shake of his head. He looked around at the humble quarters Clay presently called home, sighed. "Nobody can accuse you of living high on the hog, I reckon," he finished, sounding weary now.

Clay shoved a hand through his hair, recalling the difficult trek back from Dara Rose's place. It had taken him and Chester the better part of half an hour to cover the five hundred yards or so between the jail and that snug little house.

Once he'd warmed up, had some coffee and put on long johns and an extra layer of clothes, he meant to venture out again, track down that family Dara Rose had mentioned—the O'Reillys—and see for himself that they were warm and had something to eat. He figured it was his duty, as marshal, to see that folks made it through when there was an emergency like that snowstorm, especially women and children.

"Finding your way back to the hotel in this blizzard might be tricky," Clay told his cousin, in his own good time. "You can bunk in the cell there if you want."

One side of Sawyer's mouth quirked upward in a grin. "And give you a prime opportunity to lock me up, soon as I shut my eyes, and then drop the key down a deep well? Not likely, cousin."

"You sorely overestimate my ability to tolerate your company," Clay responded dryly. "The sooner you're on your way, the happier I'm going to be."

Sawyer didn't reply right away, which was a telling thing, because he was usually quick to shoot off his mouth. There *was* a whole other side to Sawyer, though—one nobody, including Clay, really knew much about.

"You must know I never laid a hand on your girl, Clay," Sawyer said, as a chunk of wood crackled and splintered to embers inside the stove. "So what exactly is it about me that sticks in your craw? We used to be as close as brothers."

Too warm now that he'd been standing near the stove for a while, Clay moved on to his desk, reclaimed the creaky wooden chair, sat back in it with his hands cupped behind his head. Chester, lying nearby on his blanket pile, gave a single, chortling snore, and another piece of wood collapsed in the fire, with a series of sharp snaps.

"You come here," Clay answered presently, "uninvited, I might add, and let on that I'm a grief to the family, like some prodigal son off squandering his birthright in a far country, and then you have the gall to ask what sticks in my craw? It's the hypocrisy of it. *You're a gunslinger*, Sawyer, a hired gun. Little better than an outlaw, most likely. It might even be that if I went through all these wanted posters on my desk, I'd come across a fair likeness of your face."

"I'm not an outlaw," Sawyer said flatly. "You know that."

"Do I?" Clay asked. "You blow through the Triple M every few years like a breeze—just long enough last time to turn my girl's head—and then, one fine day, a telegram comes in, and you're gone again, without a word to anybody. Like you know somebody's picked up your trail so you'd better be moving on, pronto."

Sawyer sighed again, and it came out raspy. "I don't reckon anything I say is going to get through that inch-thick layer of bone you call a skull," he said. "You made up your mind about me a long time ago, didn't you, cousin?"

There was no denying that. "I reckon I did," Clay replied quietly, feeling wrung out. "You can tell Ma and the rest of the family that you've seen me and I'm fine. Seems to me that your business here is finished."

Even as he spoke those words, Clay wondered what the *real* reason for Sawyer's visit might be. Blue River was too far out of his cousin's way for this to be about Annabel, or a favor to Clay's ma and pa.

Sawyer crossed to the door, took his hat and canvas

duster down from their pegs and put them on. Then he hesitated, one hand on the old-fashioned iron latch. "You're right," he said, with more sadness than Clay had heard in his voice since they were ten years old and Sawyer's dog took sick and died. "I guess there's no getting back on your good side. I'll be on tomorrow's train, if it gets here, and you can get on with whatever the hell it is you think you're doing."

With that, Sawyer opened the door and went out, letting in a blast of snow-speckled cold that reached into the deepest parts of Clay and held on.

He almost relented, almost called Sawyer back—but in the end, he figured it was best to let him go.

THE SNOW LAY like a thick, glittering mantle over the countryside when Dara Rose went out to feed the chickens, carrying the egg basket and a jug to refill their water pan, but the sky was the purest blue, cloudless and benign. As quickly as it had arisen, the storm was over; water dripped rhythmically from the edges of the roof, and the path to the henhouse was slushy under the soles of her high-button shoes.

Hope stirred, springlike, in Dara Rose's heart, as she crossed the yard. She could hear the chickens clucking away in the coop, wanting their breakfast and their liberty from a long night of confinement.

Using the side of her foot, Dara Rose cleared a patch of ground for the birds and let them out while she ducked inside to fetch the water pan. Pleased to see that every member of her little flock had survived, she scattered their feed and then went on to collect the eggs.

There were six—a better count than the day before, though still less than she'd hoped for—and Dara Rose set each one carefully in the basket and returned to the house.

Edrina and Harriet were up and dressed, Edrina full of glee because she didn't have to go to school that day, and Harriet equally happy to have a playmate.

Dara Rose took off her bonnet and cloak, hung them up, washed her hands at the pump in the sink and put a pot of water on to boil, for oatmeal.

In the middle of the meal, a knock sounded at the front door.

Frowning, wondering who would be out and about so early, with the snow still deep enough to make traveling through it a trial, she pushed back her chair, told the children to finish eating and behave themselves and hurried through the small parlor. On some level, she realized, she'd hoped to find Clay McKettrick standing on her tiny porch, but this only came to her when she saw Mayor Wilson Ponder there instead.

Through the glass oval in the door, the older man's face looked purposeful, and a little grim.

Dara Rose opened the door. "Mayor Ponder," she said, not bothering to hide her surprise. He'd arrived, she saw now, looking past him to the street, in a sleigh drawn by two sturdy mules. "Come in."

"I won't tarry," Ponder said gravely, with a distracted tug at the brim of his bowler hat. He remained where he was, forcing Dara Rose to stand in the bright cold of the doorway and wait to hear what business he had with her. "I know this isn't a convenient time, what with the blizzard and all, but frankly, I'm not comfortable putting the task off any longer." He reddened slightly, though that might have been because of the weather, and not any sense of chagrin, and his muttonchop whiskers wobbled as he prepared to go on. "The town purchased this house for the use of the marshal, Mrs. Nolan, and if Clay McKettrick doesn't mean to use the place, well, we—the town council, that is—would prefer to sell it."

Dara Rose felt the floor shift under her feet, but she kept her shoulders squared and even managed not to shiver at the cold, and the news the mayor had just delivered.

"Oh," she said, hugging herself and wishing for her cloak, wishing for summer and better times. "Do you have a prospective buyer?"

"Ezra Maddox wants the property," Mayor Ponder said, after more whisker-wriggling. "He's offering two hundred and fifty dollars cash money and, what with bringing in electricity, the town could use the funds."

Ezra Maddox owned a farm, Dara Rose thought, dazed and frustrated and quite cornered. What did the man want with a run-down house miles from his crops and his dairy cows?

By now, everyone knew Clay had decided to live over at the jailhouse. Could it be that Mr. Maddox was simply trying to force her hand by buying the house out from under her? Was he hoping she would give in and accept his offer of a so-called housekeeping job, possibly followed by marriage, and send her children away in the bargain?

Dara Rose seethed, even as cold terror overtook her.

"How long until we have to move?" she asked, amazed at how calm she sounded.

Mayor Ponder hesitated before he answered, perhaps ashamed of that morning's mission. On the other hand, he'd gone to all the bother of hitching mules to a sleigh to get there bright and early, which did not indicate any real degree of reluctance on his part. "Ezra's mighty anxious to take possession of the place," he finally said. "But since Christmas is just two weeks away, well, he's—*we're*—willing to let you stay until the first of the year."

Dara Rose gripped the door frame with one hand, thinking she might actually swoon. Behind her, in the kitchen, the girls' voices rang like chimes as they conducted some merry disagreement, laced with giggles.

"Well, then," Dara Rose managed, meeting the mayor's gaze, seeing both sympathy and resolve there, "that's that, isn't it? Thank you for letting me know."

With that, she shut the door in his face.

And stood trembling, there in the small parlor, until she heard his footsteps retreating on the porch.

"Mama?" Harriet, light-footed as ever and half again too perceptive for a five-year-old, was standing directly behind her. "Can we get a dog? Edrina says we don't need another mouth to feed, but a puppy wouldn't eat very much, would it?"

All of Dara Rose's considerable strength gave way then, like a dam under the strain of rising water. She uttered a small, choked sob, shook her head and fled to the bedroom.

Dara Rose seldom cried—even at Parnell's funeral

service, she'd been dry-eyed—but she was only human, after all.

And she'd come to the end of her resources, at least for the moment.

So she sat on the edge of the bed she shared with her daughters—Parnell had slept on the settee in the parlor— covered her face with both hands and wept softly into her palms.

CLAY WAS HAVING breakfast over at the hotel dining room— bacon and eggs and hotcakes, with plenty of hot, fresh coffee—when Sawyer wandered in, looking well-rested and clean-shaven, his manner at once affable and distant.

"Mind if I join you?" he said, pulling back a chair opposite Clay and sitting down before Clay could answer. He picked up the menu and studied it with the same grave concentration their illustrious granddad reserved for government beef contracts.

Politicians and pencil pushers, Angus had been known to remark, on the occasions he did business with such officials. *A man would have to be simpleminded to trust a one of them.*

"Make yourself at home," Clay said, dryly and long after the fact. He hadn't slept much the night before, thanks to Dara Rose and Sawyer's unexpected presence and the long slog through the snow to the O'Reilly place.

He'd found them huddled around a poor fire like characters in a Dickens novel, wrapped in thin blankets. They'd had fried eggs for supper, Mrs. O'Reilly had told him, and those were all gone, and he was welcome to what was left of yesterday's pinto beans if he was hungry.

Clay had thanked her kindly and said he'd already had supper, which happened to be the truth, though he would have lied without a qualm if it hadn't been, and then he'd carried in most of their dwindling wood supply to dry beside the homemade stove. Before coming to the hotel for breakfast that morning, he'd stopped by the mercantile, pounded at the front door until the storekeeper let him in, and purchased a sackful of dried beans, along with flour, sugar, a pound of coffee and assorted canned goods for the O'Reillys. He'd paid extra to have the food delivered before the store was open for business.

Now, sitting across from his pensive cousin in a warm, clean, well-lighted place where good food could be had in plenty, he felt vaguely ashamed of his own prosperity. While the McKettricks didn't live grandly, they didn't lack for money, either. Clay had never missed a meal in his life, never had to go without shoes or wear clothes that had belonged to somebody else first. Unlike the O'Reilly children, and too many others like them, he'd had a strong, committed father, backed up by three uncles and a granddad.

The cook, a round-bellied man who doubled as a waiter, came over to the table to greet Sawyer and take his order.

Sawyer simply pointed toward Clay's plate and said, "That looks good."

The cook nodded and went away.

Sawyer sat there, easy in his hide, dressed like a prosperous gambler. Instead of his usual plain shirt and even plainer denim trousers, he sported a suit, complete with a white shirt, a string tie and a brocade vest. "You look miserable this morning, cousin," he said cheerfully, "but something tells me it isn't remorse over the uncharitable welcome you offered last night."

Clay gave a raw chuckle, void of mirth. His appetite was gone, all of a sudden, and he set down his knife and fork, pushed his plate away. "It definitely isn't remorse," he said.

Sawyer helped himself to a slice of toasted bread and bit into it, chewed appreciatively. Though his eyes twinkled, his voice was serious when he replied, "You could still go back to the Triple M, you know. They'd welcome you back into the fold with open arms and shouts of 'hurrah.'"

"I'll pay them a visit one of these days," he said. "There aren't any hard feelings on my side."

"Nor theirs, either." Sawyer shoved a hand through his unruly dark-gold hair, which was always a little too long. "You're lucky, Clay," he said, his gaze moving to the window next to their table. "Pa and Granddad can't seem to make up their minds whether to kill the fatted calf in my honor or take a horsewhip to me." He frowned, squinted at the foggy glass. "I think somebody's trying to get your attention," he observed.

Clay looked, and there, on the other side of that steamed-up window, was Edrina, practically pressing her nose to the glass. She waved one unmittened hand and retreated a step.

"I'll be damned," Clay muttered, gesturing for the child to come inside.

"Who's the kid?" Sawyer wanted to know.

"Friend of mine," Clay answered, as Edrina scampered toward the entrance to the dining room.

She hurried over to the table, face flushed with cold and purpose, and stood there like a little soldier.

"Mama's crying," she said. "Mama *never* cries."

Clay scraped back his chair, took Edrina's small hands into his own, trying to chafe some warmth into them. "Where's your bonnet?" he fussed, trying to process the idea of Dara Rose in tears. "You aren't wearing any mittens, and your coat is unbuttoned—"

"I was in a *hurry*," Edrina told him, with a little sigh of impatience. She spared Sawyer the briefest glance, then looked back at Clay with a proud plea in her eyes. "You'll come home with me, won't you? Right now? Because Mama is crying and Mama never, *ever* cries."

"Go on," Sawyer said to Clay. "I'll settle up for your breakfast."

Clay got up, retrieved his duster from the back of the chair beside his and his hat from the seat and put them on. "What's the matter with her?" he asked, more worried than he could ever remember being before. "Is she sick?"

Gravely, Edrina took his hand, tugged him in the direction of the door. "I don't know," she said fretfully. "Maybe. But she was fine while we were having our oatmeal. Then Mr. Ponder stopped by, and they talked, and when Harriet asked Mama if we could please get a dog, Mama commenced to blubbering and ran right out of the room."

Outside, the snow was melting under a steadily warming sky, but it was still deep. Clay curved an arm around Edrina's waist, much as he had done with Chester the night before, and set off for Dara Rose's place with long strides.

DARA ROSE MARCHED herself out into the kitchen, pumped cold water into the basin she kept on hand and splashed her face repeatedly while Harriet watched her solemnly from the doorway.

"Are you through crying, Mama?" the child asked, very softly.

Dara Rose felt ashamed. Now she'd upset Edrina and Harriet, and for what? A few moments of self-pity?

"I'm quite through," she said, drying her still-puffy face with a dish towel. "And I haven't the slightest idea what came over me." She hugged Harriet, then frowned, looking around. "Where is Edrina?"

Harriet bit her lower lip, clearly reluctant to answer.

"Harriet?" Dara Rose said, taking her little girl gently but firmly by the shoulders. *"Where is your sister?"*

Harriet's eyes were huge and luminous. "She went to fetch Mr. McKettrick," she finally replied.

Alarm rushed through Dara Rose, and not just because a glance at the row of hooks beside the back door revealed that Edrina had gone off through the deep snow without her bonnet or her mittens. She was just reaching for her own cloak when she heard footsteps on the front porch—boots, stomping off snow.

Clay knocked, but then he came right in, carrying Edrina. His gaze locked with Dara Rose's as he set the little girl down and pulled the door closed behind him.

She'd never seen a man look so worried before, not even when Parnell came to that settlement house in Bangor, Maine, to claim her and the children. They'd been mere babies then, Edrina and Harriet, and memories of their real father, Parnell's younger brother, Luke, soon faded.

"Are you sick?" Clay demanded, in the same tone he might have employed to confront a drunk with disorderly conduct.

Dara Rose wasn't sick, except with mortification. "I'm quite all right," she said, but she didn't sound very convincing, even to herself. She shifted her attention to her elder daughter, letting her know with a look that she was in big trouble. "I apologize for any inconvenience—"

Clay's neck reddened, and his eyes narrowed. "I'd be obliged if you girls would wait in the kitchen," he said, though he never looked away from Dara Rose's face.

Edrina and Harriet, always ready with a protest when *she* made such a request, fled the room like rabbits with a fox on their trail.

"That little girl," Clay said, in a furious whisper, one index finger jabbing in the general direction of the kitchen a few times, "was so worried about you that she braved all that snow to find me and bring me here. So don't think for one minute that you're going to put me off with an apology for any *inconvenience*."

Dara Rose stared at him. "Why are you so angry?"

she finally asked. *And why does it thrill me to see you like this?*

"I'm not angry," Clay rasped out, wrenching off his Wyatt Earp–style hat and flinging it so that it landed on the settee, teetered there and dropped to the floor. "Damn it, Dara Rose, whatever went on here this morning scared your daughter half to death, and since Edrina is the most courageous kid I've ever come across, *I* got scared, too."

The thrill didn't subside, and Dara Rose prayed her feelings didn't show. "I lost my composure for a moment," she confessed, as stiffly proud as a Puritan even as her heart raced and her breath threatened to catch in the back of her throat and never come loose. "Believe me, I regret it. I certainly didn't mean to frighten the children—"

"Well," Clay said, in earnest, "you *did.* And I'm not leaving here until you tell me what Ponder said to you that made you go to pieces the way you did."

Dara Rose swallowed, looked down at the floor. Right or wrong, Clay meant what he said—that much was obvious from his tone and his countenance. He wouldn't be going anywhere until she answered him.

"Dara Rose?" He was standing close to her now, his hands resting lightly on her shoulders. He smelled of fresh air, snow and something woodsy. "Tell me."

She knew she ought to pull away from him, ought to look anywhere but up into his face, but she couldn't manage either response. "Mayor Ponder stopped by to tell me that, since you don't want this house, the town council plans to sell it to Ezra Maddox for two hundred and fifty dollars," she said. It was remarkable how calm she sounded, she thought, when her insides were buzzing like a swarm of bees smoked out of their hive. "We have to be out by the first of the year."

"That son of a—" Clay ground out, before catching himself.

Dara Rose felt tears burning behind her eyes again, and she was determined not to disgrace herself by shedding them. "I have ten dollars," she said, like someone talking in their sleep. "And I've saved some of the egg money. It won't take us far, but it's enough to leave town."

"Where would you go?" Clay immediately asked.

"I don't know," Dara Rose replied honestly. "Somewhere."

"The town isn't going to sell this house," Clay said.

"Of course they are," Dara Rose argued, though not with any spirit.

"I'm the marshal," Clay told her, "and under the terms of our agreement, I'm entitled to living quarters. It just so happens that I've decided I'd rather live here than in the jailhouse."

Dara Rose's jaw dropped, and it took her a moment to recover. A *long* moment. "But we couldn't… Where would the children and I—?"

Clay hooked a finger under her chin. "Right here," he said. "You and Edrina and Harriet could live right here, with me—if you and I were married."

Dara Rose nearly choked. *"Married?"*

"It wouldn't do for us to live under the same roof otherwise," Clay said reasonably.

"But we're nearly total strangers—"

"For now," Clay went on, when her words fell away, "it would be a private arrangement. All business. I won't press you to bed down with me, Dara Rose. This place is too small for such shenanigans, anyhow, with the girls around."

Dara Rose couldn't believe what she was hearing. It was Parnell, all over again. Clay was offering a marriage that *wasn't* a marriage, offering shelter and safety and respectability. But unless she wanted to send her children away and move in with Ezra Maddox, she couldn't afford to refuse.

"Why?" she asked, barely breathing the word. "Why would you want to do this, Clay McKettrick?"

He smiled at her. Tucked a tendril of hair behind her right ear, where it had escaped its pins. "I want a wife," he said, as though that explained everything, instead of raising dozens, if not hundreds, of new questions.

"But you said the marriage wouldn't be real."

"It won't be, at first," Clay told her. Where did he get all that certainty, all that confidence? All that *audacity*? "But maybe, with time…"

"What if nothing changes?" Dara Rose broke in, feeling almost as though she needed to shout to be heard over the thrumming of her heartbeat, though of course she *didn't* shout, because the children would have heard.

"Then there'll be no harm done," Clay said. "We'll have the marriage annulled, I'll set you and the girls up in decent circumstances somewhere far from Blue River, and we'll go our separate ways."

No harm done? He spoke so blithely.

Was the man insane?

Possibly, Dara Rose decided. But he was also an infinitely better bet than Ezra Maddox.

CHAPTER SEVEN

BY THE FOLLOWING MORNING, Sawyer was long gone and the snow had turned to mud so deep that folks had had to lay weathered boards and old doors in the street, just to get from one side to the other without sinking to their knees in the muck. Hardly anybody rode a horse or drove a wagon through town or along the side roads, either, but the sun shone like the herald of an early spring, and the breezes were almost balmy.

Clay considered all this as he stood in his small room at the jailhouse, stooping a little to peer at himself in the cracked shaving mirror fixed to the wall. He'd washed up and shaved, and then shaken out and put on the only suit he'd brought to Blue River—the getup consisted of a black woolen coat fitted at the waist, matching trousers, his best white shirt, starched and pressed for him at the Chinese laundry before he left Indian Rock, a brown brocade vest and a string tie.

He hated ties.

Hated starched shirts, too, for that matter.

He'd worn this suit exactly three times since he bought it—to one wedding and two funerals. Today, it was a wedding—his own—and even though it was his choice to get married, the occasion had its somber aspects, as well.

Up home, the ceremony would have been a community event, like a circus or a tent revival or the Independence Day fireworks, drawing crowds from miles around and working the womenfolk up into a frenzy of sewing and cooking and marking their calendars so they'd know how long the first baby took to show up. The men would complain about having to wear their Sunday duds, sip moonshine from a shared fruit jar out in the orchard behind the church after the "I do's" had been said and lament that another unwitting member of their sex had been roped in and hog-tied.

Clay smiled to think of all that nuptial chaos and was glad he'd managed to escape it, though he felt a twinge of nostalgia, too. He and Dara Rose would be married quietly and sensibly, in a civil ceremony performed by Mayor Ponder at her place, with Edrina and Harriet the only guests. There would be no cake, no photographs, no rings and no wedding night, let alone a honeymoon, because this was an arrangement, a transaction—not a love match.

Which wasn't to say that Clay didn't fully expect to bed Dara Rose when the time came, and if they got a baby started right away, too, so much the better. He figured the actual consummation of their union would probably have to wait until spring, though, when the ranch house was finished and he and Dara Rose had a room to themselves.

Fine as the weather was, spring seemed a long way off when he thought of it in terms of making love to his wife.

Resigned, and leaving his hat behind because it

didn't look right with the suit, Clay bid his dog a temporary farewell—Chester had taken to curling up on the cot inside the jail's one cell whenever he wanted to sleep, which was often—and set out for Dara Rose's little house, following the sidewalk as far as he could and then crossing the street by way of the peculiar system of planks and discarded doors and the beds of old wagons.

Mayor Ponder arrived by the same means, followed single file by a thin woman in very prim garb and one of the town council members—they'd come along to serve as witnesses, Clay supposed. Clutching a copy of the Good Book and a rolled sheet of paper as he minced his way over the swamplike road, Ponder looked none too pleased at the prospect of joining the new marshal and the pretty widow in holy matrimony.

Clay disliked the mayor, mainly because of the remark Ponder had made about not minding if Dara Rose wound up working upstairs at the Bitter Gulch Saloon, but he could tolerate the man long enough to get hitched. The rest of the time, Wilson Ponder was fairly easy to ignore.

"There's still time to change your mind," Ponder boomed out, as if he wanted the whole town to hear, when he and Clay met at Dara Rose's front gate. "Charity is charity, but I think you might be taking it a little too far in this instance."

Charity is charity.

The front door of the house was open, probably to admit as much fresh air as possible before the winter weather returned, and Clay had to unlock his jawbones by an act of will. What if Dara Rose had heard what Ponder said? Or the children?

He didn't respond, but simply glowered at Ponder until the other man cleared his throat and muttered, "Well, let's get on with it, then."

Edrina and Harriet appeared in the doorway, beaming. They had ribbons in their hair, and they were wearing summer dresses, very nearly outgrown and obviously their best.

"Mama looks so pretty in her wedding dress!" Edrina enthused, as Clay moved ahead of the others, stepped onto the porch and immediately swept both children off their feet, one in the curve of each arm.

They giggled at that, and the sound heartened Clay. Reminded him that he'd put on that itchy suit because he was going to a *wedding*, not a funeral.

Behind him, the female witness made a sighlike sound, long-suffering and full of righteous indignation.

Once again, Clay tamped down his temper. He wanted to pin that old biddy's ears back, verbally, anyhow—he'd never struck a woman, a child or an animal, and never intended to, though he'd landed plenty of punches in the faces of his boy cousins growing up—but today was neither the time nor the place to hold forth on what he thought of nasty-natured gossips.

For one thing, he didn't want to spoil the day for Edrina and Harriet. They were clearly overjoyed at the prospect of a wedding, though with Edrina, it was partly about being allowed to miss a few hours of school.

"I'll bet your mama *does* look pretty," Clay agreed,

in belated reply to Edrina's statement. "Almost as pretty as the pair of you, maybe."

That got them both giggling again, and Clay smiled as he set them on their feet.

And then nearly tripped over them when Dara Rose appeared, wearing an ivory silk gown with puffed-out sleeves and lace trim at the cuffs. Her cheeks were pink, her eyes bright with a combination of nervousness and hope, her hair done up in a soft knot at her nape and billowing cloudlike around her face.

The sight of her knocked the wind out of Clay as surely as if he'd been thrown from a horse and landed spread-eagle on hard ground.

Ponder cleared his throat again, and the wedding party assembled itself, with surprising grace, in the middle of that cramped front room.

Dara Rose's trim shoulder bumped Clay's arm as she took her place beside him, and he felt a jolt of sweet fire at her touch.

Ponder opened the book, and then his mouth, but before he could get a word said, a ruckus erupted out in the road.

Looking down at Dara Rose, Clay saw her shut her eyes, felt her stiffen next to him.

Outside, a mule brayed, and a drunken voice bellowed.

Clay took Dara Rose's hand and squeezed it lightly before turning to head for the doorway.

Edrina and Harriet were already there, staring out.

"Mama's not going to marry you, Ezra Maddox!" Edrina shouted to the stumbling man trying to free his feet from the deep mud. "She's taken, so you'd better just get your sorry self out of here before there's trouble!"

Clay had to choke back a laugh. He rested one hand on the top of Edrina's head and one on Harriet's, and said quietly, "Go stand with your mama. I'll handle this."

Maddox was a big man, broad-shouldered and clad in work clothes, and his hair and beard were grizzled, wiry. Once he'd gotten loose from the mud, he practically tore the gate off its rusty hinges, getting it open, and stormed in Clay's direction like a locomotive.

Clay stepped out onto the porch, waited.

Behind him, Ponder said, "Now, Ezra, don't be a sore loser. You're out of the running where Dara Rose is concerned, and making a damn fool of yourself won't change that."

Ezra came to a shambling stop in the middle of the path, not because he'd taken Mayor Ponder's sage advice to heart, Clay reckoned, but because he was used to folks clearing the way between him and whatever it was he aimed to have.

Clay didn't move.

The two men studied each other, at a distance of a dozen yards or so, and Maddox swayed slightly, ran the back of one arm across his mouth. His gaze narrowed.

"Did you get to the part where the justice of the peace inquires as to whether or not anybody has reason to object to this marriage?" Maddox ranted. "Because that's when I mean to say my piece."

"Let's hear it," Clay said, in an affable drawl. He hoped the situation wouldn't disintegrate into a howling brawl in the mud, with him and Maddox rolling back and forth with their hands on each other's throats, because he didn't want that to be what Dara Rose, Edrina and Harriet remembered when they looked back on this day.

Another part of him relished the idea of a knock-down-drag-out fisticuff.

Maddox straightened, swayed again and spoke with alacrity. "I have already offered for you, Dara Rose Nolan, and you belong to me," he said, as she stepped up beside Clay and put her hand on his arm.

A thrill of something rushed through Clay, though he'd hoped Dara Rose would stay inside, out of harm's way, until he and Maddox had settled their differences.

"You belong to me," Maddox reiterated.

"I belong to myself," Dara Rose informed him. "And no one else, except for my children. I want nothing to do with you, Mr. Maddox, and I'll count it as a favor if you leave, right now."

"All right," Maddox erupted, flinging his beefy arms out from his sides with such force that he nearly fell over sideways, "you can bring the girls along, and I'll marry you straight off—today, if that's what you want."

"You are too late, Mr. Maddox," Dara Rose said, in a clear and steady voice. "Please be on your way so we can get on with the wedding."

Clay wondered distractedly if Dara Rose had ever seriously considered taking up with a lug like Maddox. He couldn't imagine her parting with her children.

Maddox just stood there, evidently weighing his options, which were few, and broke the ensuing silence by spitting violently and barking out, "This feller might have a badge, Dara Rose, but he ain't Parnell come back to life."

He turned partially, as if to walk away, but he jabbed a finger in Dara Rose's direction and went right on running off at the mouth. "I'll tell you what he is, this man you're so dead set on marryin'—he's a *stranger*, a lying drifter, for all you know—and when he moves on, leavin' you with another babe in your belly and no way to feed your brood, don't you come cryin' to me!"

Clay's restraint snapped then, but before he could take more than a single step in Maddox's direction, Dara Rose tightened her grip on his arm and stopped him.

Maddox spat again, but then he whirled around and headed for the gate and the waiting mule, every step he took making a sucking sound because of the mud.

Dara Rose let go of Clay's arm and walked, with high-chinned dignity, back into the house, leaving Clay and Mayor Ponder standing on the porch.

Ponder's gaze followed Maddox as he mounted the mule to ride away. "I'd watch my back if I were you, Marshal," he said thoughtfully. "Ezra's the kind to hold a grudge, and he's got a sneaky side to him."

INSIDE, DARA ROSE was shaken, but she made sure it didn't show.

Mayor Ponder's wife, Heliotrope, was a scandalmonger with nothing better to do than spread gossip, heavily laced with her own interpretation of any given person or situation, of course, and thanks to Ezra Maddox's unexpected visit, she'd have plenty of fodder as it was.

Dara Rose wasn't about to give her more to work with.

Besides, the children were watching her, and they'd follow whatever example she set. She wanted them to see strength in their mother, and courage, and dignity.

So she straightened her spine, lifted her chin and once again took her place at Clay McKettrick's side.

Mayor Ponder opened his book again and began to read out the words that would bind her to this tall man standing next to her.

The mayor's voice turned to a drone, and the very atmosphere seemed to pulse and buzz around Dara Rose, making her light-headed.

She spoke when spoken to, answered by rote.

After three weddings, she could have gotten married in her sleep.

Questions plagued her, swooped down on her like raucous birds. *What if Ezra had been right? Suppose Clay was a liar and a drifter—or worse? Was she marrying him because some deluded part of her had him confused with Parnell?*

"I now pronounce you man and wife," Mayor Ponder said, slamming the book closed between his pawlike hands. "Mr. McKettrick, you may kiss the bride."

Clay looked down at her, one eyebrow slightly raised, and a grin crooked at a corner of his mouth.

On impulse, and to get it over with, Dara Rose stood on tiptoe and kissed that mouth, very lightly, very quickly and very briefly.

"There," she said. "It's done."

Clay merely chuckled.

She could still back out, Dara Rose reminded herself

fitfully. She could refuse to sign the marriage certificate, ask Mayor Ponder to reverse the declaration that they were now man and wife.

Was that legal?

For a moment, Dara Rose thought she might swoon, just faint dead away right there in her own front parlor. But Clay slipped a strong arm around her waist, effectively holding her up until she signaled, with a furtive glance his way, that she could stand without help.

Thoughts still clamored through her mind, though, and her hand shook slightly when she signed "Dara Rose McKettrick" on the line reserved for the bride.

What had she *done*?

Suppose Clay was really a rascal and a drunk, instead of the solid man he seemed to be? Suppose he already *had* a wife tucked away somewhere, and he'd just made them both bigamists? And what if this stranger had spoken falsely when he promised not to exercise his rights as a husband unless and until she declared herself ready and willing?

The room felt hot, even with a chinook breeze sweeping in through the open door.

Edrina tugged at Dara Rose's hand, bringing her back into the present moment. "Now you're Mrs. McKettrick," the little girl crowed. "Can Harriet and I be McKettricks, too?"

Dara Rose had no idea how to answer.

Clay, who had clearly overheard, judging by that little smile resting on his mouth as he bent to scrawl his name on the marriage certificate, said nothing. He waited while Mayor Ponder and both witnesses added their signatures where appropriate. Then money changed hands, and the ordeal was over.

The official part of it, at least.

Mayor Ponder and his companions took their leave, and Dara Rose was alone with her new husband and her delighted children.

"We want to be McKettricks, too," Edrina insisted.

"You're Nolans," Dara Rose reasoned. "What would your papa think if you changed your names?"

"*You* changed *yours*," Edrina pointed out. "And, anyhow, Papa's dead."

Harriet's eyes rounded. "Papa's dead?"

"Of course he is, dolt," Edrina snapped. "Why do you suppose we put flowers on a grave with his name on it?"

"Edrina," Dara Rose reprimanded. "Stop it."

"I can't read," Harriet lamented, looking up at Dara Rose now, with tears welling in her eyes. "You said Papa was *gone*—"

Dara Rose exchanged glances with a somber-faced Clay and then bent her knees so she was crouching before her daughter, in the dress she'd worn to marry Luke, and then Parnell, and now Clay.

"Sweetheart," she said softly, "that's what 'gone' means sometimes. I know it's hard for you to understand, but you have to try."

Harriet turned, much to Dara Rose's surprise, and buried her face in one side of Clay's fancy suit coat, wailing in despair. This was unusual behavior, especially for even-tempered Harriet, but Dara Rose put it down to all the excitement of a front-room wedding.

"There, now," Clay said gruffly, as Dara Rose

straightened, hoisting Harriet up into his arms. "You go right ahead and cry 'til you feel like stopping."

Dara Rose sank onto the settee, close to tears herself.

She was *married*, and there was so much she didn't know about Clay.

So much he didn't know about her.

Harriet bawled like a banshee—Dara Rose realized the child was going for effect now—her face hidden in Clay's shoulder.

"Here's what I think we ought to do," Clay said, to all of them. "We ought to go out to my ranch—I'll rent a buckboard and a couple of stout mules—and find ourselves a Christmas tree."

Harriet immediately stopped wailing.

Edrina lit up like a lightbulb wired to a power pole.

"A Christmas tree?" Dara Rose repeated, confounded.

"The roads are pretty muddy," Edrina speculated, but she was obviously warming to the idea, and so was Harriet, who had reared back to look at Clay in wet-eyed wonder.

"That's why we need mules," Clay replied.

"Do you believe in St. Nicholas?" Harriet asked him, in a hushed voice.

Clay looked directly at Dara Rose, silently dared her to say otherwise and replied, "I do indeed. One Christmas Eve, when my cousin Sawyer and I were about your age, we caught a glimpse of him flying over the roof of our granddad's barn in that sleigh of his, with eight reindeer harnessed to the rig."

Edrina blinked, swallowed. *"Really?"* she breathed, wanting so much to believe, even at the advanced age of six, that she'd been wrong to think there was no magic in the world.

Dara Rose's heart ached.

"Can't think what else it could have been," Clay answered, as serious in tone and expression as a man bearing witness in a court of law, under oath. "A sleigh pulled by eight reindeer is a fairly distinctive sight."

"Thunderation," Edrina exclaimed softly, while Harriet favored her older sister with a smug I-told-you-so look.

Dara Rose glared up at her bridegroom. "Mr. Mc-Kettrick," she began, but he cut her off before she could go on.

"Call me Clay," he said mildly. "I'm your husband now, remember?"

Dara Rose got to her feet. *"Clay*, then," she said dangerously. "I will have you know—"

Again he interrupted, setting Harriet on her feet and saying, "You two go on and change your clothes. Get your bonnets and your coats, too."

Edrina and Harriet rushed to obey.

Dara Rose stood there in her sorry-luck wedding dress, trembling with frustration. "How dare you get their hopes up like that?" she whispered furiously, flushed and near tears again. "How *dare* you encourage them to believe in things that aren't even real?"

"Whoa," Clay said, cupping her chin gently in one hand. "Are you saying that St. Nicholas *isn't real*?"

"Of *course* that's what I'm saying," Dara Rose retorted, under her breath but with plenty of bluster. "He *isn't.*"

Clay gave a long, low whistle of surprise, though his too-blue eyes danced with delighted mischief. "I got here just in time," he said.

Dara Rose was brought up short. *"What?"* she managed, with more effort than a single word should have required.

Clay shook his head, as though he couldn't believe another human being could be so deluded as Dara Rose clearly was. "They're only going to be little girls once," he said, "and for a very short time. If I hadn't shown up when I did, you might have ruined one of the best things about being a kid—believing."

Dara Rose's mouth fell open. Clay closed it for her by levering up on her chin with that work-roughened and yet extraordinarily gentle hand of his.

"Now," he went on decisively, "Edrina and Harriet and I are going out to find a Christmas tree. You can either come with us, Mrs. McKettrick, or you can stay right here with the chickens. Which is it going to be?"

Dara Rose wasn't about to send her children out into the countryside in a mule-drawn buckboard with a stranger, but neither did she have the heart to insist that they forget the whole crazy plan.

"Edrina and Harriet are *my* children," she said, hearing the girls laugh and scuffle in the small bedroom as they went about exchanging their wedding garb for warmer things, "and I will not have them misled."

"Fair enough," Clay said, letting his eyes drop. "Shouldn't you get out of that fancy dress before we head out?"

THE MUD WAS DEEP, but the mules that came with the hired buckboard were strong and sure-footed. Once Clay had arranged the transaction, changed his clothes and collected Chester from the jailhouse, they made the short journey to the ranch with no trouble at all— in fact, it seemed to Clay that those mules knew how to avoid the worst of the muck and plant their hooves on solid ground.

He pulled back on the brake lever and simultaneously reined in the mules right where the kit-house would go up, come spring.

He jumped down, smiling as Edrina and Harriet piled eagerly out of the back of the buckboard, Chester leaping after them and barking fit to split a man's eardrums, and went around to reach up a hand to Dara Rose.

She hadn't said two words to him since they'd left town, and her color was high, but she let Clay lift her down.

Gasped when he made sure their bodies collided in the process.

He laughed, though she'd roused an ache inside him.

She blushed and straightened her bonnet with both hands, which made her bosom rise in that tantalizing way he so enjoyed.

"You gave your word," she whispered, narrow-eyed.

"And I'll keep it," Clay assured her. This was what

he got for putting his mouth in motion before his head was in gear, he figured. A wife to contradict everything he said and no wedding night to make up for the inevitable difficulties of an intimate alliance.

If Sawyer had been there, he'd surely have called Clay crazy, denying himself the pleasures of matrimony, especially when he was married to a woman like Dara Rose.

And Clay would have had to admit his cousin was right.

He *was* crazy.

But a promise was a promise.

"Let's go," he said, reaching into the wagon-bed for the short-handled ax he'd borrowed when he rented the team and buckboard over at the livery stable. "It'll be dark in a few hours, and there's no telling when the snow will start up again, so we'd better get started."

Edrina and Harriet were practically beside themselves with excitement, and Chester trotted around them all in big, swoopy circles, livelier than Clay had yet seen him.

The "tree" they finally settled upon looked more like a tumbleweed to Clay, who was used to the lush, fragrant firs that grew in northern Arizona, but Edrina and Harriet were enchanted. So Clay chopped down that waist-high scrub pine and carried it in one hand back to the wagon.

Dara Rose bore silent witness to all this, cautiously enjoying her daughters' delight.

Edrina had noticed the stone markers Clay had set in place the last time he was there, and she squatted on her haunches to peer at one of them. Harriet and Chester stood nearby.

"What *is* this?" Edrina asked.

Clay smiled, tossed the tree into the bed of the wagon and walked back to stand over the little girl. He was aware of Dara Rose on the periphery of things, but he didn't look in her direction.

"This is where I plan to put up my—*our*—house, once it arrives, that is."

Edrina looked up at him, brow crinkling a little. "Houses don't *arrive*," she said.

"This one will," Clay replied, enjoying the exchange. "It's coming by rail, from Sears, Roebuck and Company, all the way out in Chicago, Illinois."

"A *house* can't ride on a train!" Harriet proclaimed gleefully. "Houses are too *big* to fit!"

Clay laughed, crouched between the two girls, to put himself at eye level with them. Chester nuzzled his arm and then, quick as can be, licked Clay's face.

"I guess you'd say this house is kind of like a jigsaw puzzle," Clay told the children. "It's broken down into parts and packed in crates. When it gets here, I'll have to put it together."

Edrina frowned, absorbing his words. Then she whistled, through her teeth, and said, *"Thunderation and spit."*

"Speak in a ladylike fashion, Edrina Nolan," Dara Rose interceded coolly, "or do not speak at all."

Clay tossed a look in his wife's direction and stood tall again, resting one hand on each bonneted head. "I reckon we'll head back to town now," he said. "I don't like the looks of that cloud bank over there on the horizon."

The wind was beginning to pick up a little, too.

Dara Rose shooed the girls toward the hired buckboard, but they didn't need anybody's help to climb inside. They shinnied up the rear wheels, agile as a pair of monkeys, and planted themselves on either side of the scrub pine.

Clay hoisted Chester aboard and fastened the tailgate, but before he could get to Dara Rose and offer her a hand up, she was already in the front of the wagon, perched on the seat and looking straight ahead.

"Will there be room for us in your new house?" Harriet asked, just as Clay settled in to take the reins.

Clay looked down at Dara Rose, who didn't acknowledge him in any visible way. "Yes," he said. "You and Edrina will have to share a room at first, most likely, but after a year or two, I'll be building on, and you'll each have one of your own."

"Then where will Mama be?" Harriet wanted to know. "In my room, or in Edrina's?"

"Neither," Clay said.

A flush bloomed into Dara Rose's cheeks and, even though she hastened to adjust her bonnet, Clay had already seen. "Harriet," Dara Rose said, "please sit down immediately."

Harriet sat.

Clay bit the inside of his lip, so he wouldn't smile, turned the team and wagon in a wide semicircle and headed toward town.

The girls chattered behind him and Dara Rose, in

the bed of the buckboard, Chester no doubt hanging on every word. The wagon wheels, in need of greasing, squealed as the mules pulled the rig overland, puffing clouds of white fog from their nostrils, and the harnesses creaked.

For all that, Clay would remember that trip home as a silent one, because, once again, Dara Rose didn't say a word.

When they drove on along Main Street, passing the road that fronted the house without turning in, Dara Rose nudged him lightly with one elbow but still didn't speak.

"Where are we going?" Edrina called, from the back.

"We're having supper at the hotel tonight," Clay said, with a sidelong glance at Dara Rose. "Call it a celebration," he added dryly.

"Don't be silly," Dara Rose muttered in protest, but the girls were cheering by then, causing Chester to bark, and all of those noises combined to drown her out.

What with all the planks and doors in the road, Clay had to weave the team and wagon in and out half the length of Main Street, but he finally reined in, in front of the Texas Arms Hotel and Dining Room, and set the brake.

"This is extravagant," Dara Rose whispered to Clay, when everybody except Chester was standing on the board sidewalk. "We have food at home…"

"Tonight is special," Clay replied, before shifting his attention to Chester. "You stay put, dog, and I'll bring you out some supper."

Chester seemed to understand; he settled down next

to the Christmas tree, resting his muzzle on his outstretched front legs, sighed once and closed his eyes.

Edrina and Harriet raced, giggling, toward the main entrance to the hotel.

Dara Rose hesitated, though, and took a light but firm hold on Clay's arm. "You mustn't spoil my children," she said. "I don't want Edrina and Harriet getting used to luxuries I cannot hope to provide for them myself."

Clay suppressed a sigh. "Food," he said reasonably, "is not a luxury."

"It is when it's paid for, and someone else cooked and served it," Dara Rose insisted.

Clay smiled down at his bride. "Try to enjoy it just the same," he advised, taking her elbow and gently steering her across the sidewalk.

CHAPTER EIGHT

THE SMALL RUSTIC dining establishment serving the
Texas Arms Hotel was full of savory smells, causing
Dara Rose's stomach to rumble.

Someone had hung a wreath made of holly sprigs behind the cash register, and limp tinsel garlands drooped
from the edges of a long counter lined with stools.

Only one of the six tables was in use. A man, a woman
and a little girl, probably a year or two older than Edrina,
dined in companionable silence, their clothes exceed-
ingly fine, their manners impeccable. Since Dara Rose
had never laid eyes on them before, she knew they must
have arrived on the afternoon train.

She wondered if they were just passing through, or
if they'd come to Blue River to spend Christmas with
friends or family.

Clay nodded a taciturn greeting to the man and the
man nodded back.

Edrina and Harriet, stealing glances at the little girl,
scrambled onto chairs at a table in front of the window,
sitting side by side and swinging their feet. It had been
an exciting day for them—first, the wedding, then the
expedition to find a Christmas tree, and now a restaurant meal.

By the time they tumbled into bed that night, Dara Rose thought fondly, her daughters would be so deliciously exhausted, so saturated with fresh air, that they'd sleep like stones settling deep into the silt of a quiet pond.

Clay was just pulling back a chair for Dara Rose when the cook-waiter appeared, smiling a welcome. "I hear this is a wedding supper!" the man thundered. "Congratulations, Marshal."

It wouldn't have been proper to congratulate Dara Rose, since there would inevitably be an implication that she'd somehow *captured* her new husband, rounded him up like a rogue steer, and not by pure feminine allure. While she appreciated the courtesy, she did wish the man hadn't spoken so loudly, because the woman at the other table turned in their direction, her expression impassive, her gaze flickering briefly over Dara Rose's faded cloak, with its frayed, mud-splattered hem.

"Thanks, Roy," Clay responded, addressing the cook, with whom he was obviously acquainted, and the two men shook hands.

Dara Rose was not a person to compare herself to others, but as Clay pulled back a chair for her and she sat down, she couldn't help thinking how shabby she and the children must seem, in the eyes of that elegantly dressed woman and her little girl.

"What's it going to be, ladies?" Clay asked the children, while Dara Rose perused the menu, nearly overwhelmed by all the choices. "I can definitely recommend the fried chicken dinner, and the meat loaf is good, too."

"What's meat loaf?" Harriet wanted to know.

"You'll have the chicken dinner," Dara Rose said, without looking away from the menu. "One will be plenty for both of you."

She thought she might have felt Clay stiffen beside her, but then, as though she hadn't spoken at all, he simply answered Harriet's inquiry about the nature of meat loaf.

"I want that," Harriet said, when he'd finished. "Please."

"And I'll have stew with dumplings," Edrina added, sounding like a small adult, "if I may, please."

"You may," Clay said, without looking at Dara Rose, though she *did* see his mouth quirk briefly at one corner. "This is a very special occasion," he added, after clearing his throat quietly. "And, anyhow, Chester will be pleased to accept any leftovers. He's still building up his strength, you know."

Dara Rose's cheeks flamed. She loved animals. Her rooster and hens all had names, and she went out of her way to take good care of them. But she'd been so poor for so long—since she'd "married" Luke Nolan, a few months before Edrina was born—that the idea of giving a dog restaurant food just wouldn't fit into any of the compartments in her mind.

"There are *people* in this town who could put anything extra to good use," she said, sounding way more prim than she'd intended.

"Like the O'Reillys," Edrina said, with a sigh.

"Among others," Dara Rose agreed.

Clay was watching her so directly, and with such intensity, that she was forced to meet his gaze. "Shall we just scrape it all into a pan," he began, "and set it on the floor of their shanty, the way we'd do with Chester?"

Dara Rose blushed even harder. If they hadn't been in a public place, and if she'd been given to violence, she'd have slapped him across the face.

Before she could speak, Clay summoned Roy, the cook, back to their table with a polite gesture of one hand.

The man hurried over, eager to please.

Clay placed everyone's order—except for Dara Rose's—and then asked the cook to pack up enough fried chicken, meat loaf and trimmings to feed four people. He'd pay for and collect the extra food at the end of the meal, he said, and then looked pointedly at Dara Rose.

Confounded, and a little stung, she asked for chicken.

Edrina and Harriet were watching Clay raptly—they might have expected a laurel wreath or a winged helmet to appear on his head, from their expressions—and, not surprisingly, it was Edrina who broke the pulsing silence.

"Are we taking supper to the O'Reillys?" she asked.

"Yes," Clay said.

"Harriet and I are planning to visit Addie tomorrow," Edrina said. She turned a vaguely challenging glance in Dara Rose's direction. "Mama said we could."

Dara Rose, still feeling as though she'd been put smartly in her place and none too happy about it, thank you very much, returned Edrina's look in spades. "I said *you* could visit," she reminded her child, "since you'd already promised. I did *not* give permission for Harriet to accompany you."

"What's the harm?" Clay asked mildly, though his eyes contained a challenge, just as Edrina's had before. "That little girl looked to me as though she could use some company. Especially somebody close to her own age."

"She has romantic fever," Edrina said solemnly.

"That's not catching," Clay replied, and though his tone was serious, there was a twinkle in his eyes now. "In fact, I'd say your mother is immune to it."

"Other things *are* catching," Dara Rose felt compelled to say, though she knew there was some kind of battle being waged here, and she was losing ground. Fast.

"It's probably too cold for lice and fleas at this time of year," Clay said.

Dara Rose didn't get a chance to respond. The food arrived, heaped on steaming plates, the children's first, and then Clay's and Dara Rose's.

The family of strangers, meanwhile, had finished their meal, and the man was settling the bill. The mother and the child rose from their chairs, and then the little girl walked right over to Edrina and Harriet and put out one tiny, porcelain-white hand.

"My name is Madeline Howard," she said. With her long, shining brown hair, deep green eyes and fitted emerald velvet dress, she bore a striking resemblance to the doll in the mercantile window. "What's yours?"

"I'm Edrina," answered Dara Rose's elder daughter,

barely able to see over the mountain of food before her. "And this is my sister, Harriet."

"We're going to live in Blue River from now on," Madeline said. "Mama and Papa and me, I mean. Papa's going to build an office, and we'll have rooms upstairs."

The woman approached, laid a hand on Madeline's shoulder, offered a pained smile to everyone in general and no one in particular. "You mustn't bother people when they're eating, darling," she said.

Clay stood, put out his hand, and the woman shook it, after the briefest hesitation. "Clay McKettrick," he said. "This is my wife, Dara Rose."

This is my wife, Dara Rose.

No words could have sounded stranger to Dara Rose, and she had to swallow a ridiculous urge to explain, all in a rush, that theirs was a marriage of convenience, not a real one.

She merely nodded, though, and the woman nodded back. Like her daughter, she wore velvet, though her gown and short cape were a rich shade of brown instead of green. Not only that, but the pile on that fabric was plush, not worn away in places like most of the velvet one saw in Blue River, Texas.

The man had reached the table by then, and smiled as he and Clay shook hands. "Glad to meet you, Marshal," he said. "I'm Jim Howard, and my wife is Eloise."

Another stiff smile from Eloise. "My husband is a dentist," she said. "Most people address him as 'Dr. Howard,' of course."

Dara Rose, who had been trying to decide whether

or not good manners required that she stand, like Clay, decided to stay seated.

"We could use a dentist around here," Clay said, with a grin dancing in his eyes but not quite reaching his mouth.

Madeline smiled broadly at Edrina and Harriet. "You both have very good teeth," she said admiringly. Her own were like small, square pearls, perfectly strung.

Jim Howard—*Dr.* Howard—chuckled at that. "We'll let you finish your meal in peace," he said, steering his womenfolk gently away, toward the hotel's modest lobby and then the stairs beyond.

Clay sat down. "Nice people," he said.

Madeline, Dara Rose noticed, kept looking back, her expression one of friendly longing, as though she would have liked to stay and chat with Edrina and Harriet.

"The lady is snooty," Edrina announced, holding a dinner roll daintily between a thumb and index finger. "But I like Madeline, and her papa, too."

Dara Rose was keenly aware, in that moment, that Edrina was following her lead. Hadn't she disliked Mrs. Howard almost immediately, and returned coolness for coolness instead of making an effort to be neighborly, offer a welcome to the newcomers?

It was tremendously difficult sometimes, she thought glumly, to be the sort of person she wanted her *daughters* to be, when they grew up. And she'd fallen far short of that standard tonight.

Unexpectedly, Clay reached over and gently squeezed her hand, just once and very briefly, but the gesture raised Dara Rose's flagging spirits.

It also sent something sharp and hot racing through her, a fiery ache she had to work very hard to ignore.

"Perhaps when we get to know Mrs. Howard better," she told Edrina, somehow managing a normal tone of voice, "we'll discover that she's a very nice person."

"Perhaps," Edrina agreed doubtfully.

The girls were practically nodding off in their chairs by the time the meal ended.

Clay took the leftovers out to Chester on a borrowed plate, while Roy packed the O'Reillys' supper into a large wooden crate, carefully covered with a dish towel. The bill was paid—the cost of it would have kept Dara Rose and the girls in groceries for the better part of a month—and Clay carried the crate out to the wagon, stowed it under the seat, where Chester couldn't get at it, and returned with the empty plate.

By then, Dara Rose had put on her cloak, Edrina was wearing her outdoor garb and, together, they maneuvered a sleepy Harriet into her coat and bonnet. Clay whisked the child up into his arms and carried her to the wagon.

A light snowfall was just beginning, and the wind was picking up, so Clay took Dara Rose, the children and Chester back to the house first, saw them inside, and announced quietly that he'd return as soon as he'd dropped off the food at the O'Reilly place and turned in the mules and wagon at the livery.

Dara Rose moved by rote, helping the girls prepare for bed, tucking them in, hearing their prayers.

Harriet asked for the doll again.

Edrina said she was glad to have a new papa, then promised not to forget the old one.

Dara Rose was glad she'd turned down the wick in the kerosene lantern, leaving the room mostly in shadow, because there were tears in her eyes as she told her children good-night and kissed their foreheads.

THE SETTEE IN Dara Rose's parlor was about a foot shorter than he was, by Clay's estimation, but he'd slept in less comfortable places in his time, just the same. And Dara Rose *had* been considerate enough to set out a blanket and a pillow for him.

He smiled just imagining the joshing he'd get if Sawyer and the rest of his McKettrick cousins knew he was spending his wedding night alone, with his feet hanging over one end of a short sofa. He'd be lucky if he didn't wake up with his spine in the shape of a horseshoe and his toes numb from lack of circulation.

Chester, who'd settled himself nearby on the blanket Clay had brought over from the jailhouse, watched as he sat down on the settee to kick off his boots.

"Believe it or not," he told the dog, low-voiced, "I got married today."

Chester offered no comment.

The tumbleweed Christmas tree stood undecorated in a corner of the room, stuck in a bucket of water and looking about as festive as Clay felt, but it had a nice pine scent that reminded him of home.

Because the house was small and he was mindful of the children, Clay decided to sleep in his clothes. He was about to extinguish the lantern and stretch out, as best he could, on that blasted settee, when Dara Rose stepped out of the bedroom.

Her hair was down, tumbling well past her waist, and she wore a long nightgown, covered with a plain flannel wrapper, cinched tight at her middle.

Clay's heart skipped a couple of beats, though he knew full well she wasn't there to render an annulment legally and morally impossible.

She stopped, glanced over at the hopeful tumbleweed and then stood a little straighter. This raised her to her full and unremarkable height, but whatever her errand, she sure enough looked like she meant business.

"Either you are an irresponsible man," Dara Rose said, making it clear how Edrina came by her bold certainty about everything, "or you have more money than you let on. Which is it?"

Clay stood, though he suddenly felt bone-tired, because there was a lady in the room. "I never said I was broke, Mrs. McKettrick," he replied dryly.

"Don't call me 'Mrs. McKettrick'!" Dara Rose immediately responded. "We made an agreement. This is a marriage in name only."

"Oh, I'm well aware of that," Clay responded, thinking he'd wait forever for this woman, if that was what he had to do. "But you are legally my wife, and that makes you Mrs. McKettrick."

She pulled so tight on the cinches of her wrapper then that it was a wonder she didn't split right in two, like one of those showgirls in a magician's act. "Why do you keep pointing out that we are married in the eyes of the law?"

Clay was enjoying her discomfort a lot more than was gentlemanly. "Aren't we?" he asked, raising one eyebrow.

"Yes," she retorted, setting her hands down hard on her hips now and jutting out her elbows, "but it was a matter of expediency on my part, and nothing more."

"Gosh," Clay said, playing the rube. "Thanks."

"I would do anything for my daughters!" she blurted out. "Including marry a virtual stranger. I agreed to this arrangement *because* of them, not out of any desire to be your...your wife..." She stammered to a halt and turned a glorious shade of primrose-pink.

Clay waited a few moments before he spoke again. "That was quite a scene Maddox made today."

Dara Rose hesitated, trembled once and hugged herself as if she thought she might suddenly scatter in every direction, and it was all Clay could do not to cross the room and take her into his arms. "I suppose he believed he had call to object to—to our getting married," she continued, after a few moments of miserable struggle, "and it's true enough that he proposed—sort of."

"Sort of?" He'd known about the situation between Dara Rose and Maddox from Ponder and the others, but he wanted to hear it directly from her.

It was a long time before she answered. "I was supposed to work as his housekeeper for a year, so he could be sure I'd make a suitable wife. Then, if I passed muster, he'd put a ring on my finger."

Clay felt a fresh surge of rage rise up within him, and he waited for it to subside before he said anything. "Where did Edrina and Harriet fit into all this?"

He knew the answer to that question, too, at least indirectly but, again, he wanted the first-hand truth from Dara Rose herself.

Her eyes welled, but she looked so proud and so vulnerable that Clay continued to keep his distance. He figured she *might* actually shatter into bits if he touched her.

"They didn't," she said, at long last. Then, speaking so softly that Clay barely heard her, she went on. "He wanted me to put my children in an orphanage, or send them out to work for their board and room."

That was when Clay took a chance. He held his arms out to her.

Dara Rose paused briefly, considering, and then moved slowly into his embrace.

Clay rested his chin on top of her head. "No matter how things turn out between you and me, Dara Rose," he told her, "you will never have to send your girls away, I promise you that."

She looked up at him, her eyes moist, though she still wouldn't allow tears to fall. "How can you make a promise like that, Clay?" she whispered brokenly. "How?"

At least she hadn't called him "Mr. McKettrick." Wasn't that progress?

"I just *did* make a promise like that," he replied, wanting to kiss her more than he'd ever wanted to kiss a woman before, and still unwilling to take the chance, "and you'll find that I'm a man of my word."

She blinked. "There's so much you don't know about me," she said.

He grinned, holding her loosely, with his hands clasped behind the small of her back. "There are, as it happens, a few things you don't know about me," he replied. "I didn't come to Blue River to work as the town marshal for the rest of my life, for one. I mean to be a rancher, Dara Rose—I come from a family of them. That's why I bought two thousand acres of good grazing land, and that's why I plan to build a house on the site we visited today."

"And that's why you wanted a wife," she said, almost forlornly.

"Not just any wife," he pointed out.

"Parnell and I—" She looked at the large likeness on the wall. And suddenly, she choked up again. Couldn't seem to go on.

"It's all right, Dara Rose," Clay said, kissing her lightly on her crown, where her silken hair parted. She smelled sweetly of rainwater and flowery soap. "We've both got stories to tell, but it doesn't have to happen tonight."

She sniffled, smiled bravely, but otherwise she gave no response.

"Exactly why did you come out here in the first place?" Clay asked.

Dara Rose looked flustered. "I forgot to feed the chickens," she said. "And I was hoping you'd be asleep so I could sneak past."

Clay chuckled. "Well, I have to admit, that's something of a disappointment."

"I *never* forget to feed the chickens," Dara Rose fretted, chagrined. "The poor things—"

"I fed them, Dara Rose," Clay said.

"When?"

"Before we went to find the Christmas tree," he said, with a nod toward the tumbleweed.

She seemed to realize then that he was still holding her, and she stepped back suddenly, as though startled. "About Christmas," she began.

"What about Christmas?"

"I'd really rather you didn't encourage Edrina and Harriet to entertain fanciful notions."

"Such as?" Clay asked, feigning innocence.

Dara Rose bristled up again.

He loved it when she did that.

"Well," she huffed, "there *was* that tall tale about seeing St. Nicholas flying past your grandfather's barn roof in a sleigh drawn by reindeer—"

He smiled. "Why, Mrs. McKettrick—are you calling me a liar?"

"You and your cousin must have been inebriated."

"We were eight," Clay said.

"Then you were dreaming."

"The same dream, at the same time? Sawyer and I are blood kin, but we don't share a brain."

Dara Rose sighed again. It was plain that she didn't know what to say next, or what to do, either.

Both were encouraging signs, Clay figured.

"Get some sleep," he told her. "You've had a long day."

She glanced at the settee, then took his measure with her eyes. Drew the obvious conclusion. "You are in for an uncomfortable night," she said, without any discernible concern.

For more reasons than one, Clay thought. But what he said was, "I'll be just fine. See you in the morning."

Dara Rose nodded, turned around and went back into the bedroom.

Clay watched her go, rubbing his chin with one hand, calculating the number of settee nights he'd have to put in between now and spring, when the house would be ready.

In the end, he slept on the floor, next to Chester.

At least that way, he could stretch out.

WHEN HE OPENED his eyes again, it was morning, and Edrina and Harriet were standing over him, looking worried.

"We thought you might be dead," Edrina said, with a relieved and somewhat wobbly smile.

"But you're not," Harriet added emphatically.

"No," Clay said, with a laugh, as he sat up. "I do believe I'm still among the living."

Both children were dressed for daytime, with their curly hair brushed and held back at the sides of their heads by small combs. Their faces were rosy from a recent scrubbing and their eyes shone.

"Mama is taking us over to the O'Reillys' place to visit Addie," Edrina said, "as soon as she's finished feeding the chickens and gathering the eggs and making breakfast."

Clay yawned expansively and got to his feet. "Where's Chester?"

"He's outside with Mama," Harriet replied. "She said he needed to do his business."

"What time is it?" Clay wondered aloud. He owned a pocket watch but seldom carried it; there had been no real need for that, back on the Triple M. There, where there was always a full day's work to do, you started at sunrise and finished when you finished, whatever time it was.

Before either child replied, he caught sight of the timepiece hanging prominently on the wall. Eight o'clock.

"When we get back from the O'Reillys'," Harriet piped up, "can we decorate the Christmas tree?"

Clay hesitated to answer, realizing that he didn't even know if Dara Rose *owned* any decorations, or whether she'd take kindly to his buying some for her, over at the mercantile.

Reckon you should have thought about that before you cut down that sorry sprig of sagebrush you're calling a Christmas tree, he told himself silently.

"That's up to your mama," he finally said.

Both children looked deflated.

"She'll just say it's a whole week 'til Christmas and St. Nicholas isn't coming, anyhow, so what do we need with a silly tree," Edrina said, in a rush of words.

Inwardly, Clay sighed. These were Dara Rose's children, and she had a perfect right to raise them as she saw fit, but he hoped she'd ease up on that rigid personal code of hers a little, and let them be kids while they could.

In the near distance, the back door opened, and Clay

felt the rush of cool air where he stood. Dara Rose called out, "Girls? You're not bothering Mr. McKettrick, are you?"

Chester trotted through the inside doorway, came over to greet him.

Clay smiled and ruffled the dog's ears.

"We don't want to call you 'Mr. McKettrick,'" Edrina told Clay.

"We want to call you 'Papa,'" Harriet said.

The backs of Clay's eyes stung a little. "I'd like that," he said quietly, "but that's another thing that's got to be left up to your mama."

"What's to be left up to me?" Dara Rose asked, standing in the doorway. Her hair was pinned up, unlike last night, and like the girls', her cheeks were pink with well-being.

"Whether or not we can call Mr. McKettrick 'Papa,'" Harriet answered.

"And if we can put baubles on the Christmas tree," Edrina added.

Both of them stared expectantly at their mother.

"Oh," she finally said, shifting the handle of the egg basket from one wrist to the other. Her gaze flicked to Clay's face and then back to the girls. "It's too soon to address Mr. McKettrick in such a familiar fashion," she said. "But I don't see why we couldn't get out the Christmas things."

So she *had* Christmas things, Clay thought. That was something, anyway.

Edrina and Harriet swapped glances and made what

would seem to be a tacit agreement to take what they could get.

"Breakfast will be ready in a few minutes," Dara Rose said. "And there are plenty of eggs this morning. We can each have one—Mr. McKettrick may have two, if he wishes—and there will still be enough left to sell over at the mercantile."

"One egg will suit me fine," Clay said, gruff-voiced. Soon as he'd put in a few hours over at the jailhouse and walked through the town once or twice to make sure there wasn't any trouble brewing, he'd head over to the mercantile and stock up on foodstuffs. See if old Philo would agree to deliver what he bought.

Dara Rose wouldn't like it, he supposed, when the storekeeper turned up with sugar and coffee beans and a wagonload of other goods, but he already had an argument ready. He didn't expect her to feed him and Chester; therefore, he wanted to contribute to the grubstake.

Plus, he had to have coffee in the morning, to get himself going.

So they ate their simple breakfast, the girls so excited, between the promised outing and the tree waiting to be festooned with geegaws, that they could barely sit still.

Dara Rose cleared the table while Clay donned his duster and his hat and summoned the dog. He'd left his gun belt and pistol over at the jailhouse, because of Edrina and Harriet, but he'd strap on the long-barreled .45 before he set out on his rounds. It wasn't that he expected to need a firearm, but he wanted any potential troublemakers to know the new marshal was serious about upholding his duties.

"Thanks for breakfast," Clay said, with a tug at his hat brim.

Dara Rose nodded, then looked away.

THE VISIT TO little Addie O'Reilly was necessarily brief since the child was bedridden. Last night's snow hadn't stuck, thank heaven, but there was still a bitter chill in the air, and Addie's two younger brothers sat on the bare floor near the odd, cobbled-together stove, playing with half a dozen marbles.

Peg tried to put a good face on things, but Dara Rose could tell she was embarrassed. There was no place to sit, except on one of the two beds or an upended crate—undoubtedly the same one that had contained last night's donated supper.

The girls, meanwhile, chatted with Addie.

"Somebody left a box of hot food at my doorstep," Peg said, following Dara Rose's gaze to the crate. Four clean plates, plus utensils, were stacked beside it. "We sure did have ourselves a fine feast, and there's enough left to get us through today, too."

"That's...wonderful," Dara Rose said.

"I figure it had to come from the dining room over to the hotel," Peg went on, wiping her hands down the skirt of her calico dress. "I mean to take the plates and silverware back later."

Dara Rose merely nodded. Clay must have wanted to keep his part in the enterprise a secret, so she didn't say anything.

Fortunately, neither did Edrina or Harriet. They were busy telling Addie all about the little girl, Madeline, whose papa was a dentist.

"You'll never guess who stopped by here yesterday," Peg said, taking Dara Rose by surprise.

"Who?" Dara Rose asked, simply to make conversation.

"Ezra Maddox," Peg said. "He's offered me housekeeping work, Mrs. Nolan. The job doesn't pay much, but at least there'll be plenty of good farm food for these kids, and if things work out, Mr. Maddox and me will be married come the spring." She paused. "You don't mind, do you? Now that you've married the marshal and all?"

Dara Rose smiled. "I don't mind," she was quick to say. Then, cautiously, afraid Peg O'Reilly might have misunderstood Maddox's offer, she asked, "He didn't object to your bringing the children along?"

"He did," Peg confided, in a whisper, "but I told him I wouldn't be parted from my little ones for anything or anybody, and he finally agreed to take them in."

The boys were still busy with their game of marbles, and Edrina was telling Addie that there wasn't going to be a Christmas program over at the schoolhouse this year because that last snowstorm threw everything out of whack.

"What about—?"

"My husband?" Peg asked. "Ezra knows about him, of course. Says we'll look into getting me a divorce if it comes to that."

Dara Rose's heart ached for Peg O'Reilly. "This is what you want to do?" she asked, very quietly.

"It's the answer to a prayer," Peg replied, looking a little surprised by Dara Rose's question.

Ezra Maddox, the answer to a prayer?

It just went to show, Dara Rose thought, that one woman's idea of hell was *another* woman's idea of heaven.

CHAPTER NINE

FULL OF CONSTERNATION, Dara Rose studied the Closed sign on the door at the mercantile, the handle of the egg basket looped over one wrist, and wondered what on earth could have prompted Mr. Bickham to close his establishment at midmorning. Edrina and Harriet, meanwhile, climbed onto the bench in front of the store and peered in through the display window.

"Mama!" Harriet suddenly cried, so startling Dara Rose that she almost dropped the egg basket. "She's gone! *Florence is gone!*"

Dara Rose caught her breath, the fingers of her free hand splayed across her breastbone to keep her heart from jumping right out of her chest.

Florence?

Harriet let out a despairing wail.

"Hush!" Edrina told her sister, speaking sternly but slipping an arm around the child's shoulders just the same. The two of them looked so small, standing there on the seat of that bench, like a pair of beautiful urchins.

The doll, Dara Rose realized belatedly.

Of course. Florence was the doll Harriet had been admiring—yearning after—ever since it first appeared in the mercantile window, the day after Thanksgiving. And now the doll was gone.

It would be set out for some other child to find on Christmas morning.

Although Dara Rose had never for one moment believed she could buy that doll for her little girl, Harriet's disappointment grieved her sorely. Like any mother, she longed to give her children nice things, but that was a pleasure she couldn't afford; they needed practical things, and some small measure of security, be it the egg money she squirreled away a penny at a time, or the ten dollars resting between the pages of her Bible.

Hurting as much as her child was—maybe more— and doing her best to hide it, Dara Rose set the egg basket down carefully and gathered Harriet into her arms, lifting her off the bench and holding her tightly. "There, now," she whispered, her throat so thick she could barely speak. Not that there was a great deal to say at a moment like that, anyway. "There, now."

"I should have sold my hair!" Harriet sobbed. "Then I would have had the money to buy Florence!"

Once again, Dara Rose thought of Piper's gift, safe at home, and ached.

Edrina jumped down from the bench, tomboylike, and tugged at Harriet's dangling foot. "Stop carrying on, goose," she commanded, but there was a slight quaver in her voice. "You'll have the whole town staring at us."

Harriet shuddered and buried her wet face in Dara Rose's neck. "I—really—thought—I—could—have—

Florence—for—my—very—own," she said, punctuating her words with small but violent hiccups.

"Shh," Dara Rose said gently, still holding the child. "Everything will be all right, sweetheart. We'll go home now. Edrina, bring the egg basket."

By the time the three of them reached the end of Main Street and turned toward the house, Harriet had settled down to the occasional quivering sniffle.

A buckboard stood near Dara Rose's front gate, with two mules hitched to it.

Philo Bickham sat in the wagon box, reins in hand, beaming at Dara Rose as she approached with the children.

"I was just about to unload all this merchandise and leave it on the porch," he said. "The marshal said he'd be here to accept delivery, but there's been no sign of him so far."

Dara Rose frowned, at once wary and intrigued.

Edrina bolted forward and scrambled right up the side of that buckboard, skillful as a monkey, using the wheel spokes as footholds. "Thunderation!" she whooped.

Mr. Bickham jumped to the ground, nimble for a man of his age and bulk. He strode around to the back of the wagon and lowered the tailgate. "He darned near bought the place out, your new husband," the storekeeper crowed, no doubt pleased to make such a sale. Blue River was not a wealthy community, which meant the owner of the mercantile scraped by like most everyone else.

"Mama," Edrina spouted, "there's a tin of tea...and a

big ham…and *peaches*…and all sorts of things wrapped in brown paper—"

"Edrina Nolan," Dara Rose said, setting Harriet on her feet, "get down from there this instant."

"Don't go poking around in those packages," Mr. Bickham said good-naturedly, shaking a finger at Edrina and then Harriet. "The marshal made himself mighty clear on that score. After all, it's almost Christmas, and there's a secret or two afoot."

Dara Rose was still trying to think what to say when Clay rode around the corner on Outlaw, Chester trotting in their wake.

Mr. Bickham hailed him, and Dara Rose sent the girls inside, over their protests.

"Sorry if I held you up any, Philo," Clay told Mr. Bickham, barely glancing at Dara Rose as he swung down from the saddle. "A telegram came in from Sears, Roebuck and Company. They've shipped the makings of my house out by rail, and the whole works will be arriving here in about ten days."

"You'd better get that foundation dug and that well put in, then," Mr. Bickham said, giving Clay a congratulatory slap on one shoulder. "Reckon you can round up some hired help down at the Bitter Gulch, and if this weather holds, since you've got a put-together house coming, you'll be out there on your own place in no time."

Clay nodded and, once again, his gaze touched on Dara Rose's face.

"What is all this?" she asked evenly, as soon as Mr.

Bickham had hoisted the first box from the back of the wagon and started toward the house with it.

Clay gave her a wry look and lifted out a second box. "Chester and I," he said, with a twinkle, "don't believe in freeloading. We always pay our own way."

Dara Rose opened her mouth, closed it again. "But all those packages, and the tea, and that enormous ham—"

"You like tea, don't you?" Clay teased, starting toward the house.

Dara Rose scurried to keep up with his long strides. "Of course I like tea," she said, flustered, "but it's a luxury, and we don't need it—"

"Sure you do," Clay replied, climbing the porch steps now. "What do you plan on serving all the ladies of Blue River when they start dropping by to see for themselves just what kind of mischief we're up to over here?"

Harriet and Edrina, huddled in the doorway, scattered to let them through.

Mr. Bickham was coming from the other direction, and Clay sidestepped him.

"Mr. McKettrick," Dara Rose persisted, when the two of them were alone in the kitchen, "I do have my pride."

"Yes, Mrs. McKettrick," Clay agreed. "I have taken note of that fact." He took a large tin from the box he'd carried in. "Would you mind putting some coffee on to brew while Bickham and I finish unloading that wagon? I've got a hankering for the stuff, and I like it strong and black."

Dara Rose couldn't seem to untangle her tongue.

"You do own a coffeepot, don't you?" Clay asked offhandedly.

"Yes," she managed, blushing. "Parnell drank coffee every morning."

Clay merely nodded, as though she'd confirmed something he already knew, and went out again.

Dara Rose got out Parnell's coffeepot, rinsed it at the sink and pumped fresh water into it. Then she had to ferret out the grinder, with its black wrought-iron handle.

She was wiping the dust out of the contraption with one corner of a flour-sack dish towel when Clay and Mr. Bickham came in again, both of them carrying boxes.

Edrina and Harriet were, of course, consumed with curiosity.

Harriet, though puffy-eyed, had long since stopped crying.

"Sugar," Edrina cataloged, joyfully examining each item. "And flour. And lard. And *raisins*. Mama, you could bake a pie."

"Perhaps," Dara Rose agreed, afraid to say too much because she wasn't sure she could control all the contradictory emotions welling up inside her. Her pride stung like a snakebite, but in some ways, she was as jubilant as the children.

Tea. Sugar. Flour.

A whole ham, big enough to feed half the town of Blue River.

They'd been doing without such things for so long that it was impossible not to rejoice, at least inwardly.

Firmly, Dara Rose brought herself up short. She

squared her shoulders and poured coffee beans into the grinder and began turning the handle, enjoying the rich aroma. "Mr. McKettrick has been very generous," she said, not looking at Edrina and Harriet. "But we mustn't come to expect such things—"

"Why not?" The voice was Clay's.

Dara Rose kept her back to him, spooning freshly ground coffee beans into the well of her dented pot, setting it on to boil. "Because we mustn't, that's all," she said. She bent and opened the stove door and pitched in more wood. Jabbed at the embers with the poker.

"There's some stuff for the Christmas tree in the box I left on the settee," Clay said quietly, sending the girls scampering with chimelike hurrahs into the front room.

Dara Rose, thinking Mr. Bickham must be within earshot, taking it all in, turned to look for him. He was as big a gossip as Heliotrope Ponder and, running the only general store in town, he got plenty of chances to tell everything he knew and then some.

But there was only Clay, filling the doorway, watching her. Philo Bickham must have been outside, fetching another box from the buckboard.

"It's almost Christmas," Clay said gruffly. "Just this once, Dara Rose, let yourself be happy. Let your *daughters* be happy."

Her face burned, and she couldn't help remembering all the times Parnell had splurged on some little treat for the girls, running up an account at the mercantile that had taken her months to pay off.

"Did you go into debt for all this?" she asked, keeping her voice down so the girls and Mr. Bickham wouldn't hear. Nobody knew better than she did how little the marshal of Blue River actually earned.

Clay smiled, though his eyes remained solemn, and then he shook his head, not in reply, but in disbelief. "I paid cash money," he said, turning to walk away.

By the time the coffee was ready, the kitchen and part of the front room were jammed with boxes and crates and brown parcels, tied shut with twine.

"Where's Mr. Bickham?" Dara Rose asked, when Clay returned to the kitchen, squeezed past her to wash his hands at the sink pump. "I thought he'd stay for coffee."

"He has a store to run," Clay said quietly.

In the next room, the girls giggled and Chester barked and the noise was pleasant to hear, even though Dara Rose was uncommonly jittery.

She put away the cup she'd set out for Mr. Bickham and filled the remaining one, returned the pot to the stove.

"Mr. McKettrick?"

"What, Mrs. McKettrick?" Clay countered wearily, as he drew back a chair, sat down and reached for the steaming cup of coffee.

Dara Rose brought out the sugar bowl, long unused, filled it from the newly purchased bag and set it on the table, along with a teaspoon.

"Thank you," she said meekly, not looking at him. "For all these groceries, I mean—"

That was when he pulled her onto his lap. His thighs felt hard as a wagon seat under her backside, and *that* realization started all sorts of untoward things rioting inside her.

"You're welcome," he said, in a throaty drawl.

Dara Rose's heart pounded, and she felt dizzy. "Clay—the *children*—"

He sighed. "They're busy squeezing parcels," he said.

Dara Rose sat very still, afraid to move.

Clay watched her mouth for a few moments, and managed to leave Dara Rose as breathless as if he'd actually kissed her, and soundly. Then he said, very quietly, "Just so we understand each other, Mrs. Mc-Kettrick, I do mean to bed you, right and proper, one day soon."

Dara Rose gulped, knowing she ought to pull free and get back on her own two feet but strangely unable to do so. "But you said—"

He rested an index finger on her mouth, and a hot shiver went through her. "I know what I said, Dara Rose, and I'll keep my word. But it's only fair to tell you that I'm fixing to do everything I can to bring you around to my way of thinking."

Dara Rose absolutely could not speak. She was full of indignation and longing and searing heat.

That was when he kissed her—softly at first, and then in a deep way that made everything inside her melt, including her very bones.

When their mouths finally parted, it was Clay's doing, not Dara Rose's.

She'd have been content to let that kiss go on forever, it felt so good.

"I believe I'm making progress," he said, with a certain satisfaction.

He was indeed, Dara Rose thought. If Edrina and Harriet hadn't been in the house, never mind the very next room, she might have taken Marshal Clay McKettrick by the hand and led him straight to her bed. She sighed wistfully.

It had been so long since she'd been held in a strong man's arms, reveled in the sweet responses lovemaking roused in her.

She glanced at the doorway, but her children were still in the front room, playing some game with the dog, filling that little house with barks and giggles. "Parnell and I—we weren't…we didn't…"

Clay simply listened, looking thoughtful.

"What I mean is, we were never…*intimate*," Dara Rose confessed. Even saying that much—telling such a small part of her story—was a tremendous relief. "He married me to give my children a name."

"Go on," Clay said.

Dara Rose checked the doorway again. "I was married—or I *thought* I was married—to Parnell's younger brother, Luke." She swallowed hard. "Edrina was born, and then Harriet, and then—"

Clay didn't prompt her. He was a patient man.

"And then Luke was thrown from a horse and killed, and I learned—I learned that he'd had another wife all along. A *real* wife, and several children. I'd been a—a kept woman from the first, without even knowing it, and our—*my*—children had been born out of wedlock."

Something moved in Clay's handsome face.

Pain? Fury? Pity, perhaps? She couldn't tell.

Afraid she'd lose her courage if she didn't finish the story right now, Dara Rose went on. "I had no money, and no place to go, and after his brother's funeral, Parnell came to me and offered marriage. He was such a good man, Clay." She realized she was crying. When had the tears begun? "When he died upstairs at the Bitter Gulch, everyone felt so sorry for the children and me, and there was this huge scandal, and I couldn't— I couldn't explain that I wasn't a true wife to him. He must have been so lonely…"

When she didn't go on, Clay set her on her feet, and try though she did, Dara Rose couldn't read his expression.

He got up from his chair, his coffee forgotten on the table, and whistled for his dog.

Chester came to him eagerly, without hesitation, as Clay was putting on his duster and his distinctive round-brimmed hat.

"This calls for some thinking about, Dara Rose," he said. "And I need to get Outlaw back to the livery stable, see that he's put up proper for the night."

With that, Clay opened the back door, and he and Chester went out.

Edrina and Harriet appeared in the inside doorway the instant he'd closed the door behind him.

"Aren't we going to decorate the Christmas tree?" Edrina asked plaintively.

Dara Rose didn't answer. She hurried across the kitchen and through the front room to watch through the window as Clay rounded a corner of the house, passed through the gate, gathered his horse's reins and mounted up.

"What about the Christmas tree?" Harriet trilled from somewhere behind Dara Rose.

"After supper," she heard herself say, as her heart climbed into her throat. "We'll tend to it after supper."

And Clay McKettrick rode away, Chester following, leaving Dara Rose to wonder if he meant to come back.

WHEN HE REACHED the jailhouse, Clay let himself in, started a fire in the potbellied stove and nearly fell over the large crate waiting by his desk.

He approached the box, apparently delivered while he was away, peering down at the return address: *The Triple M. Indian Rock, Arizona.*

He felt a twinge of homesickness, but it passed quickly.

Much as he loved the ranch, and his family, the Triple M wasn't home anymore. Home, for better or for worse, was wherever Dara Rose happened to be.

When had he fallen in love with her?

He wasn't sure. It might have been today, when she sat on his lap in her tiny kitchen and poured out her heart to him.

Or it might have been when he first laid eyes on her, just a few days before.

All he could say for sure was that it felt a lot like being kicked in the belly by a mule, this falling in love.

He was exultant.

He was crushed.

Dara Rose had loved another man, and that man had

betrayed her, and if Luke Nolan hadn't already been dead, Clay would have cheerfully killed him.

His deepest regret? That he hadn't been there to step in and make things right for her and for the kids, as illogical as that was. Parnell had been the one to rescue her, give his two-timing brother's family a legal right to the Nolan name.

Clay McKettrick was jealous of a dead man and, at the same time, he knew he could never have settled for the kind of empty marriage Dara Rose and Parnell had had together. He was a young man, and red-blooded, and he needed more.

He wanted everything—wanted Dara Rose's heart, as well as her body. Wanted to adopt Edrina and Harriet, change their last name for good, raise them as McKettricks.

And he surely wanted to make more babies with Dara Rose.

Oh, yes, he wanted it all.

He drew in a deep breath. *Slow down, cowboy*, he thought. *Get a grip.*

There was no telling what Dara Rose thought when he'd walked out on her that way, but he needed to sort things through, needed to *think*.

That was the kind of man he was.

He fetched a knife, pried up the lid on the crate his mother had sent from the Triple M. She must have paid a hefty freight charge to get it there before Christmas, even by train.

Inside, carefully nestled in straw, he found a dozen succulent oranges, a tin full of exotic nuts and a number of his favorite books, some of which he'd owned since he first learned to read. There was more, but Clay's eyes were so blurred by then that he was lucky to be able to read his mother's letter and, even then, he only got this word and that.

"Sawyer wired that you're married...two stepdaughters...bring them home when you can...we're all so anxious to welcome your wife and your children to the family—"

Clay closed his eyes, drew a deep breath. That was Chloe McKettrick for you. If he loved a woman, and that woman's children, then his mother was ready to enfold them in the warmth of her heart, receive them as her own.

It was the McKettrick way. Babies were born into the family, or they arrived by marriage, and it made no difference either way. Once a McKettrick, always a McKettrick.

No matter what happened between him and Dara Rose, Edrina and Harriet were part of the fold, now and forever. If he died tomorrow, or Dara Rose did, his pa and ma, his aunts and uncles and sisters and brothers and cousins—even old Angus and his wife, Concepcion—would take them in and love them like their own flesh and blood.

The knowledge made Clay's throat tighten and his eyes scald.

He wanted to go back to Dara Rose right then, wanted that more than anything, but he didn't give in to the desire.

Yes, she was his wife.

And yes, it was a safe bet that she wanted him as much as he wanted her, after that episode in her kitchen.

But what mattered now was the children.

And that was why Clay McKettrick decided to spend his second night as a married man in the spare room behind the jailhouse. If he'd gone back to Dara Rose's place, he wasn't at all sure he could have resisted her.

He needed her.

He *loved* her.

And that was precisely why he couldn't go home to that little house, with its tiny rooms and its thin walls.

Clay McKettrick knew his limits.

And, where Dara Rose was concerned, he'd reached them.

DARA ROSE LISTENED for Clay's footstep on the back porch as she peeled potatoes to fry up for supper with some of the salt pork he'd bought at the store. When the meal was over and the dishes had been washed and put away and he still wasn't back, she declared that it was time to decorate the Christmas tree.

"We'd rather wait for Mr. McKettrick," Edrina said, looking glum.

"Where did he go?" Harriet asked.

Dara Rose sighed. She'd been a fool to go against her own better judgment and marry Clay McKettrick. Men couldn't be depended upon to stick around. They lied and cheated and got themselves thrown from horses and killed, they died in the arms of prostitutes above some saloon or, like Mr. O'Reilly, they simply decided they'd rather be elsewhere and took to their heels.

Devil take the hindmost.

"To the livery stable, I think," Dara Rose finally replied.

"He left a long time ago," Edrina reasoned. "It's getting dark outside."

Harriet's lower lip wobbled. "Maybe he's not coming back," she said.

Dara Rose pretended not to hear. "I'll fetch the Christmas box from the cedar chest," she told the children, marching into the front room. "And then we'll see what we can do with this tree."

The girls didn't speak, so she turned her head to look at them.

They stood side by side, arms folded, expressions recalcitrant.

"That wouldn't be right," Edrina said staunchly. "Mr. McKettrick cut that tree down himself. We wouldn't even have it if it weren't for him."

Harriet nodded in grim agreement.

Dara Rose thought fast. "Wouldn't it be a nice surprise, though, if he came home to find it all sparkling and merry?"

Edrina, self-appointed spokeswoman for her little sister as well as for herself, stood her ground. "We'd rather wait," she reiterated.

Dara Rose shook her head, proceeded into the bedroom to give the children a chance to change their minds and lifted the lid of the cedar chest at the foot of the bed. She kept the few simple ornaments they owned, most of them homemade, tucked away there, inside an old boot box of Parnell's.

There was a shining paper chain, made of salvaged foils of all sorts.

There were stars, cut from tin, with the sharp edges hammered down to a child-safe smoothness, and ribbons, and Parnell's broken pocket watch.

And there were two tiny angels, sewn up from scraps of calico and embroidered with Edrina's and Harriet's names, their wings improvised out of layers of old newspapers, cut out and pasted together.

Dara Rose had always treasured these humble decorations, as had the girls, but now, in the dim light of the rising moon, falling softly through the window, they looked humble indeed. Nearly pitiful, in fact.

She swallowed, straightened her spine, and returned to the front room with the dog-eared carton, only to find Edrina and Harriet busy with the one Clay had spoken of earlier.

There's some stuff for the Christmas tree in the box I left on the settee, he'd said.

The children looked wonder-struck as they lifted one glistening item after another out of the box—a porcelain angel with feathers for wings and a golden halo fashioned of thin wire; shimmering baubles of blown glass in bright shades of red and blue and gold and silver; a package of glittering tinsel that flashed in the lamplight like a tiny waterfall.

Dara Rose spoke in a normal tone, but it was a struggle. "Shall we decorate the tree after all, then?" she asked.

But Edrina and Harriet shook their heads.

Slowly, carefully, they put all the exquisite ornaments Clay had purchased back into the box from the mercantile.

"We'll wait," Edrina said.

And that was that.

The girls went off to get ready for bed, without being told.

Dara Rose, not quite sure *what* she was feeling exactly, put on her cloak and went outside to make sure the chickens were safe in their coop, with their feed and water pans full.

When that was done, she tarried, looking up at the silvery stars popping out all over the black-velvet sky, hoping Clay would step through the backyard gate.

He didn't, of course.

So Dara Rose went back into the house, to her children, to oversee the washing of faces and the brushing of teeth and the saying of prayers.

Edrina, hands clenched together and one eye slightly open, asked God to make sure Mr. McKettrick and Chester found their way back home, please, and soon.

Harriet said she hoped whatever little girl had Florence would take good care of her and not lose the doll's shoes or break her head.

Dara Rose offered no comment on either prayer.

She simply kissed her precocious children goodnight, tucked them in and left the room.

In the kitchen, she brewed tea, and sat savoring it at the table, with the kerosene lantern burning low on the narrow counter.

After Luke, and again after Parnell, Dara Rose had

solemnly promised herself she would never wait up for another man as long as she lived.

And here she was, waiting for Clay McKettrick.

HAVING MADE HIS DECISION, Clay locked up the street door and banked the dwindling fire, and he collapsed onto the bed in the back room of the jailhouse, not expecting to sleep.

He must have been more tired than he thought, because he awakened with sunlight streaming into his face through the one grimy window, and Chester snoring away in the nearby cell.

Clay got up, made his way into the office, made a fire in the stove and put on a pot of coffee. He let Chester out the rear door and stood on what passed for a porch, studying the sky.

It was bluer than blue, that sky, and the day promised to be unseasonably warm.

Even with half his mind down the road, following Dara Rose around that little house of hers, there was room in Clay's brain for all the things that needed to be done before the kit-house arrived.

He heated water on the stove top, once the coffee had come to a good boil, and washed up as best he could, but his shaving gear and his spare clothes were stashed behind the settee at Dara Rose's.

In the near distance, church bells rang, and Clay realized it was Sunday.

The good folks of the town would be settling themselves in pews right about now, waiting for the sermon to start—and then waiting for it to end.

The ones who wouldn't mind working on the Sabbath Day, on the other hand, were probably gathered down at the Bitter Gulch Saloon, defiant in their state of sin.

Since he needed a well dug, and a foundation, too, Clay figured he'd better get to the latter bunch before they got a real good start on the day's drinking.

An hour later, Chester stuck to his heels the whole time, he'd hired seven men, roused a blinking and grimacing Philo Bickham to open the mercantile and sell him picks and shovels, a pair of trousers and a plain shirt, and rented two mules and a wagon from the livery to haul the workers and the tools out to the ranch.

For a pack of habitual drunks, those men got a lot of digging done.

Clay worked right alongside them, while Chester roamed the range, probably hunting for rabbits. He'd make a fine cattle-dog when there was a herd to tend.

At noon, Clay drove the team and wagon back to town, Chester along for the ride, bought food enough for an army at the hotel dining room and returned to the work site and his hungry crew.

He'd felt a pang passing the turn to Dara Rose's place, having finally remembered that he'd promised Edrina and Harriet that they'd decorate the Christmas tree the night before, but he'd make that up to them later.

Somehow.

Just about supper time, Clay called a halt to the work, satisfied that the foundation was dug and they'd made good progress on the well. The crew climbed into the back of the wagon, as did Chester, and the marshal of Blue River, Texas, turned the mules townward.

He paid the men generously, turned the team and wagon in at the livery and took his time tending to Outlaw, lest the horse feel neglected after being left to stand idle in his stall all day.

Too tired to bother with supper, and too dirty to stand himself for much longer, Clay returned to the lonely jailhouse, lit a lantern, fed Chester some leftovers from the midday meal and commenced carrying and heating water to fill the round washtub he'd found hanging from a nail just outside the back door.

The new clothes he'd bought that morning were stiff with newness and smelled of starch.

Once there was enough hot water in the washtub to suit him, Clay stripped off his filthy clothes, climbed in and sat down, cross-legged like an Apache at a campfire, sighing as the strain eased out of his muscles. He was no stranger to hard physical work, coming from a family of ranchers, but it had been a while since he'd swung a pick or wielded a shovel.

He was sore.

As the water cooled, Clay scoured off a couple of layers of grime and sweat and planned what he'd say to Dara Rose, later tonight, when he intended to knock at her kitchen door and ask if he and Chester could bunk in her front room again. In the morning, they could talk things through.

Only it didn't happen that way.

Clay was just coming to grips with the fact that he didn't have a towel handy when the jailhouse door flew open and Dara Rose stormed in, wearing her cloak but no bonnet and, temper-wise, loaded for bear.

Seeing Clay sitting there in the washtub in the alto-
gether, she stopped in her tracks and gasped.

"You're just in time, Mrs. McKettrick," he said. "It
seems I'm in something of a predicament here."

Dara Rose blinked and looked quickly away, keeping her head turned and not asking what the predicament might happen to be.

"My children," she said, "refuse to decorate the
Christmas tree unless you're there."

"If you'll fetch me a towel, Mrs. McKettrick," Clay
drawled, enjoying her discomfort more than he'd enjoyed much of anything since yesterday's kiss at her
kitchen table, "I'll make myself decent, and we'll at-
tend to that Christmas tree."

Dara Rose kept her face averted. "Where...?"

"The towel? It's hanging from a hook next to my
shaving mirror, in the back room."

"I meant to say," Dara Rose sputtered, still not looking in his direction, "*where have you been* since last
night?" She gave him a wide berth as she went in search
of the towel.

"I'm glad you asked," Clay said, smiling to himself
as he waited for her to come back, so he could dry off
and get dressed in his new duds. "It shows you care."

She returned, flung the towel at him and turned her
back. "Nonsense," she said. "Edrina and Harriet were
very disappointed when you left—that's the only reason I'm here."

Clay rose out of the tub, the towel around his middle,
and sloshed his way into the spare room, where he hast-
ily wiped himself dry and put on the other set of clothes.

Dara Rose had her eyes covered with both hands when he came back. "Are you dressed?" she asked pettishly.

"Yes, Mrs. McKettrick," he said easily. "I am properly attired."

She lowered her hands, looked at him with enough female fury to sear off some of his hide and repeated her original question, dead set on an answer.

"Where *were* you, Clay McKettrick?"

CHAPTER TEN

WHERE WERE YOU, Clay McKettrick? Clay crossed to Dara Rose, laid his hands gently on her shoulders and felt a tremor go through her slight but sumptuous body. "First," he began, his voice low, "I'll tell you where I *wasn't*, Mrs. McKettrick. I wasn't with a secret wife, and I wasn't upstairs at the Bitter Gulch Saloon, enjoying the favors of a dance-hall girl. I'm not Luke, and I'm not Parnell. I'm *Clay McKettrick*, and it would behoove you to get that straight in your mind. As for where I was, I slept right here last night, and this morning I hired a crew and went out to the ranch to start digging a foundation and a well. The makings of our house will be here right after the first of the year, as I told Philo Bickham yesterday, in your presence and hearing. And as long as the weather cooperates, I plan to spend as much time as I can out there, making the necessary preparations, because the sooner we can move into a place of our own, the better."

She looked up at him, confused and probably startled by the uncommon length of the speech he'd just given. He could see that she was still afraid to hope, afraid to trust, when it came to any personal dealings with a man. She bit down on her lower lip but didn't speak.

Clay smiled, kissed the top of her head. She wasn't wearing her bonnet, and her hair was coming loose from the knot at her nape, tendrils falling around her cheeks and across her forehead.

I love you, he thought. He was ready to say it right out loud, but he wasn't sure Dara Rose was ready to *hear* it, so he put the declaration by for later.

"I think we'd better get over to the house and decorate the Christmas tree," Clay drawled, enjoying the soft, pliant warmth of her, standing there in his arms, innately uncertain and, at the same time, one of the strongest women he'd ever encountered. "You see, Mrs. McKettrick, if we stay here much longer, I'm liable to seduce you, and I surely do not want our first time together to happen in a jailhouse."

She pinkened in that delightful way that only made him ache to see the rest of her, bare of all that calico, and mischief danced in her upturned eyes. Every signal she was sending out, however subtle, said she was a woman who enjoyed the intimate attentions of a man, who wasn't afraid or ashamed to uncover herself, body, mind and spirit, and then lose herself in the pleasures of making love.

Glory be.

"You seem to have a great deal of confidence in your powers of seduction, *Mr.* McKettrick," she remarked, after twinkling up at him for a few spicy moments. "What makes you think you could persuade me to give in?"

He cupped her chin in his hand, bent to nibble briefly at her mouth. Another shiver went through her at his touch. "Trust me," he said gruffly, after drawing back. "I am a persuasive man."

She sighed. "Yes," she admitted. "I believe you are."

He steered her in the direction of the door, whistled for Chester, took his hat and coat from their pegs. "For instance," he teased, as they stepped out onto the blustery sidewalk, the dog following, "I talked you into marrying me, when we'd only known each other for a few days. And I didn't even ask you to work as my housekeeper for a year before I decided whether to keep you or throw you back."

Dara Rose elbowed him, walked a little faster. "I agreed to your proposal," she whispered, though there was no one on the street to overhear, "*only* because I was desperate to keep my family together, with a roof over our heads."

"Speaking of your children," Clay drawled, "did you leave them home alone to come over here to the jail and hector me?"

She stopped, right there on the sidewalk, with Clay between her and the empty street. "Of *course* not," she said, as indignant as a little hen with her feathers ruffled. "Alvira Krenshaw is with them."

"The schoolmarm?"

Dara Rose nodded pertly. "The woman you probably considered courting before you turned your charms on me," she said.

Clay slipped an arm around Dara Rose's small waist and got her moving again, in the direction of the house where he'd be spending another night on the front room floor, with his dog. "Miss Krenshaw," he said, "was never in the running. And how did you manage to wrangle a woman who herds kids for a living into looking after those two little Apaches of yours?"

"Alvira dropped by with a book she wanted to lend to Edrina. A thick one, with lots of pictures, likely to keep that child busy until school takes up again, after New Year's. Anyhow, I made tea." Dara Rose continued to walk, but she'd turned thoughtful. "Alvira sat down to talk and, well, there's something *about* tea, it seems, that causes a person to drop her guard, at least a little. The whole story—most of it, anyway— just poured out of me."

Clay suppressed a chuckle, knowing it would not be well-received. *Remind me to dose you up with tea first chance I get*, he thought. But, "Go on," was what he said, as they started across the street, his hand resting lightly at the small of her back now, barely touching, but still protective.

"I didn't tell Alvira about Luke, or even how it really was between Parnell and me," Dara Rose confided. "But I *did* say that you and I had had a disagreement and I couldn't stop thinking about where you might be or what you might be doing."

Even in the near darkness, Clay saw her blush. It had cost her, pride-wise, to make that admission, even to a good friend, and it was costing her still.

"I see," he said.

They'd rounded the corner now, and Dara Rose's house was just ahead, so she hastened to finish. "Alvira said I'd better come and find you, then, to settle my mind, while she looked after Edrina and Harriet."

"Is it?" Clay asked.

"Is *what*?" Dara Rose retorted, sounding a mite testy. "Is your mind settled, where I'm concerned?"

They stood in front of her gate by then, light spilling out of the windows into the darkened yard. The apple tree was a spare shadow, etched into the night.

"Where you are concerned, Mr. McKettrick," Dara Rose finally replied, "*nothing* is settled. I don't know what to think, what to believe—"

He kissed her then, deeply, the way he would have done if they'd had the whole world to themselves. Adam and Eve, in Texas instead of the Garden.

"Believe *that*," he said, when he'd caught his breath. "And the rest will take care of itself."

Dara Rose just stood there, looking dazed. Even in the poor light, he could see that her lips were swollen, still moist from his kiss.

Calmly, Clay opened the gate, held it for her and shut it after they'd gone through, Dara Rose and Chester and, finally, himself.

At the base of the porch steps, Dara Rose stopped and sort of bristled, about to make some delayed response to being kissed, Clay supposed, but she didn't get the chance, because the front door sprang open and Edrina and Harriet burst out, barely able to contain their glee.

"*Now* can we decorate the Christmas tree?" Harriet demanded.

Miss Krenshaw stood, smiling, on the threshold behind them, already buttoning her practical woolen coat, ready to leave.

"Yes," Dara Rose confirmed, fondly weary in her tone. "We can decorate the Christmas tree." Her gaze shifted to Miss Krenshaw. "You're not leaving, are you?"

"I have a few letters to write, back at the teacherage," Miss Krenshaw replied, sparing a polite nod of greeting for Clay. And with that, she was past them, down the steps, striding along the walk toward the gate. There, she turned back. "Don't forget about the party at the schoolhouse," she called, most likely addressing Dara Rose.

"WHAT PARTY AT the schoolhouse?" Clay asked, as Edrina and Harriet beset him with hugs, in their joy at his return. Without missing a beat, he scooped them up, one in each arm, and the sight struck a deep and resonant chord inside Dara Rose.

She led the way into the kitchen, where she'd stowed a plate of supper in the warming oven, in hopes that Clay would be around to eat it.

"After the blizzard," Dara Rose explained, wadding up a dish towel to use as a pot holder and taking Clay's meal from the heat, "Miss Krenshaw decided to call off the Christmas program at school. Now, with all this springlike weather and Pastor Jacobs called away because of an illness in his family, so there won't be a church service, she's had second thoughts. There's no time for the children to memorize recitations and the like, but we can still have some sort of informal gathering on Christmas Day, for the community—sing a few hymns and carols…"

She paused, glanced back at him, felt a thrill as he set the girls down, then removed and hung up his hat and coat. His movements were easy and deliberate, and he looked from her face to the plate in her hands and back again.

"You must be hungry, after a hard day's work at the ranch," she said, suddenly and desperately shy.

"I am indeed hungry, Mrs. McKettrick," he said, in a throaty voice, letting his eyes move over her once before heading to the sink to wash his hands. Everything about him was so masculine—his stance, the movement of his powerful shoulders, the back of his head where his dark hair curled against the neck band of his collarless shirt. He turned, damp and handsome, his sleeves rolled up to his elbows, water spiking his eyelashes. "I am indeed."

"Eat fast!" Edrina urged Clay, as he sat down at the table. "We've been waiting *forever* to decorate the Christmas tree!"

"Forever," Harriet testified.

"For that," he said, "I do apologize." Clay looked down at the simple but plentiful meal Dara Rose had prepared—boiled potatoes, the last of the preserved venison and green beans she had grown in her own garden the summer before and subsequently put up in jars for the winter. He favored her with a slight, appreciative smile, and then spoke again to the children, who were fairly electrified with energy. "Settle down now," he said quietly. "We'll get to that tree, I promise."

They subsided, dragged themselves melodramatically out of the kitchen, portraying despondency, Chester tagging along, his ears perked up in anticipation of some new and wonderful game the three of them might play.

Clay ate at his own pace, the way he did everything, and seemed to savor the food Dara Rose had put aside for him, with no real conviction that he'd be around to eat it.

Once he'd finished, Dara Rose offered coffee, but Clay shook his head, said, "No thank you," and started for the front room. When Dara Rose lingered to clear the table, Clay shook his head a second time and beckoned politely for her to follow.

Edrina and Harriet had been busy, Dara Rose discovered. They'd taken every single ornament out of the boxes and laid them in neat rows on the settee.

Later, out in the woodshed behind the house, working by lantern light and supervised by two very lively little girls and an eager dog—Dara Rose spent the time fussing over her chickens—Clay cobbled together a stand to support the small tree and they all went back inside.

To Dara Rose, the thing looked more like a shrub than a tree, but both Edrina's and Harriet's eyes glowed with awe as one decoration after another was reverently added to this bough or that one. The homemade ornaments held their own against the store-bought ones, in Dara Rose's opinion, and she had to admit that, when finished, the effect was very nearly magical—especially when the porcelain angel with the wire halo and the feather wings seemed to hover over the whole of it, offering a blessing.

"Thunderation," Edrina breathed, reflected light from the colorful blown-glass ornaments shining on her face.

"It's bee-you-tee-ful," Harriet pronounced.

Even Chester, sitting between the children and gazing at the shining display, seemed spellbound.

"It's enough to make a person believe in St. Nicholas," Clay said quietly, for Dara Rose alone to hear. "Isn't it?"

"No," she said promptly, but without her usual conviction.

Only days ago, Dara Rose reflected dizzily, she'd been alone in the world, with two children to support, winter coming on and the threat of eviction hanging over her head. She might well have lost Edrina and Harriet forever, the way things were going.

But then Clay McKettrick had arrived by train, with his handsome horse, and pinned on the marshal's badge, and turned her entire life upside down.

The man had even managed to turn a scrub pine into a more-than-respectable Christmas tree.

It was hard, under such circumstances, *not* to believe in magic.

Christmas Eve

THE CLOCK ON the front room wall chimed ten times, and the lantern light wavered as Clay came out of the bedroom, shaking his head.

"Not yet," he said to Dara Rose, who was waiting to fill the pair of small stockings she'd allowed the girls to hang from the knobs on the side table. She'd sent him in to see if Edrina and Harriet were really asleep, or just pretending. "Those two are playing possum, for sure."

Dara Rose had an orange to drop into the toe of each stocking, thanks to the box from Clay's people up north, along with a bright copper penny and the new mittens she'd bought at the mercantile a few days before.

These things alone would delight the children, she knew, but there was so much more; she'd splurged on shoes and ready-made coats for her daughters, and Clay's packages—still wrapped in their brown paper and tucked beneath the lowest boughs of the tree—contained numerous mysteries.

They retreated into the kitchen, Clay drinking luke-warm coffee left over from supper, and Dara Rose sipping tea. She'd felt downright reckless, spending Piper's ten dollars so freely, and it still made her breath lurch to think how she'd spent some of it.

Idly, Clay took a small package from the pocket of his shirt, and set it down next to Dara Rose's teacup.

She looked up at him, but she didn't—couldn't—speak.

"Open it," he urged, with that crooked grin tilting his mouth upward at one side, in the way she'd come to love.

Dara Rose hesitated, drew a folded sheet of paper from her skirt pocket and handed it to Clay. "This is for you," she said, so softly that he cocked his head slightly in her direction to catch the words.

"You go first," he said, holding the paper between fingers calloused from working practically every spare moment to prepare for the arrival of the Sears, Roebuck and Company house, all while tending to his duties as town marshal.

Dara Rose's fingers trembled as she opened the little packet, folding back its edges.

A golden wedding band gleamed inside, sturdy and full of promise.

"Will you wear my wedding band, Dara Rose?" Clay asked.

In some ways, it would always seem to both of them that *that* was the moment they were truly married, there at the kitchen table, in the light of a single lantern, on Christmas Eve.

She nodded, murmured, "Yes," all the while blinking back tears, and allowed him to slip the ring onto her finger. It was a perfect fit.

Clay sat watching her for a few moments, his gaze like a caress, and then, very slowly, he opened the sheet of paper she'd given him.

His eyebrows rose slightly as he read, and then a grin spread across his face, lighting him up from within.

She'd given him a receipt for a night's lodging at the Texas Arms Hotel—for two.

"Does this mean what I hope it does?" Clay asked.

Dara Rose had been blushing a lot since she met Clay McKettrick, but at that moment, she outdid herself. Her whole face caught fire as she nodded.

Clay still didn't seem convinced. "You're giving me a wedding night for a Christmas gift?"

She blushed even harder. As her legal husband, he was *entitled* to a wedding night, their bargain notwithstanding. Maybe she should have waited, given him socks or a book or perhaps a fishing pole...

Meanwhile, his golden band gleamed on her left ring finger, simple but heavy.

"Yes," she forced herself to say.

"Hallelujah!" Clay replied, and then he got up from his chair and pulled her into his arms—clear off her feet, in fact—and kissed her so thoroughly that she was gasping when he let her go.

Dara Rose dashed out of the kitchen, afraid of her own scandalous tendencies, and went to look in on the children.

Certain that Edrina and Harriet were at last asleep, she returned to the front room just in time to see Clay set the exquisite doll from the mercantile window squarely in front of the Christmas tree, next to a stack of storybooks that must have been meant for Edrina.

Dara Rose drew in her breath.

"Oh, Clay," she whispered. She hadn't dared think, or hope, that he'd been the one to buy Florence.

But he had.

He waggled an index finger at her and spoke gruffly. "Don't you dare tell me I shouldn't have done this, Mrs. McKettrick. I might not be Edrina and Harriet's real father, but I couldn't love them more if I were, and besides, after all they've been through in their short lives, they deserve a special Christmas."

Dara Rose was fresh out of arguments. She simply went to Clay, slipped her arms around his lean waist and let her head rest against his chest. She could feel his steady, regular heartbeat under her cheekbone.

"I love you, Clay McKettrick," she heard herself say.

Clay drew back just far enough to tilt her face upward with one curved finger. "Do you mean it, Dara Rose?"

"I never say anything I don't mean," she replied, quite truthfully.

He grinned. "I meant to be the first one to say 'I love you,'" he told her, "and darned if you didn't beat me to it."

"Hold me," Dara Rose said. "Hold me tightly, so I know this isn't a dream."

"It isn't a dream," he told her. His breath was warm in her hair. "I love you, Dara Rose. I think I have since I first laid eyes on you that first day, when I brought Edrina home on Outlaw and you were so riled up, you were practically standing next to yourself."

She clung to him, with both arms, and her body ached to receive his, but that would have to wait.

Still, it was Christmas Eve, and Clay was holding her, and in a few weeks, they'd be settled in their new house, with a room to themselves and all the privacy a married couple could want.

She'd waited a long time for Clay McKettrick, and she could wait a little longer.

ON CHRISTMAS DAY, in the early afternoon, members of the community began arriving at Blue River's one-room schoolhouse, some on foot, some on horseback, others riding in wagons or buggies.

Miss Alvira Krenshaw had done a fine job decorating the place with paper chains and the like, and everyone who could afford to brought food to share with their neighbors. Clay carefully carried in the huge ham, arranged on a scrubbed slab of wood and draped in clean dish towels, and set it on top of one of the bookcases, with the mounds of fried chicken and the beef roasts and various other dishes already provided by earlier arrivals.

Edrina, preening a little in her new coat and shoes, carried another of her gifts, a game of checkers in a sturdy wooden box, under one arm, hoping, Dara Rose supposed, to find some unsuspecting child to challenge to a game.

Harriet, also sporting a new coat and lace-up shoes—the first pair she'd ever owned that hadn't belonged to Edrina first—held Florence tightly against her side. The doll came with a small wardrobe, neatly folded inside a travel trunk, and Harriet had changed its clothes three times before they left home.

Everyone was there, including Dr. Howard, his wife, Eloise, and little Madeline, the newcomers.

People laughed and talked, often-lonely country folks crowded together in small quarters, and eventually Miss Krenshaw sat down at the out-of-tune piano and launched into a lively version of "God Rest Ye Merry Gentlemen."

Just about everybody sang along; though, of course, some voices were better than others. Some hearty, some thin and wavering.

"Hark, the Herald Angels Sing" followed, and then "Silent Night."

Snow began drifting past the windows, and Ezra

Maddox showed up, along with Peg O'Reilly, her two boys and little Addie, bundled warmly in a quilt.

Holding the child in his strong farmer's arms, Mr. Maddox looked around at the assemblage, as though daring anyone to question his presence.

"Come in, come in," Miss Krenshaw sang out, from the piano seat, "we're just about to start supper."

Dara Rose immediately approached Peg, though she gave Mr. Maddox a wide berth, and hugged her friend warmly. Peg had obviously made an effort to dress up, and the children looked clean and eager to share in festivities.

"Happy Christmas, Peg," Dara Rose said, smiling.

"Ezra didn't say we ought to bring food," Peg whispered, looking fretful, as though she might be poised to flee.

"Never mind that," Dara Rose assured the other woman. "There's plenty to go around. In fact, I wouldn't be surprised if we wound up with as many leftovers as the Lord's disciples gathered up after the feast of the loaves and fishes."

Peg managed a tentative smile. "Addie shouldn't be out—she's been running a fever. But the little ones were so pleased to have some kind of Christmas…"

Dara Rose couldn't help seeing some of herself in Peg O'Reilly. After her husband's desertion, and all the struggles to keep body and soul together, for her children and herself, Peg barely believed in good fortune anymore, or human generosity. If, indeed, she'd *ever* believed.

Putting a hand on the small of Peg's bony back, she

steered her friend toward the part of the schoolhouse where the food awaited, helped her to fill plates for Addie and the little boys and find places for them to sit.

After that, everyone sort of stampeded forward, and there was much merriment and laughter as the people of Blue River, Texas, shared a simple Christmas.

Although she made sure Edrina and Harriet had supper, Dara Rose barely saw her husband for the rest of the evening. He was always on the other side of the crowded schoolhouse, it seemed, but each time she found him with her eyes, he smiled and winked and made her blush.

They finally converged at the cloakroom—Clay and Dara Rose, Edrina and Harriet—and the girls, probably exhausted, seemed unusually reticent.

Harriet tugged at Dara Rose's skirt and said, "Mama, bend down so I can speak to you."

Smiling, Dara Rose leaned to look directly into her youngest daughter's face.

"We have lots of presents at home," Harriet said, with a rueful glance at her lovely doll, which was now looking a bit rumpled from being clenched so tightly in her arms.

"And the O'Reillys didn't get anything at all," Edrina added, shifting her checkers game from one arm to the other. "They didn't even have a *tree*."

Clay had joined them by then, and he'd managed to collect their coats from the conglomeration in the cloakroom, but he didn't say anything.

"Do you think St. Nicholas would be sad if I gave Florence to Addie?" Harriet asked, her eyes luminous as she searched Dara Rose's face.

"And her brothers would probably like this checkers game," Edrina added.

Dara Rose's vision blurred.

She looked helplessly up at Clay.

He laid a hand on Edrina's shoulder, smiled down at Harriet. "I think a thing like that would make St. Nicholas mighty happy," he said.

Both girls shifted their gazes to Dara Rose.

She could only nod, since her throat had tightened around any words she might have said, cinching them inside her.

Edrina and Harriet raced off, beaming, to give away their Christmas presents.

EPILOGUE

December 26, 1914

CLAY GAVE DARA ROSE plenty of time to settle into their room at the Texas Arms Hotel that evening, making his usual rounds as marshal, tending to Outlaw in his stall at the livery stable and the chickens in the backyard at home. The children were spending the night with Miss Krenshaw, in the teacher's quarters behind the schoolhouse, and the thought made her smile every time it came to her. After all the times Edrina had played hooky, it was ironic, her being so pleased by the idea of sleeping there.

At her leisure, Dara Rose unpacked her tattered carpetbag, took a long, luxurious bath in the gleaming copper tub carried in, set down in front of the room's simple fireplace, the hearth blazing with a crackling and fragrant fire, and filled with steaming, fragrant water. She soaked and scrubbed and dreamed, and when she heard Clay's light knock at the door, she started.

She'd lost track of time. Meant to be properly clad in the lovely lace-trimmed nightgown and wrapper Clay had given her for a private Christmas gift, presented when the children were asleep and they were alone. Instead, though, here she was, stark naked, her skin slick with moisture, her hair still pinned up in a knot at the back of her neck. She stood, trembling, not with fear, but with anticipation, and reached for her towel.

"It's me, Mrs. McKettrick," Clay said, from the other side of the door. "May I come in?"

Dara Rose gulped hard. "Yes," she said.

His key turned in the lock, and the door opened, and Clay stepped inside. His eyes drank her in even as he shut the door again. Slowly, he took off his hat and then his coat, with its star-shaped badge, unbuckled the ominous gun belt he wore when he was working, set it aside.

"Do you really need that towel?" he asked, with a hint of mischief in his eyes, as he ran a hand through his dark hair.

Dara Rose, feeling deliciously reckless, let the towel drop.

Clay looked at her frankly, his gaze touching her bare breasts, rousing her nipples to peaks, gliding like reverent hands down the sides of her waist and over her hips and even to the silk thatch at the juncture of her thighs.

He swallowed visibly. "Mrs. McKettrick," he said, in a rumbling drawl, "you are unreasonably beautiful."

What did one say to that? Dara Rose didn't know, didn't try.

She simply waited to be touched.

Clay approached her then, lifted her out of the tub by her waist and set her in front of him. Kissed her until she felt drunk with the sensation of his mouth on hers, the radiant heat and hard substance of his body promising so much to her soft one.

"You have me at a disadvantage, Mr. McKettrick," Dara Rose managed, free to be the temptress she was at long last, and exulting in that.

"How's that?" he asked, arching one dark eyebrow and running his hands lightly up and down, along her ribs.

"You, sir," she replied, breathless at his touch, wanting more, so much more, "are fully dressed, while I am quite naked."

"Indeed you are," he agreed huskily, using one hand to loosen her chignon and send her heavy hair spilling down her back.

In the next moment, Clay lifted her again and, secret vixen that she was, Dara Rose locked her bare legs around his hips, tilted her head back with a slight groan when she felt the length of his shaft against her. That made him chuckle, and find her mouth with his, and kiss her into another, even deeper daze of jubilant need.

Suddenly, she landed, with a soft but decisive bounce, on the hotel bed, looked up at Clay as he unbuttoned his shirt, tossed it aside. Instead of stretching out beside her, though, he knelt at the side of the bed, gently parted her legs and kissed his way, very lightly, up the inside of her right thigh.

She gasped and arched her back when he conquered that most intimate place, and took her fully into his mouth.

Suckled, lightly at first, and then with increasing hunger.

Dara Rose, twice married, had never been so deliciously ravished, never felt so beautiful or so womanly, never known such a wild and frantic greed for pleasure.

Instinctively, she arched her back, and Clay slipped his hands under her buttocks, now quivering with the strain of making an offering of her entire self, and feasted on her until her body buckled and undulated in fierce spasms of celebration and she cried out.

The sound was low and long and husky, part howl and full of triumph that must have sounded, instead, like agony.

"That—" Clay chuckled against her still-tingling flesh "—is why we need our own bedroom, Mrs. Mc-Kettrick. One with thick walls."

Dara Rose laughed, or sobbed, or both. She couldn't tell which, didn't care.

All that mattered, for the moment, was that she loved this man, and he loved her, and she could, at last, abandon herself completely to this one someone, leave behind her practicality and her fears and simply *be*.

How odd, she thought, that there could be such freedom in surrender.

Still soaring from that first shattering release, Dara Rose was only dimly aware of Clay rising, removing the rest of his clothes. But when he lay down with her, on the turned-back sheets, the deepest satisfaction she'd ever known instantly gave way to the deepest *need*.

It was primitive, urgent, that need. It rocked her.

Desperate, she tried to pull Clay on top of her, feverish to take him inside her. Hold him there, to please him and be pleased *by* him.

Her body, one with his.

Her soul, one with his.

But Clay was as deliberate about making love as he was about everything else he did. He moved with slow confidence, every kiss, every caress, backed with certainty.

He enjoyed her breasts freely, and for a long time.

She moaned, her nipples pebble-hard and wet from his tongue, his lips.

He teased her. He whispered in her ears, and nibbled at her lobes, and traced the length of her neck with the tip of his tongue, leaving a line of sweet fire behind.

And when he finally lay down flat on the bed, his hands strong, he set her astraddle of his mouth and devoured her all over again, until she was rocking on him, clenching the rails in the headboard of the bed, damp with perspiration, her head tipped back in a low, guttural cry of relief as he finally allowed her to crest the pinnacle and let go.

As she descended, he told her quietly that he had not yet begun to make love to her, that they'd be at it for a lifetime.

He told her all the places he would have her, all the times and ways. She reveled in the knowledge.

"Suppose someone hears?" she fretted, when Clay laid her down again and, at last, poised himself above her.

"Suppose they do?" Clay countered hoarsely, with a grin. And then, in one long, fiery thrust, he was finally inside her, deep, deep inside her.

Part of her.

And all the flexing and needing and carrying on started all over again.

Just as Dara Rose's *life* had started all over again, with the arrival of this man, with his quiet, steady ways and his strength, so at home in his own skin.

It was the beginning of forever, for both of them.

And a fine forever it would be.

* * * * *

COMING HOME

CHAPTER ONE

As THE BUS from Phoenix chortled away, dust and exhaust fumes billowing in its wake, Cassidy McCullough left her suitcases unattended on the tarmac in front of Hennipen's Gas & Grab, an establishment that definitely lived down to its name, and approached the familiar sway-backed mare standing peaceably in the shade of what was probably the only deciduous tree in the whole town of Busted Spur, Arizona.

The horse was loosely tethered to a rusted pump handle, and there was a water bucket in easy reach.

"This is some kind of joke, right?" Cassidy muttered, knowing full well that it wasn't. This was her Uncle Duke's idea of expediency; meaning, he was busy elsewhere, and either unable or unwilling to drop whatever he was doing to meet her in front of Hennipen's, like a civilized person.

She loved her uncle, her only remaining blood relative, as far as she knew, anyway, but, since tumbling out of bed at the figurative crack, back in Seattle, rushing to the airport, where she waited through no less than three delayed flights, and then traveling north via Greyhound, she was tired and frazzled and, yes, cranky.

Annabelle Hennipen startled her with a throaty chuckle and, "It's no joke."

She stood in the station's open doorway of the Gas and Grab, a voluptuous woman with pencil-thin eyebrows and clouds of bottle-blonde hair. "Your Uncle Duke," she went on cheerfully, "he rode in an hour or so ago, on one of his cow ponies, leadin' old Pidge there behind him. Duke said his truck was broke down again, but it was probably temporary, so he'd come back here and pick up your suitcases soon as he and G.W. got the rig running. In the meantime, he didn't want to leave you waiting around, so he brought the horse."

The mention of G.W. Benton, her uncle's best friend, caused a very unexpected pinch in the pit of Cassidy's stomach. Sure, she'd had a crush on G.W. since she hit puberty, but she was all grown-up now, with a fiancé and a great job as a television reporter and occasional anchorwoman. She'd thought she was past such visceral reactions to his name, even mild ones.

Cassidy turned to face Annabelle, and shook her head. "Sometimes I wonder if that man ought to be allowed to live alone," she remarked.

"I been sayin' the very same thing for years," the other woman replied, with a wide grin. Annabelle was a voracious reader with a top-notch vocabulary, but she liked to "talk country," as she might have phrased it, provided she knew the other person pretty well. Claimed it felt more natural. "'Duke McCullough,' I tell him, 'you need a wife and I need a husband, so why don't we just go ahead and hitch ourselves to the same wagon? Two can pull twice as far as one.' He just smiles in that knee-meltin' way he has and says something like, 'One of these days, Annabelle, I'm gonna take you up on that offer, and it'll serve you right when I do, because then you'll be stuck with me for the duration.'"

Cassidy had heard it all before, of course; Duke and Annabelle had been flirting with the idea of marriage for as long as she could remember. The truth was, Duke wasn't the only one with a chronic case of cold feet—Annabelle could be pretty skittish herself. They never seemed to be on the same page, those two, when it came to tying the knot; if one was ready, the other wasn't. Thinking about the slow, plodding horseback ride ahead of her, all five dusty, sweltering miles of it, Cassidy didn't reply right away.

She'd just have to bite the bullet, she guessed. Open one of her suitcases, slip into the rest room, and swap out her tailored beige crepe pantsuit and matching strappy shoes for jeans, a tank top, and a pair of sneakers. And mount up.

It wasn't as if she had any other choice, there were no taxis in Busted Spur, since it barely qualified as a wide spot in the road, let alone a town. Annabelle had a car, but she couldn't be expected to close up shop, even for the fifteen or twenty minutes the trip out to the ranch would take. The Gas & Grab was a one-woman operation, and customers were few and far between these days. Every sale counted, however small.

Cassidy's best friend, Shelby, would have been glad to provide transportation, except that she was in Nogales for the day, buying folk art and silver jewelry for her online shop. The reality: Pidge was parked outside and the poor horse had to get home somehow.

"Don't stand out there in the heat," Annabelle scolded affectionately. "Come on inside and cool off before you and ole Pidge start for home."

Cassidy's mind had drifted, and she realized Annabelle had been talking for a while now. Though she'd missed the middle part, it didn't take a psychic to fill in the gap. Annabelle had been pondering the mystery that was Duke McCullough.

"You're right, of course," she said, without much conviction.

Annabelle stood with one shoulder braced against the doorframe now, her arms folded. She had muscular biceps and a small, colorful tattoo of a dragonfly just above her right wrist.

"You reckon Duke's ever gonna change?" she asked, as she stepped back to allow Cassidy to enter the store, and it was clear from her tone that she didn't really expect an answer.

Cassidy gave her one anyway. "No," she said, sighing with relief in the air-conditioning. "Would you want him to?"

Annabelle pondered for a few moments, looking solemn, then shook her head. "Probably not," she admitted. "If he was different, he wouldn't be Duke."

"There you have it," Cassidy replied. Just then, the bell over the front door jingled, and Annabelle's whole face brightened.

"Customer," she chimed.

Cassidy grinned. "Take care of business," she said.

"I'll be fine." Annabelle nodded in an of-course-you-will kind of way, returned Cassidy's grin, and greeted the newcomer.

After lugging both her suitcases into the "staff" rest-room, a cubicle with a sink and a toilet, Cassidy took out a change of clothes, and swapped out her pantsuit and pricey shoes for denim, cotton and sneakers. She'd worn her shoulder-length brownish-blonde hair in a loose chignon for the trip; now, she let it down, did a little finger-combing, folded her dressy jacket, pants and sleeveless top, and packed them away, along with the heels.

Within a few minutes, she'd tucked her luggage and laptop case into a corner of the storage room, among crates of soda and other products, picked up her shoulder bag, which contained the main necessities of life: her cell phone, an iPad, a hairbrush, a wallet, a small bottle of hand sanitizer, and a travel-size package of tissues.

Good to go.

She called a cheerful "see you later" to Annabelle and went out the back door.

Pidge raised her big head from the water bucket, nickered a greeting, and waited. Cassidy reached her side, threw both arms around the animal's sweaty, horse-scented neck, and hugged it. "I've missed you," she said, in a murmur, feeling strangely tearful.

Pidge nickered again and headbutted Cassidy a couple of times, though gently, as if to ask, *Where have you been?*

She untied Pidge, pressed her shoulder bag against her side with one arm, gripped the saddle horn with her free hand, shoved one foot into the stirrup, and swung up into the worn saddle. She'd forgotten how good it felt, sitting on a horse's back, and she took a few moments to savor the sensation and allow muscle memory to kick in. Then she said softly, "All right, girl. Let's go home."

Before they could start, though, Annabelle rushed out with a wide-brimmed straw hat in one hand.

"Wait," she said, careful not to spook the horse as she came closer. "Take this."

Cassidy smiled, accepted the hat and plopped it onto her head. "Thanks," she told Annabelle, who was already hurrying back toward the door of the Gas and Grab.

Pidge didn't need much urging.

Once Cassidy nudged the mare's sides gently with the soft heels of her sneakers, Pidge snorted, let her belly swell and then contracted it again, and finally set out in the direction of home, her movements as slow and steady as if she'd been pulling a plow.

"WELL, NOW," SAID G.W. BENTON, straightening his back and then adjusting his hat, when his seven-year-old son, Henry, tugged at his shirt sleeve and pointed out the horse and rider coming up Duke's driveway. "Would you look at that?"

The question was rhetorical, of course, but Henry answered it just the same.

"I *am* looking, Dad," he said, since, like most kids, he was a literalist. Then, just as unnecessarily, he added,

"Cassidy's back." There was a note of wonder in his voice.

"Duke," G.W. said, to get his friend's attention.

Duke came out from under the hood of his beat-up old truck, smeared with motor oil and grinning like a fool. Wiping his hands on his pant legs, he strode off toward Cassidy, took hold of Pidge's bridle, and waited for his niece to step down from the saddle.

"Where's her stuff?" Henry wanted to know. He looked and sounded worried. "Duke said Cassidy would be sticking around here for a while."

G.W. ignored the odd spark of excitement he felt as he watched Cassidy slip out of the saddle, nimble as ever, let out a laugh, and accept Duke's greasy hug.

"I don't imagine she wanted to ride all the way from town with a suitcase in each hand," he told the boy.

Henry didn't reply; he just bolted in Cassidy's direction, full-tilt.

She saw him coming, dropped to one knee, right there in the dirt, and opened her arms to catch him.

While Duke looked on, still grinning, Cassidy laughed and practically hugged the stuffing right out of the kid.

For his part, G.W. didn't move a muscle at first; he just looked on. The spark he'd felt before flared up again, and he wondered what it meant, if anything.

He'd known Cassidy McCullough all her life. She didn't look much different than the last time he'd seen her, back at Thanksgiving, but something had changed since then. It was unsettling, that something, and it felt almost like an ambush.

In the next instant, he decided the idea was crazy

and shook it off. He joined the welcome party, put out a hand to Cassidy just as she got back on her feet, one arm still looped around Henry's skinny, little-boy shoulders, holding him close to her side.

She looked at G.W.'s hand, then his face. A smile quirked at the corner of her mouth, but she didn't move otherwise. "Hello, G.W.," she said, very quietly.

G.W. let his hand fall back to his side. That sensation of being taken by surprise washed over him again, and he didn't like it one damn bit.

"Hello," he replied, and the word came out sounding dry as sawdust.

What the devil was wrong with him, anyhow? Sure, Cassidy was all grown-up, and she was beautiful, too, but both those things had been true for some time now. There was no good reason for his reaction.

Fortunately, she didn't seem to notice. She just inclined her head toward Duke's ancient pickup, with its raised hood, rusty patches, and broken tailgate. Except for a good set of tires, the rig was a wreck. "Next time I visit," she said, "I'll rent a car."

According to Duke, Cassidy had come home to plan her fancy wedding.

Therefore, the next time she visited, G.W. reflected, nonplussed, she'd be married to that city dude, Michael-somebody.

Since that thought didn't set well with him for reasons he didn't care to explore further, G.W. swung a glare Duke's way.

He was irritated with Duke, had been all morning.

He was tired of helping to fix that old rust-bucket of a truck.

Duke wasn't poor, for God's sake. He could afford a decent truck—a whole fleet of them, if the notion struck him. After all, Duke had enjoyed more than his fifteen minutes of fame during the very profitable three seasons his reality show, *Man Seeks Monster*, had been on the air.

An acknowledged expert on cryptids, such as Bigfoot, he was still making money in his sleep, now that the series was being streamed on the internet, and then there were the fees he collected for speaking engagements and personal appearances at various conventions.

On top of all that, Duke sustained a weekly vlog on YouTube, posted a regular podcast with listeners numbering in the tens of thousands, and collected advertising revenues on both fronts.

The man had plenty of money.

What he *didn't* have, it seemed to G.W., was the sense God gave a fence post.

If he had, he'd have met his niece at the airport, like a normal human being would have done. Instead, he'd left Cassidy a horse.

Why all this ought to piss G.W. right off the way it did was anybody's guess. It just did, that's all.

"Now why would you want to rent a car?" Duke asked Cassidy blithely, already leading Pidge toward the barn.

Cassidy made no reply, knowing her uncle didn't expect one; she just watched them go, her uncle and the tired horse, shaking her head and smiling a little.

Henry was still clinging to her, both arms wrapped around her waist, his blond, buzz-cut head tilted back so he could look up into her face.

G.W., still exasperated and not having a clue why, since he'd grown up with Duke and nothing the man did ever surprised him, no matter how off-the-wall crazy it was, slapped his hat against his right thigh and then slammed it back on his head.

"Is that truck going to be running anytime soon?" Cassidy asked mildly, indicating Duke's disabled pickup with a nod of her head.

If she'd noticed G.W.'s fractious mood, she gave no sign of it.

"God knows," G.W. said, thrusting the words out on a long breath, like a sigh. Then, somewhere inside himself, he stumbled across a smile and dredged it up to the surface. "I didn't know about the horse," he said.

In fact, though Duke had mentioned that Cassidy was coming home to plan her wedding, G.W. hadn't known when she was due to arrive, either.

"If I had, Henry and I would have met your bus."

Cassidy's smile seemed to wobble a little. She looked tired, overheated, and pretty dusty, too. "That's okay," she said, very quietly. "I kind of enjoyed riding Pidge again. It's been too long."

Henry finally released his hold on Cassidy's middle, but immediately grabbed her hand and started tugging her toward the house. He had a thing about women, Henry did; his mother had been gone almost three years by then, and he still missed her.

So did G.W., of course, though the raw ache had worn off at some point.

Now, when he thought of Sandy, the memories were almost always good ones, from before she got sick.

Cassidy allowed Henry to haul her over to the side porch, and the door that led into the kitchen, and G.W. just naturally followed along.

He and Henry washed up at the sink while Cassidy slipped away to the downstairs bathroom, ostensibly to do the same thing.

By the time they all reconnected in the kitchen, Duke was back from the barn.

Once he'd scrubbed the grease off his hands and forearms, he opened the fridge door and rummaged around until he came up with two cans of beer, a soda for Henry, and a bottle of store-bought iced tea, the kind Cassidy liked.

At least he'd made some kind of preparation for company, G.W. thought, still a mite sour.

Unless, of course, the stuff was left over from Cassidy's last visit, in which case it had to be way past its expiration date.

"How was your flight?" Duke asked his niece, joining the rest of them at the round oak table that had been sitting right where it was for the better part of a hundred years.

Cassidy unscrewed the cap on her iced tea and raised the bottle as if making a toast. "Can't complain," she replied. "Security was a total pain, like it always is, but I had an aisle seat and there wasn't much turbulence. As for the bus ride from Phoenix, well, I could complain about that, but I'm not going to."

Duke chuckled, raised his beer in acknowledgment of her gesture, and said, "Well, it's over now. You're here, safe and sound."

"Not to mention saddle-sore," G.W. observed dryly.

Duke slanted a glance his way, and temper flashed in his dark gray eyes. He opened his mouth, remembered Henry's presence, and shut it again, but G.W. had a pretty good idea what his friend had been about to say—something along the lines of, *What's your problem, Asshole?*

Since G.W. couldn't have said what his problem was, precisely, he was glad the question hadn't been put to him.

"I'm going to be in second grade when school starts again," Henry announced, after taking a long slug of cola. He never got the sugary kind unless Duke gave it to him; at home, he drank milk, water, or unsweetened fruit juice, so he was making the most of the opportunity.

Cassidy widened her eyes—they were blue, her eyes, thick-lashed and bright as a star-spangled sky, in spite of her obvious fatigue—and gave a low whistle of exclamation. A few tendrils of her dark blonde hair tumbled down and clung to her neck.

"Seriously?" she replied. "*Second grade, already?* Why the last time I saw you, Henry Benton, you were only in *first* grade."

"That was way last year," Henry said soberly. "At Thanksgiving."

"Right," Cassidy said, drawing out the word.

"You hungry?" Duke asked, all solicitous now that Cassidy had made her own way home.

Was there no end to Duke's hospitality? G.W. wondered, still grumpy. What other grand surprises awaited Cassidy—clean sheets on her bed? Freshly laundered towels in the upstairs bathroom?

Not that any of it was his business, one way or the other.

Duke's previously unasked question suddenly had merit.

What the hell *was* his problem?

Actually, he knew what it was, but he wasn't ready to admit that, even to himself.

"I'm starving," Cassidy said, with feeling. "The six pretzels I was served on the plane wore off a long time ago, and I had to hurry to catch the bus."

The bus.

That, to G.W.'s mind, was even worse than the horse. Why hadn't Duke at least borrowed a rig, if he wouldn't buy one, and met Cassidy's flight down in Phoenix?

Stop it, G.W., he told himself silently. *You are an asshole.*

"Well, then," Duke said, pleased with himself, "I guess it's a good thing I whipped up a batch of my special chicken-and-wiener spaghetti casserole a while back and shoved it in the freezer. Half an hour in the oven, and supper's on the table."

Cassidy laughed, and the sound reminded G.W. of the bell in the country church down the road, back when it still had a clapper. Used to float on the air, the peal of that bell, summoning the faithful—or the merely resigned—from far and wide.

"Sounds good to me," she said. "In the meantime, I could use a shower."

Duke was already out of his chair, turning stove knobs, cranking up the oven.

Cassidy got up, too, ruffled Henry's stubbly hair as she passed him, and headed for the back stairway. "You two are welcome to stay and eat with us," Duke told G.W., once she was gone.

"Gosh," G.W. said. He'd been standing since Cassidy rose from her chair. "Much as I enjoy your amazing culinary skills, old buddy, Henry and I have other plans."

Henry looked downright discouraged. "*You* have other plans," he said, leveling his gaze at G.W. for a moment before turning his attention to Duke. "Dad has a date."

"It's not a date," G.W. said, too quickly.

Duke's mouth twitched. He opened the freezer above his refrigerator and rooted around until he'd managed to extract a casserole dish wrapped in tinfoil and secured with a few strips of duct tape.

"Your loss," he told G.W.

"If it's not a date," Henry persisted, "how come I have to be babysat?"

"You're spending the evening with your grandma," G.W. reminded his son. "That doesn't qualify as being 'babysat.'"

Henry rolled his eyes dramatically. "She'll make me watch *Dancing with the Stars*," he protested. "She has a whole huge bunch of episodes saved up on her TV.

And most of the dancers aren't even stars—not really. They're just people who get their pictures on the covers of those little newspapers at the supermarket all the time."

"Life is hard," G.W. said, suppressing a smile, "and then you die."

"I hate it when you say that," Henry replied.

"I'll save you some chicken-and-wiener spaghetti casserole," Duke promised the kid, all sympathy. In a good-cop-bad-cop scenario, he would have been the good one, while G.W. got to be the mean guy.

Eff that, he thought.

Thanks," Henry answered, ignoring his dad.

Then he stomped outside, slammed the screen door behind him.

G.W. sighed. Squeezed the bridge of his nose between a thumb and forefinger.

"You could use some sensitivity training," Duke remarked affably, peeling the duct tape off the casserole.

G.W. opened his mouth, closed it again, and followed the trail Henry had just blazed.

Only difference was, he didn't slam the screen door.

Much as he would have liked to do just that.

REVIVED BY HOT water and soap lather, barefoot and clad in a faded pink and white polka-dot sundress she'd found in the back of her bedroom closet, Cassidy returned to the kitchen, drawn by the scent of supper.

Duke hadn't heard her coming down the stairs, so she paused at the edge of the room, watching as he lifted the spaghetti casserole from the oven.

The concoction, innovative as it was, would probably taste even better than it smelled.

Standing there, unnoticed as yet, Cassidy let her thoughts drift back over the years she'd lived in this sturdy, roomy old house, and the people with whom she'd shared the space—Duke, of course, and her late grandmother, Molly.

Twelve years Cassidy's senior, Duke had always been more like a big brother to her than an uncle. Molly, widowed young, had been strong, forthright and beautiful, through and through.

The situation had been complicated, right from the beginning.

Cassidy felt a pang of sorrow, the nostalgic kind.

Her bio-mom, Heather Lawrence, hadn't planned on getting pregnant at the age of eighteen, but she had.

Already on her own, she'd married Cassidy's father, Jack McCullough, Duke's older brother, who was barely twenty at the time.

In short, it didn't last.

One day, Heather had written the briefest of notes— *"So long"*—on a scrap of paper and taped it to the refrigerator door. Then, leaving her child and most of her belongings behind in the cramped apartment above the abandoned movie house in Busted Spur, she'd boarded the 4:00 bus for Phoenix and subsequently vanished.

For a while, Jack had been sure she'd come home.

Instead, she'd stayed gone.

There had been postcards now and then, always mailed from a different place. The last one—Cassidy had found it among her grandmother's things, years after Molly's death—had simply announced that she'd remarried and wouldn't be getting in touch again.

True to her word, she never did.

Jack had tried to fill the gap Heather left, in those early weeks after her departure, but in the end, he couldn't hold down a job and look after a small, baffled child, constantly crying for her mama.

Oh, he'd sent home most of his pay and called regularly.

After more training and a brief visit home, he'd been deployed, sent to North Africa. He wrote often, and the allotment checks arrived on schedule.

A little over a week before Jack's tour of duty would have ended, he was killed in action.

Naturally, Molly had been devastated, but she'd carried on—she'd had a ranch to run, after all, as well as a young son and a granddaughter to raise.

Stoic in that way country women often are, especially when they've been raised on the land, Molly had simply kept on keeping on. She bought and sold cattle, helped to mend fence lines, repaired leaky roofs and broken pipes, raised a garden in summer, and still managed to smile a lot more often than she cried.

When Cassidy was seven, Molly came down with a case of pneumonia, entered the hospital, spent nearly two weeks there, and finally came back to the ranch to recover.

Instead of getting well, though, she'd gotten sicker.

Finally, Duke had had to drive her to the hospital again.

This time, she didn't come home.

So many people attended Molly's funeral that the services had to be held outside, since the church couldn't hold them all.

Only twenty at the time, Duke had carried on as best he could, running the family ranch, looking after Cassidy, a kid at the time, probably with a lot of help from his girlfriend, Annabelle.

Despite their best efforts, letters from the county began to arrive, then phone calls, then visits.

Social workers had scoured the country for Heather, it turned out, but they'd had no luck finding her or any of her kin. That was when they'd started making noises about putting Cassidy in foster care.

Duke—he'd been christened "Pernell," but he'd refused to answer to any variation of that from day one, so everybody had finally given up and let him name himself after John Wayne—was too young, certainly, to take proper care of small child.

One thing about Duke, though: he was bone-stubborn. He and Cassidy added up to a family, by his calculations, and nobody was going to split them up.

Somehow, he'd prevailed against the system and, with considerable help from Annabelle, neighbors and friends, he'd raised his niece to adulthood.

Back in the day, he'd helped Cassidy with her homework every night. He'd sat through every school program, every Christmas pageant at church, every dance recital, dressed up in his best jeans, a white shirt starched stiff, with shiny boots on his feet.

Smiling wide, and proud as all get-out, he'd been as devoted as any father.

At home, he'd combed the tangles out of Cassidy's hair, bandaged her skinned knees, seen her through her teenage years. When she earned a full-tuition scholarship and went off to college, Duke had taken a night job as a mechanic, in addition to his ranch work, and helped with her living expenses.

And when she'd graduated with a degree in Media Arts and promptly landed an entry-level job as a reporter at a Seattle TV station, he'd been thrilled for her.

So, she thought, re-entering the present moment, standing there in that familiar kitchen, with the linoleum floor cool beneath her feet, if he'd left her a horse as transportation that day instead of coming to fetch her himself, it was no big deal.

Suddenly, Cassidy's eyes burned, and she sniffled.

Alerted by the sound, Duke set the casserole dish in the middle of the table, turned to her, and smiled, his handsome head tilted slightly to one side. "Hey," he said. "You're not crying, are you? Because there's no crying in baseball."

She laughed moistly at the ancient joke. "This is baseball?" she countered.

"Might as well be," Duke replied.

Then he put his arms out wide, and Cassidy went straight into them, held on tight. He'd had a shower of his own, and exchanged his work clothes for a clean shirt and jeans that looked new. And he smelled of spray starch and sunshine and his chicken-and-wiener spaghetti casserole.

Propping his beard-stubbled chin on top of her head,

he said, "I'm glad you're home, Little Bit. I am surely glad you're home."

"Me, too," Cassidy said. The hug ended, and she pulled back a chair at the table to sit.

Duke sat down across from her.

"Guess we'd better say grace," he said.

"Grace," Cassidy said, straight-faced. They laughed again.

And that was the moment Cassidy truly came home.

G.W. FELT UNCHARACTERISTICALLY AWKWARD, standing on the bumpy sidewalk outside Becky's Coffee Bar, on Main Street, with his hat in one hand.

Five minutes before, he'd dropped Henry off at Sandy's mother's place; the boy had sulked all the way into town, his earlier accusation in Duke's kitchen occupying the space between father and son like a third person.

Dad has a date.

"This," G.W. protested now, under his breath, "is not a date."

Not that either of them had raised the subject since they left Duke's place.

Okay, yeah. He *had* asked Alice Fletcher to meet him at Becky's for coffee at a specific time—tonight.

He liked Alice well enough; she was new in town, would be teaching fifth grade at the local elementary school in the fall.

They'd met at the social gathering following a school-board meeting a few days before and G.W. had to admit, to himself if no one else, that he'd been attracted to the woman—kind of. She was pretty, she was smart, and she seemed like a good sport.

Plus, he'd been feeling a mite lonesome lately.

He wouldn't call meeting for coffee a date, but it was possible Alice might be of another opinion entirely.

He swore silently.

He'd been looking forward to this evening—until Cassidy McCullough came riding back into his life on an ancient horse named Pidge.

Something had shifted, deep inside him, the moment he caught sight of her.

And that something, whatever it was, whatever it meant, was there to be reckoned with.

In the moment, all G.W. wanted to do was get back in his truck, drive over to his mother-in-law Myrna's place, rescue Henry from an evening of *Dancing with the Stars*, and head for home.

Once he'd wrangled the boy through the evening ritual: bath, pajamas, bedtime story, prayers, and, finally, an exchange of "good-nights," he'd be able to think.

G.W. always thought more clearly on his own land—whether sitting in his front room, out riding fence lines, fishing down at the creek, or standing under that familiar patch of stars arching between one red mesa and another.

He squared his shoulders, reached for the door handle.

He couldn't just walk away without an explanation; Alice had surely seen him by now. He might make some excuse, say he had trouble out on the ranch—a sick horse, maybe. Crazed cattle running amok. The crash of an alien spacecraft.

He opened the door and stepped inside. The place was full but, then, it only had six tables, each one topped with Formica and surrounded by mismatched chairs.

When it came to public gathering places, besides the churches and the schools, Busted Spur boasted one diner, three taverns, and Becky's hole-in-the-wall java joint. The aromas of freshly brewed coffee and baked goods greeted him right away, and, looking around, he soon spotted Alice, sitting alone at a corner table, her head bent over a book, the fluorescent light catching in her sleek cap of dark hair.

As G.W. approached, she looked up, closed her book, and smiled.

He smiled back. "Am I late?"

Alice shook her head. She had navy blue eyes, high cheekbones and very good teeth. "You're right on time, G.W."

He didn't sit. There were no waitresses at Becky's; if you wanted something, you went up to the counter, waited your turn, and asked for it.

The tabletop was clear except for Alice's book and a glass of ice water.

"What can I get you?" he asked, with a slight nod toward the chalkboard menu on the wall behind the cash register.

"Just plain coffee," Alice said. "I'll doctor it myself."

G.W. nodded again, made his way to the counter.

There, he ordered two coffees and, realizing he was ravenous, two good-sized cranberry scones as well.

Becky herself poured the coffee, placed the scones on separate plates, and asked if he wanted them "nuked." G.W. had gone to school with Becky; she'd been Sandy's best friend, maid of honor at their wedding.

G.W. said no, he'd just take the scones as they were, thanks.

Becky, a petit force of nature with a headful of red dreadlocks, a turned up nose and mischievous green eyes, pretended to peek around G.W.'s right shoulder for a look at Alice.

As if she hadn't already checked her out.

"It's about time you got yourself a life, G.W. Benton," she whispered, with a grin. "She's real pretty, that new teacher."

Yes, G.W. thought, Alice was easy on the eyes, all right.

She was probably lots of other good things, too.

Unfortunately, she wasn't Cassidy.

CHAPTER TWO

MORNING SUNLIGHT SLANTED through Cassidy's bedroom window, found her face, turned the insides of her eyelids bright pink.

She stretched, luxuriating in her girlhood bed, allowed herself to pretend, for just a few seconds, that she'd never left home in the first place.

A chirp from her cell phone wrenched her out of the brief fantasy; she sat up, scrabbled for the device on her nightstand, peered at the screen. The text was from Michael Brighton-Stiles, the man she was going to marry.

Marry.

The word fell through her brain like a dark meteorite, landed hard and spiky in the pit of her stomach. She blinked a couple of times.

Focus, she told herself. *Focus*.

Although Cassidy was a morning person, she usually needed at least half an hour and a mug of strong coffee to resurface from the depths of sleep.

Wake up, sleepyhead, the message read.

Using her thumbs and biting her lower lip, Cassidy fumbled out a response.

Easy for you to say. You've probably been up since daybreak.

After a brief pause, a line of smiley faces appeared inside a small comic-book style bubble on Cassidy's phone. Then more words appeared:

I miss you.

A lump formed in Cassidy's throat, and she was glad the conversation was virtual.

Me, too, she wrote. Not very romantic, she thought, but she was still shaking off last night's dreams. Surely, that was it.

I'll call you later, Michael replied, rapid-fire. He was a morning person, too, but he started early. In a meeting now.

Okay, Cassidy replied.

Suddenly, she was almost overwhelmed by a strange, unfounded feeling of guilt, as if she'd told a lie.

A thumbs-up icon served as Michael's goodbye.

She'd showered and dressed before the realization struck her—neither she nor Michael had used the word "love," even once.

Now that she thought about it, she couldn't recall the last time either of them had used it, except in a very superficial way.

Michael, though handsome and a very successful attorney, was something of a Mama's boy, and that fact was getting more and more difficult to ignore.

Cassidy's mood took a dive, and the backs of her eyes scalded.

Downstairs, the kitchen door opened and closed, and familiar voices rose through the planks of the floor.

Her gloom evaporated instantly.

Grinning, she raced for the rear staircase, down the steps, into the morning smells of coffee brewing, eggs frying, bread toasting.

Her very best friend, Shelby, ponytailed and beaming, was just looping the handle of her shoulder bag over one of the hooks beside the back door.

Duke, looking as pleased as if he'd arranged the reunion personally, stood at the stove, spatula in hand, overseeing breakfast.

Shelby and Cassidy hugged, both teary, both laughing. "Girlfriend," Shelby trilled, "it is *so* good to see you!"

Cassidy hugged her friend again, too happy to speak.

Shelby smiled and cupped Cassidy's face in her hands. "Repeat after me," she said. "Say, 'it's good to see you, too, Shelby.'"

Cassidy smiled back. "What you said," she replied.

Shelby rolled her dark brown eyes. "You haven't changed a bit," she said.

Duke set another place at the table, dished up the eggs. "I'd say she's changed plenty," he put in. His tone was amicable, but there was an edge to his words. "Time was, I thought Cassidy would get her fill of the bright lights and the big city and come on back to Busted Spur, where she belongs. Instead, she's marrying some yahoo with a hyphenated last name."

Cassidy glanced quickly at her uncle, and just as quickly looked away.

"Don't start," she said evenly. "You don't even know Michael, and Seattle happens to be a very beautiful place."

Shelby's gaze tripped from Cassidy's face to Duke's and then back again. "Can we skip this part?" she asked.

She'd always been the peacemaker.

"Sit down and eat," Duke ordered gruffly, the underside of his jaw going red. He kept his eyes averted. "Both of you."

Nobody argued.

The toast was buttered, then slathered with blackberry jam. The coffee was poured. The food was delicious, plentiful and loaded with fat grams. Cassidy ate anyway.

Normally, living her regular life in her tiny apartment in downtown Seattle, she'd break into a carton of Greek yogurt, the diet kind, and nibble at half a banana, saving the other half for a mid-morning snack at her desk.

Michael was big on healthy choices; after all, his mother was a nutritionist.

"So, where do we start, with this wedding thing, I mean?" Shelby asked, when Duke left the table to answer the wall phone on the other side of the room.

Although he was a technological wizard by anybody's definition, there was one, count 'em, one, landline in the entire house.

Again, Cassidy felt that dropping sensation, a sort of freefall from her head to her pelvis, but she answered blithely. "Let's not worry about the wedding right now. I was thinking we could go for a horseback ride, or drive to Sedona and take in a movie or—"

Shelby's eyes were solemn. "Or?" she prompted, when the silence stretched past the three-second mark.

"We have plenty of time to make plans," Cassidy said, looking away.

On the far side of the kitchen, Duke was discussing the logistics of an upcoming expedition in search of his favorite monster, the legendary Bigfoot.

Shelby touched Cassidy's hand.

"Sure," she agreed gently. "We have all kinds of time."

The visit was supposed to last a week, and the proverbial clock was ticking. Not exactly an eternity.

Still, it seemed to Cassidy that a little procrastination couldn't hurt.

Duke finished his call, hung up, and returned to the table. Scraped back his chair.

The look he gave Cassidy was sheepish, but there was a gleam in his eyes and his mouth tilted up at one side. "When you marry this guy," he ventured, "are you planning to hyphenate again?"

Cassidy relaxed. "Cassidy McCullough Brighton-Stiles?" she said, as though trying out the name. "That would be a real mouthful."

Duke chuckled. "That it would," he agreed. Then, mercifully, he changed the subject. "I got the truck running this morning, by the way. Do you want me to pick up your stuff at the Gas & Grab, or were you planning on fetching it yourself?"

"On Pidge?" Cassidy rejoined. "At the moment, she's all the transportation I've got."

"We'll use my Blazer," Shelby said.

"Truck's running again," Duke reiterated. "I'll be glad to make the trip to town."

"You just want an excuse to see Annabelle," Cassidy teased.

Duke cleared his throat. "I happen to have an important meeting," he said, very soberly. Then, like sunshine parting clouds, his grin flashed. "And I don't need an excuse to see Annabelle."

Thus, the matter was decided.

They finished breakfast, Duke left for town, and Shelby and Cassidy washed the dishes and tidied up the kitchen.

After some discussion, they decided against both the horseback ride and the movie in Sedona and settled on going to Shelby's place instead.

The buying trip to Nogales had been a good one, Shelby said, and she wanted to show Cassidy the loot. Afterward, Shelby would whip up a batch of her famous nachos, and they'd talk and talk, catch up on everything that had been going on in their lives since the last time they were together.

No mention of the wedding was made.

G.W. STILL CONSIDERED himself a rancher—he owned five hundred acres, maybe a hundred head of cattle, a sturdy house and a good barn—but ranching was a hardscrabble enterprise at best, there in the red-rock country of Arizona.

He made most of his living by designing and building websites at one or the other of three computers set up in his home office and by investing and reinvesting his net profits. He wasn't rich, but he didn't owe a dime to anybody, and Henry, at seven, already had a hefty college fund.

So far, so good.

That morning, with the first round of chores done and Henry clothed, fed and outside playing with Chip, the dog, G.W. was having a hard time keeping his mind on the business at hand. If he was going to be preoccupied, it seemed to him, he ought to be thinking about Alice.

Instead, he couldn't get Cassidy out of his head.

Cassidy. His best friend's niece.

Until yesterday, he'd thought of her as a kid, if he'd thought of her at all. He'd watched her grow up, for God's sake. As a child, she'd been a pesky little monkey, following him and Duke pretty much everywhere they went. Then, right on schedule, she'd morphed into a gawky adolescent, all knees and elbows, with braces on her teeth.

Naturally, Cassidy had gone right on evolving, transforming into a college coed, and finally, unquestionably, a woman.

He'd loved his late wife, Sandy, worked hard building a life with her.

And then she died.

After that, practically consumed by grief, G.W. had done all he could just to keep getting up in the mornings. If it hadn't been for Henry, he suspected, he might have shut down entirely, turned into one of those crusty old codgers who hoard catalogs and newspapers and soup cans until they have to make their way along winding paths to get from one room in their house to another.

Devastated as he'd been, though, throwing in the towel hadn't been an option. He'd had a son depending on him.

So he'd taken hold. Held on.

Always good with computers, he'd taught himself to build websites.

With Henry's future in mind, he'd invested the proceeds from Sandy's modest life insurance policy.

He'd herded cattle, hauled hay onto the range when the grass gave out, fed and exercised his horses.

Most importantly of all, he'd overcome an ongoing, bone-deep urge to withdraw into himself, close off his deepest emotions, and make sure Henry and everybody else in the world stayed on their own side of the barricade.

Making the decision to go on had been one thing, and living up to it had been another. It had been a process, not an event, a series of efforts, wrong turns, and fresh starts.

If it hadn't been for Duke, showing up on his doorstep with a six-pack or a pan of that god-awful chicken-and-wiener spaghetti of his, inviting Henry to go fishing or camping or some such, thus ensuring that he, G.W., would go, too, well, he still might have folded up.

Looking back now, G.W. knew he wouldn't have looked twice at any woman during those years.

Over time, however, the wounds had closed.

These days—and nights—he could remember Sandy without wanting to drink himself stupid, drive his truck off the highest cliff he could find, or go outside, dig in his heels, and bellow insults at God until a retaliatory lightning bolt put him out of his misery. He did the only thing he knew to do—he kept putting one foot in front of the other, literally and figuratively.

For all the healing he'd undergone, though, there were still scars. G.W. loved Henry with his whole heart; it was involuntary, almost a reflex. He'd loved Sandy in the same all-encompassing way. And losing her had damn near killed him.

Love was a risky thing, he'd learned that the hard way. He heard the back door open, heard Henry's sneaker-padded steps and Chip's toenails clicking across the kitchen floor.

"Dad?" The boy spoke from the doorway to G.W.'s office. G.W. closed the program he'd been working on and swiveled in his chair.

"That would be me," he said, with a grin.

When Henry was younger, he'd have hurtled across the room and flung himself into G.W.'s lap, but those days were already gone, apparently. A shred of an old song played in G.W.'s head: *turn around*...

"Are you finished working yet?" Henry's knees were grass-stained beneath the hems of his summer shorts and the laces of his seemingly oversize sneakers were untied.

G.W. shoved a hand through his hair, sat back in his chair. "Truth is," he said, "I'm not getting much done. You hungry?"

Henry shook his head.

Beside him, Chip, a lop-eared black Lab, watched G.W. with interest.

"Could we go over to Uncle Duke's?"

"Duke's probably busy, and besides, he's got company, remember?"

Henry's grin practically blinded him. "Yeah," he said. "Cassidy's there."

"Most likely, she's busy, too," G.W. said carefully.

"She might need a ride to town or something," Henry insisted, with enthusiasm.

G.W. hated to dampen his son's spirits, especially after the little tiff they'd had the night before over his "date" with Alice Fletcher, but reality was reality. "We can't just drop in, son," he replied.

"We do that all the time," Henry pointed out reasonably. "Are you mad at Uncle Duke or something?"

"No," G.W. said, "I'm not. Why do you ask?"

Henry screwed up his freckled face, considering.

In that moment, G.W. thought his heart might burst, trying to contain everything he felt for this boy. He was mighty glad it wasn't his turn to speak, because he'd sound like a bull frog if he tried.

"You were sort of cranky," Henry said, finally. "Soon as Cassidy got there, you were in a bad mood. Don't you like her?"

G.W. sighed. He had overreacted when Cassidy showed up on horseback the day before, getting all bent out of shape at Duke's failure to act like an uncle, but he wasn't about to try explaining that to a seven-year-old—

especially when he couldn't explain it to himself. "I like Cassidy fine," he said moderately.

"Then you must have been mad at me," Henry concluded, looking pretty annoyed himself.

"I wasn't mad at you, Henry."

"Then why did you make me go to Gramma's and watch *Dancing with the Stars* for three hours?"

"You know why. I was having coffee with a friend."

"You were on a date."

G.W. templed his fingers in front of his chest. "We've had this discussion," he reminded the child. "But suppose, just for a minute, that it was a date. What's so terrible about that?"

Henry flushed, folding his skinny kid-arms in front of his skinny kid-chest.

Beside him, Chip thumped the floor with his tail, absorbed by the drama. "You were with that woman you met at the schoolboard meeting," the boy accused.

"And?"

"She's not mommy material!"

G.W. suppressed a smile. "Whoa back, boy. Nobody said anything about mommies. It was no big deal."

"Grown-ups always say stuff like that," Henry protested vigorously. "Next thing you know, some woman is moving in, bossing everybody around, hanging her underwear on the shower rod."

Where did he get this stuff?

"Henry," he said, "Ms. Fletcher and I had coffee together. That's all." A pause, a breath. *Steady now.* "Trust me, she won't be moving in with us or hanging her underwear on the shower rod."

Henry remained doubtful. His arms, still folded, looked rigid, and his chin was set at an obstinate angle. "My friend Mark's dad said that about his girlfriend, and guess what? Now she's Mark's stepmother and she gets to tell him what to do and he's seen her bras and her panties, because she wears fancy ones that cost a lot of money and she rinses them out in the bathroom sink all the time."

"Horrifying," G.W. said.

"You think it's funny!"

"Well," G.W. mused aloud, "yeah. I guess I do."

"It's not funny! It's embarrassing."

"I hate to break this to you, kid, but you won't always feel that way. Someday, in fact, some good-looking woman will be sudsing up her undies in your bathroom, and you'll be just fine with the idea."

Henry reddened with righteous conviction. "Never," he said.

God, he was stubborn.

Like his daddy, he heard Sandy say.

G.W. put out a hand. "Bet you five bucks," he said.

"Not unless you allow for inflation," Henry told him. "By the time I'm grown-up, and you have to pay me, five dollars won't be worth much."

"You've got me there," G.W. said.

Henry huffed out a sigh. "You're really bullheaded sometimes, Dad."

G.W. chuckled. "And you're half again too smart for your own good." He leaned forward, resting his forearms on his thighs. "The way I see it, what we have here is a standoff. We'd better just agree to disagree and be done with it, don't you think?"

Another sigh, though less gusty than before. "Well, if you're not going to work, and we're not going over to Uncle Duke's place, can we at least go somewhere? 'Cause I'm really bored and so is Chip."

G.W. thrust himself to his feet. "In that case, I guess we'd better come up with a plan."

Henry looked hopeful now. "Like what?"

"I'm thinking we could head for the swimming hole. Cool off a little."

Henry beamed. "Yes!" he yelled.

Chip let out an excited yip. Whatever was coming down the pike, the dog was ready to participate, no holding back.

"Let's get going, then," G.W. said. "We're burning daylight."

SHELBY LIVED IN the same small house she'd grown up in, on Pine Street.

Her parents, both retired postal workers, had purchased an RV and hit the road three years before.

Shelby, an only child, had been going through a bad divorce at the time, so she'd moved back to Busted Spur from Phoenix—temporarily, she insisted—to house-sit and figure out what she wanted to do next.

As it turned out, Shelby's mom and dad loved the gypsy life. They came back a couple of times a year, stayed a week or two, and then took off again.

Shelby, always an enterprising type, had adopted a couple of dogs, lived frugally on her savings from her last job, and slowly but surely built herself an eclectic online business. She sold folk art, inexpensive jewelry, and what she called upcycled furniture, carefully restoring chairs and small tables and wooden chests she found at flea markets and garage sales and thrift stores.

Except for a nonexistent love life, she claimed, she was perfectly happy, and Cassidy, perched on a stool at Shelby's kitchen counter and munching her delectable nachos, believed her.

"What about you?" Shelby ventured. "Are you happy, Cass?"

"Of course I am," Cassidy said, a little too quickly. "I'm about to marry a fabulous man. I have a great job. Why wouldn't I be happy?"

"You tell me," Shelby said, reaching for her glass and rattling the ice inside before taking a swig of diet soda. "I look at you, my friend, and I don't see happiness. I see uncertainty. I see sadness. But I sure as heck don't see a bride-sparkle in your eyes or a flush of excitement in your cheeks." She bit into a tortilla chip dripping with melted cheese, salsa, and other good things, chewed and swallowed, and then went on, her tone thoughtful. "If I were getting married in a few months, I'd be over the moon. I'd be talking about nothing but the guy and what I was planning to wear, what color my brides-maids' gowns would be, the sort of flowers I'd have in my bouquet, where we were going on our honeymoon. You haven't said one word about any of those things."

"There's time," Cassidy said, but it was a weak argument and she knew it.

"What's the problem?" Shelby persisted. From kindergarten days, she'd been able to see right through Cassidy, but this was the exception to the rule. Or, at least, that was what Cassidy told herself.

"I'm crazy about Michael," she said.

"Are you?" Shelby asked quietly. "Or are you just feeling stuck?"

Cassidy bristled. "No, I'm not *feeling stuck*."

"Yes, you are," Shelby replied. "Since when does a person planning a country club wedding in a world-class city like Seattle have to come back to little ole Busted Spur, Arizona to decide on the details?"

"Maybe I wanted to consult my best friend?"

"Oh, save it, Cassidy," Shelby said gently. "God knows, I'm glad to spend time with you, but it's not as if we live on separate planets. We email, we text, we FaceTime. We could decide on dresses and all the rest through the miracle of technology. You came home because you wanted to *be* home."

Cassidy's cheeks were hot by then, but it wasn't because she was flushed with prenuptial excitement. "I love Michael," she insisted.

Calmly, Shelby licked a dollop of cheese from the tip of one finger. "Not G.W. Benton?"

"G.W. Benton? You've got to be kidding!"

Shelby's shoulders moved in a casual shrug. "Kidding? Hardly. The man is drop-dead gorgeous, your classic cowboy, in every sense of the word. He's smart, he's honest and he's obviously capable of long-term commitment. If I thought I had a chance with the guy, I'd be all over him in a hot minute."

Cassidy opened her mouth, closed it again. Thought

seriously of making an indignant exit until she remembered that she'd ridden to town in Shelby's Blazer, and it would be a long, hot walk home to the ranch.

Shelby smiled. "You were crazy about G.W. from the day you hit puberty. No matter who you went out with, you compared the poor guy to him. Don't you think I remember?"

"Oh, for heaven's sake, Shelby," Cassidy sputtered. "You and I were kids. He was a grown man. And, yes, I had a crush on G.W., but so did every other female within a hundred-mile radius of Busted Spur."

"You cried for a week when he and Sandy got married," Shelby recalled.

"That was a long time ago."

"I'll bet you even compare Michael to G.W.," Shelby went on.

"I do not."

"So tell me about him. Michael, I mean."

"You know all about Michael. I've told you everything."

Shelby gave a slight nod, of the complacent variety. "You've told me more than you think you have, Cass."

"What is that supposed to mean?"

"Last month, for example, you said he wanted you to lose five pounds. The month before that, you told me Michael's mother—*his mother*—chose your wedding gown. And before that—"

"Stop," Cassidy broke in. "Michael's mother has good taste. The dress is beautiful."

"Michael's mother has no business picking out your wedding dress, Cassidy. Plus, you always planned on getting married here, didn't you? In that little country church your grandmother attended?"

"Can we not talk about this?"

"I think we have to talk about this. Marriage is serious business, my friend. And trust me, if you get it wrong, the fallout can be wicked. Believe me, I've been there."

Feeling cornered, and strangely defensive, Cassidy braced both elbows on the counter top and rested her head in her hands.

"Not now, Shelby," she said, grimly. "Please. Not now."

Shelby reached out, patted Cassidy's shoulder. "When?" she asked, very softly.

Cassidy merely shook her head.

"Okay," Shelby said. "I'll wait. The last thing I want to do is upset you, believe it or not. So from here on out, even if it kills me, I'll keep my opinions to myself until you ask for them. Deal?"

Cassidy swallowed hard. Lowered her hands. "Deal," she replied.

After that, there didn't seem to be much to say. They gave up on the nachos; Shelby put the leftovers in the fridge, and reached for her car keys.

So much for togetherness.

THE SWIMMING HOLE sparkled like liquefied crystal, spangled with moving flashes of sunshine, filtering through the leaves of cottonwood trees. The pool was spring-fed, so the water would be ice-cold, even in the heat of midsummer, but Henry didn't care, and G.W. hadn't either, when he was his son's age.

Chip leaped from the truck as soon as an opening appeared, a glossy black streak of dog shooting over stones and patches of grass, dashing onto the same fallen log that had served as a footbridge for as long as G.W. could recall.

Henry, wearing cutoff jeans, a T-shirt and flip-flops, and carrying a rolled-up bath towel under one arm, gave a hoot of laughter when Chip reached the middle of the log and hurled himself into the water.

A great, sparkling splash rose around the animal, and he surfaced, paddling gleefully toward the bank. Hauling himself out of the drink, Chip shook, slinging gleaming droplets in all directions.

"Dumb dog," Henry crowed, with great affection, dropping his towel on the flat surface of a boulder.

Chip gave a couple of eager barks, then dashed back out onto the log and flung himself off it again.

G.W., shirtless and, like Henry, making do with a pair of cutoffs, wasn't quite so anxious to take the plunge.

Henry waded right in, shivering and delighted, while Chip swam in a wide circle, yipping encouragement.

They were a sight to remember, the dog and the boy, awash in dappled sunlight and spring water.

A memory sneaked up on G.W. just then; he saw Sandy, slim and shapely in her two-piece swimsuit, standing waist-deep in the swimming hole one summer day, teaching a younger, smaller Henry to float on his back. She'd taught the boy well; by the time Henry was four, he was as agile in the water as a baby seal.

G.W. waited for the pang to pass, then hung his own

towel from a low-hanging cottonwood branch and grinned as he approached the edge of the swimming hole. Henry was treading water, while Chip paddled toward shore, where he promptly shook himself off again, baptizing G.W. in the process.

G.W.'s laugh was part howl.

To get it over with, he stepped into the water and immediately dunked himself to the shoulders. The cold bit into him like sharp teeth. Stole his breath.

Henry, blue-lipped and bright-eyed, swam over, set his feet on the stony bottom, and windmilled his arms, splashing G.W. unmercifully.

G.W. grabbed the boy around his waist and hauled him close to stop the assault, laughing the whole time.

Chip, still on the bank, stood with his back to G.W. and Henry, dripping wet and barked, once, twice, a third time.

Henry watched the dog, squinting in the bright glare of the afternoon, then started toward him. Chip was fairly obedient, as a general rule, but if he bolted in pursuit of a jackrabbit or some other critter, they might spend the rest of the day tracking him down.

Just then, a horse and rider appeared on the bank, a single shape against the light.

"Duke!" Henry called, shading his eyes with one hand.

G.W. felt a brief, sharp stab of jealousy.

Duke swung down from the saddle as Chip scrabbled up the bank to greet him. He bent to ruffle the dog's sodden ears.

"You gonna go swimming?" Henry asked eagerly, as Duke, leaving his pinto cowpony to wait, reins crisscrossed over its neck, sidestepped down the rocky incline, Chip hopping gleefully at his side.

Duke shook his head. "Not today," he said. "I'm a warm-water man, myself. Cold makes my bones ache."

G.W., willing himself not to shiver with the cold, waded back to shore. "What's going on?" he asked his friend.

"I spotted your truck and decided to stop by and say howdy," Duke replied. "Annabelle's cooking supper tonight, after she closes up the store, of course, and she gave me strict orders to invite the two of you."

The way Henry whooped and punched the air with one miniscule fist, a person would have thought he hadn't had a decent meal in weeks.

Something about his eagerness chapped G.W.'s hide, and he wasn't proud of that. He held his tongue and looked down at Henry.

The boy was practically jumping up and down. "Can we go, Dad? Can we go?"

G.W. smiled, ran a hand over Henry's spiky hair. "Sure," he said.

He'd have preferred to keep his distance from Cassidy, at least until he got some perspective, and, at one and the same time, he looked forward to being near her, even if they didn't so much as look at each other.

"Great," Duke said, taking off his hat, running an arm across his forehead and putting his headgear back on again. "See you around six-thirty."

"See you then," G.W. replied.

"Can Chip come, too?" Henry called out, as Duke was turning to head back to his horse.

Duke paused, adjusted his hat, and grinned. "He's welcome," he told the boy. "Hope he likes barbecue."

A few moments later, Duke was back in the saddle and riding off.

"We'd better go home and get ready," Henry announced.

G.W. glanced at the sun. "Six-thirty is still a long way off," he said.

But Henry was already reaching for his towel, covered in goose-bumps, teeth chattering. He draped the thing around him like a cape. "Chip needs time to get dry," he reasoned. And then he started up the hill, the dog trotting alongside.

CHAPTER THREE

Even in her bedroom, with the door and both windows closed, Cassidy could smell the smoke wafting up from the brick barbecue grill in the backyard, and it made her stomach rumble. She'd offered to help with the preparations, but Annabelle had shooed her away, saying cheerfully, "Let us fuss over you a little."

Now, Cassidy sat cross-legged in the middle of her bed, her iPad in her lap.

Her suitcases, delivered by Duke while she was still munching nachos with Shelby, had been unpacked and tucked away in the back of her closet. The few articles of clothing she'd brought along were neatly hung up or arranged in her dresser drawers.

Her laptop remained in its case, under her desk. Her cell phone, plugged into its charger, rested on the nightstand. It was stubbornly silent.

She considered texting Michael, just to say hello, but decided against it. It was six-twenty, but he often worked late, and even if he'd escaped the office early— he was a junior partner in his grandfather's law firm— he'd most likely be pumping iron at the gym or jogging around Green Lake.

Or visiting his mother.

He'd promised to get in touch "later."

Did she even want him to call?

Silly.

Of course she wanted him to call.

Cassidy tried to be annoyed with Shelby, for planting doubts in her mind, but she couldn't quite get there.

Her crazy, mixed-up feelings were her own responsibility, not her friend's.

She lifted the tablet in both hands and peered at the screen. She'd already read her email, such as it was.

Her neighbors, Jim and Sarah, who lived in the apartment across the hall from hers, said the weather was glorious and they were bringing in Cassidy's mail every day. Magazines, flyers and bills. They were watering her plants and they missed her, but they hoped she was having a really good time way down there in Broken Spur.

She replied with a thank-you and a few chatty remarks, didn't bother correcting the name of her hometown.

An assistant producer at the station where Cassidy read the news and covered the occasional "personal interest" story, informed her that her temporary replacement, Jessica, was working out just fine. Cassidy shouldn't worry about a thing; why, they'd barely noticed she was gone.

"Great," Cassidy murmured.

She deleted a dozen sales pitches, stopped on a notice that someone had posted on her wall at the social media site she generally ignored, since it had been engineered by the public relations people at the station.

Probably a faithful viewer, she thought, perhaps asking where she'd disappeared to.

She opened the site, found herself looking at a smiling photo Michael, with his arm resting loosely around the slim waist of a tall, well-toned blonde with too many glistening white teeth.

Cassidy squinted, held the tablet about an inch from the tip of her nose. There was no caption, no post. Just the picture.

Something quivered in the pit of Cassidy's stomach.

She wasn't the jealous type—Michael had never given her any reason to be—but the image made her uneasy, just the same. The woman in the picture was probably an old friend, or perhaps a client.

No big deal.

Suddenly, her phone jangled, startling Cassidy so completely that she nearly dropped the iPad.

She groped for the phone, saw Michael's aristocratic face on the screen.

She felt relief. And something else that wasn't so easy to identify.

"Michael," she said, and she knew she sounded surprised.

He laughed. "Hello, Funny-face," he replied.

"Who's the blonde?" The question was out of Cassidy's mouth before she'd consciously framed the words.

Immediately, she was mortified, wanted to hide somewhere, anywhere. Under the bed. Behind the clothes in her closet.

Michael was silent for a long moment. Then, cautiously, he asked, "What blonde?"

"I'm sure she's—" Cassidy blurted, her face hot. "I mean, I don't think—"

"What blonde?" Michael repeated. This time, he didn't sound cautious, he sounded irritated.

"The one in the photo somebody posted on my page," Cassidy said, strangely calm now, though her cheeks still throbbed with heat. "Tall? Gorgeous? Wearing a black cocktail dress with a plunging neckline?"

"Cassidy," Michael said, "what are you talking about?"

She clicked on a couple of links, forwarding the photo. "You tell me," she said.

He was quiet again, probably scrolling through the messages on his phone. More than a minute passed before he let out a grim-sounding laugh.

"Oh," he said. "That's just Angela. She's on one of Mother's committees." A pause. "There was a charity benefit last night, at the club, and Mom introduced us. You know how those events are, Cass—people take random pictures, put them on the internet."

Just-Angela, Cassidy reflected, was standing so close to Michael that she was practically resting her head on his shoulder.

"Cass?" Michael prompted. "You're not going to turn into one of those suspicious types, are you?"

"Er—no," Cassidy said. "No, of course not."

"Good," Michael said finally, his voice husky, a little brisk. He sounded peevish, indignant. Coldly controlled. "Mother's getting annoyed, Cass. She says she's left you several messages about the guest list, and you haven't responded."

Cassidy had ignored the messages, though she didn't say so. "I'll check later," she said.

"This conversation is going nowhere," Michael said, with a lightness that didn't quite ring true. "Suppose we speak again tomorrow?"

"Right," Cassidy replied, already dreading the call. It seemed there was a wall between her and Michael, and there was no scaling it. "Tomorrow."

A knock sounded at her bedroom door. "I'm supposed to tell you supper's ready," called a childish voice.

Henry.

Her spirits immediately rose.

"On my way," she called out.

Michael disconnected then, without saying goodbye.

The door opened a smidge and Henry's small, freckled face appeared in the crack.

"I brought my dog," he said. "Uncle Duke said it was okay."

Cassidy set her phone aside, logged off the internet, and tossed her tablet to the foot of her bed, grinning at the boy. "How about introducing us?" she asked.

Henry's brow furrowed slightly. "But you already know Duke."

Cassidy laughed, standing up. "I meant the dog, Bucko," she said.

Henry brightened. "Oh." He sounded pleased.

Cassidy offered her hand, and Henry took it, shyly but firmly. Then he led her downstairs, through the kitchen, and out the back door.

She saw Duke and Annabelle standing shoulder to

shoulder at the grill, conferring over the food, chicken, coated in sauce and sizzling deliciously.

G.W. was sitting at the nearby picnic table, turning his phone end over end in one hand while he smiled at something Shelby said.

Shelby, meanwhile, was petting Henry's dog.

Seeing Cassidy, she smiled, bunched one shoulder in a brief shrug, as if to say, *what-can-you-do*?

"Annabelle invited me," she said, as though an explanation was needed.

"I'm glad," Cassidy replied, and it was true. She and Shelby had had their tiffs over the years, mostly while they were in high school, but the bond between them was strong.

G.W., standing now, gestured for her to have a seat. He looked cowboy-handsome in his jeans and long-sleeved Western shirt, open at the neck. Glancing down, she saw that he'd polished his boots.

Not that that meant anything.

Cassidy hesitated, caught the look of good-natured challenge in Shelby's eyes, and finally sat down.

G.W. did, too, close but not too close. He smelled of fresh air, soap and spring water, and when his elbow bumped against Cassidy's, she flinched as if he'd goosed her with a cattle prod.

Out of the corner of one eye, she saw his mouth twitch.

Shelby smiled broadly from the other side of the table, looking smug, and Cassidy made a face at her.

Annabelle left Duke's side and disappeared into the house, gesturing for Henry to accompany her. A few minutes later, the two of them emerged onto the patio, Annabelle toting a huge stoneware bowl covered in cellophane, while Henry followed proudly behind her, carrying a second, smaller bowl.

Duke speared chicken pieces onto a waiting platter, piled foil-wrapped corn on the cob on another.

"This is my special potato salad," Annabelle said, plunking down the crockery and peeling away the cellophane. Henry's bowl contained heat-and-serve rolls, protected by a checkered dishcloth.

Once everything was on the table, and everyone was seated, Annabelle next to Duke, on one side of the picnic table, along with Henry, Cassidy, G.W. and Shelby on the other.

Annabelle nudged Duke until he offered a short prayer of thanks.

Plates were filled, and there was some chatter.

"You've got a video to record tonight, don't you?" Annabelle asked Duke, once things settled down.

He nodded, indicating with a gesture of one hand that his mouth was full, so he couldn't answer just yet.

"Are you going to talk about Bigfoot?" Henry asked eagerly.

Duke chewed, swallowed. "Who else?" he countered, with a grin.

"Have you ever seen a Sasquatch, Uncle Duke? For real, I mean?"

"Up close and personal," Duke answered solemnly, but his eyes were twinkling, the way they always did when he talked about his mysterious monsters.

He'd told Cassidy plenty of stories over the years,

and she'd listened, wide-eyed and fascinated, wishing she'd seen them, too, terrified that one day, she would.

To this day, she didn't know if Duke had really encountered such creatures, as he claimed, or if he was just spinning yarns.

To Duke, making up tall tales wasn't the same thing as lying. He'd probably see it as a public service at best, and a harmless form of entertainment at worst.

One thing was for sure, tens of thousands of people listened to his podcasts and followed his blog. He'd been the one to call a halt to the reality show, not the network; said it kept him away from home too much and, besides, he'd had to wear makeup on camera. A man can only handle that kind of humiliation for a certain length of time, he'd told Cassidy.

Now, Duke did the occasional personal appearance, acted as an "expert" on similar programs to his own, and guided Bigfoot tours in the wooded areas around Flagstaff and in parts of Colorado and Montana, too. He had "proof"—recordings of bone-chilling shrieks, chest-pounding, barrages of stones striking the walls of some isolated hunting cabin or hastily-assembled lean-to, photographs of huge trees splintered to toothpicks, videos of dozens of boulders rolling down slopes for no explicable reason.

"I hope I see one someday," Henry said earnestly, swatting at a mosquito.

"Be careful what you wish for, young fella," Duke counseled, with a merry twinkle dancing in his eyes.

Henry gave a delicious little shudder and sneaked

a morsel of barbecued chicken to the dog. Everybody noticed, nobody commented.

"I wouldn't be scared," Henry said, squaring his small shoulders.

Cassidy narrowed her eyes at her uncle, a silent suggestion that he shut up.

"Maybe you wouldn't," Duke said. "I can tell you're a brave one. Here's the thing, though—sometimes, it's smart to be scared." His gaze slid, just briefly, to Cassidy's, then moved away again. "This critter, Bigfoot, I mean, keeps to himself, for the most part, and he doesn't much care for trespassers, not when they're on his turf. A full-grown Sasquatch might be twelve feet tall, and they're fast on their feet, too."

"Duke," Cassidy said pointedly, afraid the boy would have nightmares.

"Does Bigfoot like dogs?" Henry asked, ignoring everybody but Duke. As he spoke, he stroked Chip's head, resting on his small lap.

"Nope," Duke replied seriously. "It's better to keep dogs and Sasquatch apart, I think."

Henry leaned forward to make eye contact with his father. "Did you ever see a Bigfoot, Dad?" he asked.

"Guess I must have been looking the wrong way every time one showed up," he said, with a straight face. Cassidy liked that answer, though she wasn't sure why.

Henry's glance swung to Cassidy. "What about you?"

"What about me?" Cassidy teased, wanting to pull the child close and hold him tight for as long as he'd allow.

"Do you believe in Bigfoot?"

Cassidy considered the question. "I *don't not* believe," she answered presently. "I've never actually seen one—and, frankly, I hope I never do—but that doesn't mean they don't exist."

While they were talking and eating, that subtle shift happened, and daylight gave way to dusk. Stars began to pop out all over the sky, like the points of silver needles poking through black velvet, and the moon was a transparent crescent, riding low over the row of red hills in the distance.

"Getting late," G.W. remarked, rising from the bench, his empty plate and silverware in hand. "Let's help with the cleanup, son, and be on our way."

"I'm not even tired," Henry complained.

"Well," G.W. responded, "I am. Get with it, buddy."

Everybody stood up then, and the clearing away began.

Duke bid the others good-night and disappeared into the detached garage he'd converted to a state-of-the-art recording studio with some of the proceeds from his TV series to film his video for YouTube.

After a quick edit, he'd be beaming the program to all parts of the planet.

The others bumped into each other in the kitchen, putting away leftovers, washing dishes.

Annabelle wrapped generous portions of chicken, potato salad, rolls and corn on the cob for G.W. and Henry to take home.

Henry's battery ran down, all of a sudden, and he fell asleep on the kitchen floor, resting his head on Chip's

furry back. G.W. scooped the child up with a tender-
ness that struck Cassidy to the heart.

The dog lumbered to its feet, ever ready to follow his
people wherever they happened to be headed.

"You carry the food," Annabelle told Cassidy briskly,
shoving a stack of plastic containers into her hands.
"G.W.'s got his hands full, as you can see."

Cassidy knew she was being set up, but she didn't
bother to argue. She accepted the leftovers and followed G.W. out of the house, being careful not to trip
over the dog.

Henry, zonked out, didn't stir in his father's arms.

G.W. led the little procession to his truck, parked
in the gathering darkness, opened the rear door on the
passenger side of the extended-cab and eased Henry
into his car seat. The boy opened his eyes briefly, then
dropped off again.

It struck Cassidy then, a fierce rush of love for the
child. And it didn't subside.

She waited while G.W. fastened Henry in for the ride
home, shut the door, and finally rounded the rig to open
the driver's side. He stepped back, and Chip sprang past
him, scrambling across to the other seat.

With a sigh and a half grin, G.W. turned to Cassidy,
took the pile of leftovers from her hands. "Thanks," he
said, very quietly.

Cassidy didn't trust herself to speak just then, so she
merely nodded. G.W. leaned in to set the containers on
the console, turned back to her again.

"I know this is none of my business, Cassidy, but—"

"But what?" Cassidy prompted.

"This guy you're about to marry," he said. "Do you love him, Cassidy?"

She opened her mouth to answer, but nothing came out. Not even a squeak.

G.W. smiled again, almost sadly, touched her hair, and withdrew his hand.

The night sky, thick with stars, framed him.

Cassidy's heart clenched, relaxed again.

"It's real nice to have you back," he said, in parting. Then he climbed into the truck, started the engine, flipped on the headlights, and drove away.

Cassidy stood completely still in the wide gravel driveway for longer than she should have, oddly stricken by the encounter. G.W.'s words echoing in her brain. *This guy you're about to marry. Do you love him, Cassidy?*

Did she love Michael? Or had he simply been a substitute for the man she'd never dared to believe she could have? She hugged herself, tilted her head back. Overhead, the stars blurred.

She wasn't the least bit surprised when Shelby turned up at her elbow.

"You all right, Cass?" she asked gently.

Cassidy nodded, but saying anything still seemed risky. With the back of one hand, she wiped her eyes.

"When you're ready to talk," Shelby said, "I'll be ready to listen."

Cassidy merely nodded again. A part of her wanted to admit to Shelby that, suddenly, she felt hollow inside every time she thought about Michael.

Just a few days before, she had loved her fiancé, with

her whole heart, or thought she did. Now, she wasn't so sure.

"See you tomorrow," Shelby told her. Then she walked over to her aging Blazer, climbed in, and left.

Cassidy waved until she knew Shelby couldn't see her anymore, then turned and went slowly into the house.

Annabelle was sitting at the kitchen table, a cup of coffee steaming in front of her.

She looked tired—her mascara was smudged and her lipstick had worn away—but she seemed happy, too.

"Spending the night?" Cassidy asked, not unkindly.

"Haven't decided yet," Annabelle replied, with a soft smile. "Would it be a problem if I did?"

Cassidy returned the smile, wondering if her eyes were puffy from the tears she'd shed outside. "Not for me," she replied honestly.

She liked Annabelle, wished Duke would just go ahead and marry the woman, already. They weren't getting any younger, as the saying went, and they obviously loved each other—so what was the holdup?

Early on, she supposed, she'd been the main reason for the delay. As much help as Annabelle would have been, especially when Cassidy hit her teens, it would be like Duke to decide the responsibility for his niece was his and his alone.

But Cassidy had been grown-up and on her own for a while now. Where she was concerned, Duke was out of excuses.

Annabelle watched her for a moment or so. Then she said, "Shelby's worried about you, and so's Duke."

"I'm fine," Cassidy said, more weary than irritated. Annabelle arched one eyebrow.

"Are you?"

"I'm really tired," Cassidy said, dodging the question.

That much, at least, was true. On impulse, she crossed to the table, kissed Annabelle lightly on the forehead, and went upstairs.

There were several texts waiting on her phone, all from Michael, all short to the point of abruptness. What happened to "let's talk about this tomorrow"?

Cassidy, call me.

Hello? I'm waiting.

Fine. Have it your way.

Etc.

She knew there was no emergency. Michael would have called the landline, when she didn't get back to him right away. He had the number.

Besides, she didn't have the emotional energy to deal with Michael at the moment.

Instead, she took a long bath, dried herself off with a towel, brushed her teeth, and slathered her face with moisturizer and her arms and legs with body lotion. Then she put on her nightgown and went to bed.

She was exhausted, but sleep eluded her. Ironic.

She lay in the darkness, staring up at the ceiling, gnawing on her lower lip.

After an hour or so, she heard Duke come in. Heard the murmur of voices as he and Annabelle talked.

Go to sleep, Cassidy ordered herself sternly. But it was no use.

She kept thinking about G.W., when she should have been thinking about *Michael*.

She wasn't a cheater, or a sneak, which meant she was going to have to make a choice: get serious about her relationship with Michael, or walk away.

Her feelings for G.W., dormant since he'd married Sandy, had returned, full force. And, most likely, he still loved his late wife, even though she'd been gone for three years.

Finally, Cassidy reached for her cell, swiped a finger across the screen to access the icons behind it.

Still ignoring the texts from Michael, she brought up YouTube instead, tuning in to Duke's latest production.

Somewhere between a story about a creature he called "Dog-man" and a caller's account of a ghostly encounter, Cassidy slipped away into sweet, peaceful sleep.

EARLY THE NEXT MORNING, rested and incapable of staying in bed, she rose, dressed, and crept out of the house, headed for the barn. In the shadowy predawn light, she greeted each of Duke's horses by name, pausing to stroke their impossibly soft noses and listen to their nickered "hellos." She'd ridden all of them, at one time or another.

That day, she chose Skye, a dapple-gray mare, sure-footed and agile, but gentle, too. "Not today, old girl," she told a watchful Pidge. "You get to sleep in until room service arrives."

With that, she fetched the appropriate gear from the tack room, placed everything within easy reach, led Skye out of her stall, and saddled her in the dim breezeway. The ordinary, earthy smells of horse and straw and even manure heartened Cassidy, just because they were so familiar.

When the mare was ready to ride, Cassidy led the animal outside and mounted up. Annabelle's car, an elderly station wagon, was parked over by the woodshed. She smiled, reining Skye toward the open range.

When she looked back at the house a few moments later, the kitchen light was blazing, too. The sun was just beginning to stain the eastern sky, but on ranches, morning arrives early. Cassidy imagined Duke and Annabelle brewing coffee, making breakfast, talking over their plans for the day. Annabelle usually opened the Gas & Grab by six, and today would be no exception.

There was considerably more daylight by the time Cassidy and Skye splashed across a narrow spot in the creek and started up the bank on the other side. She was on G.W.'s land by then, since the creek marked the border between his place and Duke's, but she wasn't worried about running into him. He was probably up and around, but he'd be close to the house, either making breakfast for himself and Henry, or feeding his horses. Like Duke, G.W. ran cattle, but, also like Duke, it was more about heritage and habit than paying the bills. It was hard to make a living, just by ranching, unless the operation was big enough to be called a corporation.

Breaking through a line of cottonwood trees, Cassidy saw G.W.'s low-slung log ranch house in the distance. Sure enough, lights glowed in a few of the windows, and the barn was lit up, too. Cassidy drew back on the reins, sat still for a little while, taking in the scene. In winter, there would be acres of glittering snow draping the countryside, spilling from the roofs of the house and barn, lining the rough-hewn windowsills, cloaking the rural mailbox at the base of the gravel driveway.

It would be like stepping into a living Christmas card.

Cassidy felt her throat tighten even as something softened inside her. She'd missed this place, and the people who lived here—not just Duke, not just Shelby and Annabelle and various other longtime friends, but everybody who called Busted Spur home.

She thought about what Shelby had said the day before, in her kitchen. *You came home because you wanted to* be *home.*

She had yearned for this place, there was no denying that. She liked Seattle, but everything moved so fast there; somehow, she always felt out of step with things.

There was always that strange undercurrent of urgency—go, go, go—even when she was sound asleep.

But coming back for a visit was one thing. Staying for good was a whole other matter.

How would she earn a living, for one thing? There weren't any TV stations in Busted Spur of course—jobs of any kind were scarce—and she didn't have Shelby's entrepreneurial talent.

Next question: Where would she live? She was an

adult now. She couldn't stay with her uncle indefinitely. The ranch house would always be home, but she didn't belong there anymore. Not on a long-term basis, anyhow.

She rode for another hour or so, turning things over in her head, allowing herself to be saturated by sunrise and quiet and miles of open country, and then she turned back.

MYRNA SHOWED UP on G.W.'s doorstep as soon as breakfast was over, smiling broadly when G.W. let her in. She was nothing like Sandy, with her bubble of dyed blonde hair, her outdated makeup, her mood swings.

Today, she was cheerful. "Is there coffee?" she asked.

G.W. smiled. "Sure," he said, gesturing toward the table. "Have a seat and I'll get you some."

Myrna plunked her giant purse on the floor beside a chair and dropped into the seat, looking around. "Where's that grandson of mine?" she asked.

"Probably hiding," G.W. said dryly, setting a full mug of java in front of his mother-in-law. "He'll turn up once he's sure you aren't planning a marathon of *Dancing with the Stars* or some show involving housewives."

Myrna waved off the remark with a perky gesture of one manicured hand. All in all, she was a good sport. "Someday, when it's time for Henry's first prom, he'll thank me for exposing him to the finer things in life."

"I wouldn't bet on that," G.W. grinned, hauling back a chair and sitting down across from her. He'd always liked Myrna; as mothers-in-law went, she was all right. She'd been a single mom, way before it was fashionable, and she'd done a good job raising her only child, Sandy. She'd earned a decent living operating a hair salon out of her basement—still did, though she only worked part-time these days—and her love for her daughter, if a little rough around the edges, was plain to see.

Before Myrna could offer a comeback, Chip burst into the kitchen, closely followed by a reticent Henry. The kid was literally dragging his feet.

"Come over here and give this old woman a hug," Myrna commanded, spreading her arms wide.

Henry crossed the room and allowed himself, reluctantly, to be hugged. "Hey, Gramma," he said. "What's up?"

Myrna chuckled, rubbed the top of his bristly head. "My hopes," she replied. "Ready for our shopping trip to Flagstaff?"

A blank expression crossed Henry's small, freckled face, and then he gulped. "Shopping?" he croaked.

Myrna looked from Henry to G.W. and back again. "Don't tell me you've both forgotten?" she cried cheerfully. "We've been planning this forever!"

G.W. remembered—belatedly.

Last year, in the middle of summer, Myrna had stormed the malls, Henry in tow, outfitting him with new clothes for school. Socks and underwear. T-shirts and jeans. Shoes, snow boots, a jacket for fall, a warm coat for winter, the whole shebang. She'd enjoyed the expedition so much that she'd declared it an annual event and, sure enough, the time for Round Two was upon them.

According to Myrna, all the best sales were underway. G.W. was no shopper, but he would have bitten the bullet and taken Henry on a buying-spree himself, if necessary.

The thing was, the task seemed to mean a lot to Myrna; maybe it was a way to feel close to Sandy. God knew, G.W. couldn't begrudge her that.

He half-expected Henry to balk, and he was prepared to take the kid aside and talk him into going along with the plan, so Myrna wouldn't be disappointed.

To his surprise, however, Henry tilted his head to one side, musing, and finally asked, "Can we go to lunch and a movie afterward, like we did last year?"

Myrna beamed. Maybe she'd been bracing for an argument herself. "You can pick the restaurant and the movie," she replied.

Henry gave a celebratory yelp. Then he turned solemn, shifting his attention to G.W. "Will you pay lots of attention to Chip while I'm gone, Dad?" he asked. "He's gonna miss me something awful."

G.W. smiled, his heart swelling in his chest, fit to burst. "We'll both miss you," he said, "but we'll be all right, so don't go worrying about us. Concentrate on having fun with your grandmother. Got it?"

Henry grinned. "Got it," he said, and bounded off to his room to swap out his superhero pajamas for regular clothes.

As soon as he'd gone, Myrna picked up her coffee mug and took a sip. "I hear Cassidy McCullough's back home for a while," she said brightly. "She's getting married soon, I'm told."

G.W.'s gaze was level. "Yeah," he said, wondering

where this conversation was headed, exactly. And afraid he already knew.

"Folks are saying it's a big mistake," Myrna went on. "There are people who can't be truly happy anywhere but here, and the general consensus is that Cassidy is one of them."

G.W. unclamped his back molars. "Folks say a lot of things," he replied moderately.

"Not that it's anybody's business who Cassidy marries, God knows. Or where she chooses to live, for that matter. I've never put much store in gossip, myself."

G.W., being nobody's fool, didn't comment. He just stood up, crossed to the coffee maker, grabbed the carafe, and offered to refill Myrna's cup.

"G.W.," she said, very quietly.

He turned his head, looked back at her over one shoulder. "What?"

"Sandy would want you to get on with your life. You know that, right?"

G.W. stiffened. Kept his face averted, this time. "What are you getting at, Myrna?" he asked, none too patiently.

"I'm not 'getting at' anything."

G.W. made a skeptical sound, shoved a hand through his hair, and turned to meet Myrna's gaze. "I loved Sandy," he said, his voice hoarse.

"So did I," Myrna replied gently. "But I've had to go on anyhow."

G.W. said nothing.

"When my daughter died," she went on, "I wanted to lie in that grave right alongside her. Failing that, I wanted to crawl into a bottle of Jack Daniels and stay there for the duration." She paused, drew a breath, let it out slowly. "Right from the beginning, though, I knew Sandy would have wanted me to go on, to live life to the fullest." Another pause, then. "And she'd want that for you, too, G.W. You and Henry both."

"Food for thought," G.W. admitted.

Deep down, he knew Myrna was right.

CHAPTER FOUR

"YOU CAN'T IGNORE the man's texts forever," Shelby said.

It was Saturday, Cassidy had been back home for three and a half days, and she and her BFF still hadn't gotten around to making wedding plans. And, true to her word, Shelby hadn't mentioned Michael—until this morning.

She'd picked Cassidy up at the ranch twenty minutes before, and they were waiting in the drive-through at Busted Spur's only fast-food joint for sausage biscuits with egg, hash browns compressed into squares the size of a pack of playing cards, and coffee.

Cassidy, slumped in the passenger seat of Shelby's Blazer, had just looked at the screen of her phone for about the hundredth time, and, frustrated, she'd tossed the thing into the depths of her purse and muttered, to no one in particular, "Why can't I just answer him?" Hence Shelby's words of wisdom about ignoring texts.

"Don't start," Cassidy said now, with a mock glare at her friend's profile.

Shelby pretended to zip her mouth shut, but she was definitely smirking a little. Cassidy could tell, even with just a side view to go on.

The line moved, one pickup truck shorter now, and Shelby pulled forward a foot or two.

"This is ridiculous," Cassidy said. Basically, she was talking to herself, since Shelby had zipped her lips, but at least she could serve as a sounding board. She leaned over, ferreted through her handbag for her phone, and scrolled through the long series of messages. She touched Reply under Michael's most recent text and thumbed in, "Hope you're doing well. Everything is fine on my end."

Was that true? Cassidy decided it wasn't, and deleted the statement without hitting Send.

She tried, "Relax," and rejected that, too.

They moved up by a car-length or so.

"Let's hope we get to the window before they switch over from breakfast to lunch," Shelby said. "It's too early for a hamburger."

After dining in the parking lot, they'd be on their way to Flagstaff, where Cassidy intended to rent a car. She had access to Duke's truck, when it was running, but shifting gears was a battle, she needed all her upper body strength to turn the steering wheel, and all her lower body strength to work the clutch and the brakes.

In essence, driving the thing was too damn much work. On the upside, it probably qualified as a bonafide workout.

Cassidy was rereading Michael's texts. They were terse. Impatient. Not that she could blame him.

In his place, she'd have been furious, too. And hurt. Michael didn't sound hurt, though. The messages were brief—three words, max—and Cassidy found herself wanting to duck them, the way she'd dodge flying bullets.

She drew a very deep breath, let it out slowly. Glanced Shelby's way. "I don't know what to say to him," she confessed miserably.

Shelby kept her gaze on the car ahead. "You're not asking me for suggestions, I'm sure."

"No," Cassidy said pointedly. Stubbornly. Even though she wanted to do exactly that. "I'm not."

They rolled forward again. Two SUVs and a pickup truck, and they'd be at the window.

Shelby smiled, though she still didn't look at Cassidy. Her hair was piled on top of her head, held loosely in place with a huge plastic squeeze-clip. "This is taking too long," she said. "I should have cooked, but it seemed so drastic."

"Hmmm," Cassidy said. She was still staring at her phone, trying to figure out a diplomatic way to tell Michael she needed space.

"By the time our turn comes," Shelby observed, the words accompanied by an audible stomach-rumble, "we'll both be eligible for Medicare."

Cassidy chuckled, though she might just as easily have cried instead. "I haven't been very good company lately," she said. "I'm sorry, Shelb."

"Does that mean I can talk now?"

"I hadn't noticed that you'd stopped," Cassidy pointed out.

"Very funny," Shelby responded.

"Go ahead, tell me what you think."

"Gee, thanks. Don't mind if I do."

Cassidy glared at her phone again. Since she hadn't been able to come up with anything better, she typed in, Michael, I need space. Then, holding her breath, she sent the message hurtling through the ether.

The data must have had a clear shot to the appropriate satellite and zipped from there to its target, because Michael responded in about ten seconds.

"Space?" Are you kidding me? We have to talk, Cassidy. Now. I'm dialing your number, and don't even think about letting my call go to voice mail.

Their turn had come at last; Shelby had reached the drive-through window. She placed the order she and Cassidy had already agreed upon.

Cassidy's phone rang in her hand at the same moment. She considered hitting the Decline button, but that seemed cowardly.

While Shelby chatted with the person in the window, Cassidy whispered into the phone, "Hello? Michael?"

"Who else?" Michael demanded. She could picture him shoving splayed fingers through his hair. "Cassidy, what the hell is going on with you? Is this about that stupid picture on the internet? Because, if it is—"

"Michael," Cassidy said, trying to whisper while Shelby pretended not to be listening, "calm down, okay? It's just—"

He didn't let her finish. "Calm down? You fly off to Cowpattie, Arizona and leave me hanging—won't even answer my texts, for God's sake—and I'm supposed to 'calm down'?"

"Michael," Cassidy repeated, closing her eyes. "Stop. You're blowing this whole thing way out of proportion—"

"Am I? Try to see this from my viewpoint, will you? Just for a nanosecond? You're freezing me out, Cassidy, and, damn it, I want to know why."

I wish I could tell you, Cassidy thought glumly. *Trouble is, I have no clue.*

Shelby was handing money to the cashier, receiving change. Pretending not to listen.

"I just need some space, time to think," Cassidy said. The answer was a lame one, she knew, but it was all she could come up with.

"You want space?" Michael boomed. "You want time? Fine. You can have all the time you want. How does forever sound?"

Cassidy knew she should have seen that coming, but she hadn't. She felt as though she'd been punched in the solar plexus. "Michael—"

"I'm done," Michael said. "Done." And then he was gone.

Cassidy stared at her phone.

Shelby set their coffees in the cupholder on the console and handed her a bulging paper bag, grease-dappled and smelling like heaven.

Cassidy couldn't believe she still wanted to eat, considering the circumstances, but she did.

Shelby pulled ahead, parked the Blazer, and shut off the engine. "What just happened here?" she asked, her tone mild. She wasn't smirking anymore.

"I've been dumped," Cassidy said. She was shocked. Amazed. And, well, maybe she felt slightly relieved, too, like a freshly-caught fish tossed back in the water to swim free.

"Seriously?" Shelby asked. She unbuckled her seatbelt and turned slightly, so she could look straight at Cassidy.

"Seriously," Cassidy confirmed. She opened the bag, took out a wrapped breakfast sandwich and a hashbrown brick and handed them both to her friend before rummaging for her own food.

"You seem remarkably calm," Shelby said. "For somebody who's supposed to be planning a wedding, I mean."

"I think I'm in shock," Cassidy replied. She unwrapped her sandwich and took a bite. Chewed and swallowed.

"It doesn't seem to be affecting your appetite," Shelby remarked.

Cassidy laughed. Then she cried. Then she alternated between the two extremes for a couple of minutes. And all the while, she was devouring the sandwich.

Shelby probably wanted to say about a million things, but she concentrated on her breakfast and waited out Cassidy's emotional jag. She wasn't the kind of friend who shoved tissue at a person when they lapsed into mild hysteria and told them cheer up, that everything would be fine, that they were making a big deal out of nothing.

Cassidy appreciated that quality, especially then.

When they'd finished their deliciously unhealthy meal, Shelby wadded up the bag and the wrappers and got out of the Blazer to deposit them in a trash bin. By the time she returned, Cassidy had recovered a little. She was sipping coffee.

"Do you still want to go to Flagstaff?" Shelby asked.

"Yes." Cassidy put her cell phone back in her purse, pulled out her sunglasses, put them on.

"Are you—okay?"

"I'm not sure," Cassidy answered, in all honesty. "But I know one thing for certain: I don't want to drive that stupid truck of Duke's ever again, if I can avoid it. My own wheels are more than a thousand miles away at the moment, which means I need to find myself some interim transportation."

Still, Shelby hesitated, clearly concerned. "Michael will probably apologize," she ventured. "Send flowers—"

Cassidy said nothing.

Shelby faced forward, snapped her seatbelt back in place, reached to adjust the rearview mirror. "Let's roll," she said.

Five hours later, when Cassidy returned to the ranch, driving a sporty little rental with a retractable roof, she found Duke, G.W. and Henry gathered around Duke's truck. The hood was up.

Déjà vu all over again, Cassidy thought. All day, she'd been waiting for depression to set in—after all, she and her fiancé had officially broken up—but it hadn't happened. She wasn't sad, but she wasn't happy, either. She was just—numb.

It was probably a coping mechanism.

Spotting her, Henry raced over, Chip bounding alongside. "Is that your car?" the boy cried, delighted.

Cassidy, getting out, hated to burst his bubble. "It's a rental," she said.

Henry seemed a little deflated. "The kind you give back when you don't need it anymore?"

Cassidy squeezed his shoulder. "That's the idea," she said gently. She found herself wanting to explain that she didn't need a car, since she had one, back in Seattle, but that would have been too much information for sure. She nodded in the direction of Duke's truck. "Another breakdown?"

Henry nodded importantly. "Dad says it threw a rod."

Cassidy was no mechanic, but she figured that the prognosis was grim indeed.

Chip, standing so close to Henry that they were nearly holding each other up, wagged his tail, panting. He seemed fascinated by the whole exchange.

"Yikes," Cassidy said, though secretly, she was hoping Duke would finally junk that old rust bucket and buy himself a new truck. And behind that thought was another: G.W. looked almost as good from the back as he did from the front.

He turned just then, almost as if he'd heard the gears turning in her head, nodded a greeting.

"Can I have a ride sometime?" Henry wanted to know. He was checking out the car now, standing on tiptoe to peer through the driver's side window.

"Sure," Cassidy said, distracted.

G.W. walked toward her, wiping his hands on a rag. He wasn't wearing a hat, and his hair was attractively rumpled. "That pile of rusty bolts is a goner," he said, jabbing a thumb over one shoulder to indicate Duke's rig. "Talk some sense into your uncle, will you? Tell him it's time to bust out his wallet and buy a new one."

Cassidy smiled. "This is Duke McCullough we're talking about," she reminded him. "He won't listen to a word I say."

Henry was back. "Did you tell Cassidy about the flowers?" he asked his father. Then he looked up at Cassidy and piped, "Somebody sent you flowers. They're real pretty, too. A woman brought them all the way from Flagstaff, and Uncle Duke gave her a big tip for going to all the trouble."

"Slipped my mind," G.W. told the boy. Then he met Cassidy's eyes and said dutifully, "Somebody sent you flowers."

"Oh," Cassidy said.

Brilliant.

Henry was tugging at her hand. "Don't you want to look at them? Don't you want to smell them or something?"

"Absolutely," she said. "Who do you suppose sent them?"

G.W. raised one eyebrow, and his mouth tilted up at one side. His expression said, *Who indeed?*

"Let's have a look," Cassidy said, and rushed toward the house. Henry and Chip were right behind her.

Sure enough, a massive bouquet awaited her in the middle of the kitchen table, spilling from a beautiful cut glass vase.

Roses, pink and white, at least two dozen of them, plus baby's breath and lots of greenery.

So, Shelby had been right. Michael was sorry for

blowing her off the way he had. He wanted to make up. Cassidy waited to feel something, but she was still numb. Her hand shook slightly as she reached for the card, opened the tiny envelope, read the words inside.

At first, they didn't register. She read them again. The flowers weren't from Michael, after all. They were from his mother.

It's all for the best, the card read. Evangeline Brighton-Stiles had dictated the message to some hapless florist in Flagstaff.

It's all for the best? Cassidy nearly laughed aloud. As kiss-offs went, this one was in a class by itself.

"Are they from that guy you're gonna marry?" Henry asked innocently, examining the impressive bouquet.

"No," Cassidy said, carefully tucking the card back into the envelope.

"Then who sent them?"

How was she supposed to answer that? She couldn't say, "a friend," because Michael's mother wasn't one. She'd never actually liked the woman, and she'd known all along that the feeling was mutual.

So she finally settled on, "Just someone I know in Seattle."

"Oh," Henry said, clearly confused but willing to take her word for it.

"How about that ride?" Cassidy asked. "We can leave right now, if your dad says it's okay."

Henry's face lit up. "In your car?" He wanted clarification.

"In my car," Cassidy affirmed. It was back, that urge to hug the little guy.

"Can Chip come with us?"

"Yes," she replied. "But remember—we have to get the go-ahead first."

"Dad will say yes," Henry said, with exuberant confidence, running for the back door, bursting through the opening, Chip behind him, like always.

Cassidy lingered for a while, looking at the roses. They were beautiful, however venomous the intention behind them.

She reached into her bag, found her cell, checked the screen. Nothing from Michael.

Well, he hadn't wasted any time bringing his mother up to speed on the situation, had he? Who else had he told? If she checked his social media page, would she find an anti-Cassidy rant posted there?

Cassidy decided that none of it mattered.

She turned her back on the bouquet and followed Henry outside. G.W. had evidently given his permission, because Henry was in the process of lugging his booster seat across the yard, headed for the rental car, and Chip was already ensconced in the back seat. "We have to use this stupid chair until I get taller," Henry explained, breathless with the effort. "It's the law."

Hiding a grin, Cassidy helped him install the apparatus across the seat from Chip.

When they'd finished, Henry climbed in, buckled up, and beamed with anticipation.

Cassidy got behind the wheel, fastening her own seatbelt, and tooted the horn at Duke and G.W.

They'd evidently given up on the old truck by then,

closed the hood and stepped away. Duke, shaking his head, looked like a bystander at the scene of an accident.

G.W. lifted a hand in farewell.

Cassidy's heart did that fluttery thing again as she backed up the rental car and turned it around. Some of the numbness subsided, leaving room for a flash of guilt.

She should be inconsolable, or at least blue.

After four years, she and Michael were over.

There wasn't going to be a wedding.

Shouldn't she be devastated? Shouldn't she be sobbing and raging, throwing things, or listening to sad music in a dark room, or swilling beer in some seedy bar while Shelby sat across from her, elbows propped on a sticky tabletop, chin in her hands, all sympathy?

Instead, Cassidy realized, she was barely holding back a resounding, "Whoopee!"

THE WAY DUKE ACTED, G.W. thought, you'd have thought somebody died. They were at Duke's kitchen table, drinking beer.

"I've had that truck for twenty years," Duke lamented. "Twenty years."

Cassidy's bouquet of pink flowers added a funereal touch, and their heady scent made him want to open a window or two.

"Well," G.W. said carefully, "you have to admit, you got your money's worth. How many rigs last that long?"

Duke actually sniffled, and his eyes were moist. Duke, who spent a good deal of his time trying to run monsters to ground. "It had a name," he confided. "It was Doris."

G.W. suppressed a groan. He wasn't without sympathy—he knew a man could develop what amounted to a relationship with a good truck—but, Doris? Come on.

"Annabelle and I went on our first date in that truck," Duke reminisced.

G.W. couldn't help it. He sighed. "Duke," he said. "You can afford a new one. And if your first date with Annabelle was that long ago, well, maybe that's what you ought to be thinking about."

Duke looked surprised. And injured. "You know, I sort of expected a little more understanding. From my best friend, I mean."

G.W. did what he should have done a few moments before; he kept his mouth shut.

Duke's shoulders slumped slightly, and he gave a sigh of his own. "Truth is," he said, "I'm pretty sure Annabelle would say no if I asked her to get married after all this time. She might take it as an afterthought."

Two decades, G.W. reflected. That was some afterthought. But he was touched, too.

"If she did turn you down—and that's pretty unlikely, if you ask me—you'd survive it. Chances are, the two of you would just go right on the way you have been. Would that be so terrible?"

Duke was quiet for a long time. "I'm a damn fool," he said, just when G.W. was starting to feel a little uncomfortable. "Running on about the truck, and Annabelle, when you—after what happened to Sandy—"

G.W. said nothing. Shutting down was his default

reaction, whenever her name came up. He did it automatically.

Something was different this time, though. There was no pain, just a flood of happy memories. Sandy, radiant and rumpled, fresh from the delivery room, holding their newborn son. Sandy, laughing, teaching Henry to swim, turning the hose on G.W. in the front yard, shrieking with joyful indignation when he took it away, drenched her in the spray.

The years with Sandy had been good ones, better than good, but they were gone, and so was she.

"I'll move on if you will," Duke said.

Sometimes, he saw too much; G.W. guessed that was a hazard of long-term friendships. "There's one flaw in your logic," G.W. replied. "The kind of 'moving on' you're talking about requires a woman. You've got one. I don't."

"Cassidy's not going to marry that Michael yahoo, you know," Duke informed him. He nodded toward the roses, clearly disgusted. "Those flowers? They're from his mother."

G.W. glanced at the bouquet, frowned. "Okay. That's weird. I'll give you that. But where are you getting your information?"

Duke grinned. "I read the card. As for the breakup, well, Shelby told me. Called me on her way back from Flagstaff. She was worried about Cassidy."

G.W. was mildly alarmed, but he managed to hide it. Or, at least he hoped he had. "She was that upset? Cassidy, I mean?"

"Did she look upset to you?" Duke asked.

G.W. considered. Shook his head. "I guess not."

"You guess right," came the answer. "Cassidy didn't want to marry this guy; I knew it all along. She'd just painted herself into a corner, that's all. Gotten in over her head. She came home so she could think things through."

"You've got it all figured out," G.W. said, unconvinced. For once in his life, though, he'd have liked to be wrong. "And you're not giving Cassidy a whole lot of credit here, it seems to me. She's a woman, not a kid. She knows her own mind. It follows that, if she accepted the man's proposal in the first place, she planned on following through." He paused. Looked at the flowers again. "Couples fight. Then they make up. My guess is, this whole thing will blow over and the wedding will be on again."

The sound of tires on gravel alerted them to Cassidy's return from the ride with Henry and the dog. Conversation over.

"NICE FLOWERS," DUKE COMMENTED that night, as he and Cassidy shared a light supper, just the two of them.

Cassidy merely nodded, chewing. They were having chili, the kind that comes in a can. It was a favorite of theirs from way back.

"Guess I'll be getting a new truck," Duke persisted. For a man, he talked a lot. What ever happened to that Mars/Venus thing?

"Seems like a good idea."

"Are you going to tell me what's going on, Cassidy?" She smiled. "Sure. First, though, you have to tell me the truth about your alleged encounters with Bigfoot and his ilk."

"Honey," Duke said, with a twinkle, "Bigfoot has no ilk. And what's this 'alleged' stuff?"

"Tell me," Cassidy said. "Did you really see a Sasquatch?"

Duke thought for a few moments.

"I saw him," he said, at some length and very seriously.

Cassidy waited.

Duke shook his head, looking reflective. Even solemn. "I saw *something*. Heard it, too." He paused, reached for another piece of corn bread.

The silence stretched so far that Cassidy finally had to prompt her uncle to go on, albeit gently. "And?"

"I have my theories," he said, after another bemused silence.

"Such as?"

"The human mind is a powerful and mysterious thing, Cassidy," he answered. "I wonder sometimes if the things people see—angels, demons, ghosts, the monster in the closet—I wonder if they're not—well, projecting them somehow."

"You mean, they're hallucinating?"

But Duke shook his head again. "No," he said. "I think they might be creating these phenomena, externalizing some part of their own psyche. That's not the same as imagining them. Something has to be making all that noise, doing all that damage. So, I guess what I'm saying is, I think maybe most people's definition of the word 'real' is way too limited."

"But you actually saw a Bigfoot," Cassidy pointed

out. Maybe, she thought, she didn't want to give up all belief in the critter's existence herself. Did everything have to have an explanation? What kind of a world would it be with no mystery, no magic?

"I did," Duke agreed. "But that doesn't mean I wasn't seeing some aspect of my own subconscious mind."

She knew all the stories. Some of Duke's sightings had been all his own, but others had been shared with as many as half a dozen other people. "Your monster-hunting friends, though. What were they seeing? Hearing?"

"Who can say?" Duke replied. "Seeing is a subjective thing, and so is hearing. Maybe their experience was different from mine, their own version of whatever these things are. Since I can't get into their heads, I can't be sure how closely their vision matches up with mine."

"Maybe," Cassidy agreed thoughtfully.

"You could come along on this next expedition," Duke suggested, finished with his meal but making no move to rise from his chair. "Find out for yourself."

"Not a chance," Cassidy said.

"Why not?"

"Well, for one thing, I'd be absolutely terrified."

"Aren't you the least bit curious?"

She shook her head, smiling. "I'll take your word for it," she responded. "Besides, I kind of enjoy wondering and, judging by the size of your vlog following and all those loyal podcast listeners you have, I'm not the only one."

Duke was quiet for a few moments. He pushed his empty chili bowl to one side and rested his hands on the table, fingers interlaced. "You could work with me,

Cass. On the videos, I mean. The show could use a feminine touch. I'd pay you a salary, of course."

"You're still trying to take care of me," Cassidy said.

"Sue me. You're my only brother's only child. I happen to love you. And, anyway, it's true that you'd be an asset to the operation."

Cassidy thought the idea might grow on her, but she wasn't ready to commit, so she just said, "Okay, I'll give it some thought."

A comfortable silence fell, but it didn't last long.

"It's your turn," Duke said, when Cassidy didn't immediately volunteer anything about her canceled wedding.

"You're not going to let me off the hook, are you?" she asked.

Duke smiled. "Nope," he said. "A deal's a deal, sweetheart. I answered your questions. Now, you'll have to answer at least one of mine."

Cassidy's shoulders sagged with the heavy sigh she uttered, then straightened again. She managed a tentative smile in response to Duke's. "How do I plan to vote in the next election?" she spoke lightly, stalling.

"Nice try," Duke countered. "What happened between you and Michael?"

"We broke up."

"Why?"

"That's two questions. I only promised to answer one."

"Come on, Cassidy. How can I help you if you won't talk to me?"

She straightened her spine, lifted her chin, and

smiled again, though her mouth didn't wobble this time, like it had moments before. "You want the truth? Okay, here it is. I'm not very proud of myself at the moment. I'm supposed to be this strong, independent woman, smart, sensible."

"So far, you're right on. Except for the part about not being proud of yourself, that is."

Duke's words warmed Cassidy's somewhat bruised heart, but her self-esteem was still suffering. "Thanks, but you're biased," she said. "Anyway, if I'm so smart, how come I fooled myself into believing I loved a man I sometimes don't even like very much?"

She put up both hands, palms out, to stop her uncle from answering. She'd come back to Busted Spur, back to the ranch, she knew now, not to prepare for a wedding, not even to get a little perspective before she took a profound step, as she'd thought.

No, she was here to choose between more than getting married or not getting married—a lot more. She was here to choose between one life and another.

"Somewhere along the way," she went on, finally, and with a sort of broken resolution, "I misplaced myself. Oh, I had a great time in Seattle, at least at first. Everything was new and different. I met Michael. I created a role for myself, and then I played it."

Duke patted her hand. "What's next?"

"First," Cassidy said, making the decision in that moment, "I'm going back to Seattle."

CHAPTER FIVE

"YOU'RE DOING WHAT?" Shelby asked, when Cassidy showed up at her house bright and early the next morning, bearing doughnuts and specialty coffee.

"I think you heard me the first time," Cassidy said sweetly. "I'm going back to Seattle."

Shelby's mouth dropped open. Then she snapped it shut again. "Why?"

"Actually, there are a number of practical reasons."

"Cassidy."

Cassidy relented. "Some things," she said, with a note of sadness, "have to be done in person."

"For instance?"

"For instance, Michael and I need to talk. Face-to-face. I can't simply turn my back on what we had together, even if it was mostly a fantasy on my part."

"That's it? You're going all that way to break up with the man? Excuse me, but am I missing something here? Because I really thought you'd already done that."

"No, that's not it, not all of it, anyway. I have to give my notice at the station, pack up my apartment, and say goodbye to my friends."

Shelby looked hopeful again. "And then you'll come back here?"

"That's the idea," Cassidy answered. "God knows how I'm going to earn a living, and where I'm going to live, but this is where I want to be, Shelb. Here, I'm the person I want to be. Somehow, I'll find my way."

Shelby beamed, threw both arms around Cassidy, and hugged her hard. "I'll help you," she said.

"I'm counting on that." Shelby was gripping her shoulders by then, holding her at arms' length, her eyes bright with happy tears. "I'm going with you," she announced.

When Cassidy, as pleased by the idea as she was, started to protest, Shelby shushed her and went on. "Don't argue. I'm going. I'll help you pack, and ride shotgun on the way back, share the driving."

"What about your business? Your dogs?" The dogs in question, a pair of elderly mutts distantly related to the terrier breed, were lying nearby, on their bed in Shelby's studio/office, lifted their heads and perked up their ears.

"Annabelle will take care of Charles and Camilla while we're gone," Shelby answered. "Where do you think they stay when I'm away on buying trips?"

Cassidy nodded. "And the business? You have orders to fill."

"I can run the shop from my laptop," Shelby said. "I get to set my own hours, remember. It's one of the perks of being self-employed. Besides, I might come across some great stuff while we're on the road."

Cassidy was choked up for a few moments. "You'd really do this?"

Shelby laughed. "Of course I'd really do it. *I am* doing it."

"You are one amazing friend," Cassidy said, after swallowing hard.

"And don't you forget it," Shelby replied.

Three weeks later

TWILIGHT WAS GATHERING AS G.W. left his barn, the horses put up for the night and fed, Chip at his side. He reckoned the dog was feeling a little lonesome at the moment, with Henry gone for a sleep-over at a friend's house.

G.W. could identify; for him, nightfall was the time he was most conscious of being alone. By then, supper was usually over, and Henry, though not quite ready for bed, was especially quiet, worn down by a full day of being a kid.

Once the going-to-bed rituals were over, the dog nestled at Henry's feet, muzzle on paws, G.W. was on his own. He could keep busy for a while, working on one of his projects in the office, reading or listening to talk radio—he wasn't much for TV, as a general rule—but, eventually, he ran out of distractions.

Then, yet again, he had to come to terms with the fact that, basically, he was alone.

As the years passed—and G.W. had already figured out that they'd go by more quickly than he would have thought possible—as Henry grew and became more and more independent, as his life expanded, his own would be shrinking at a corresponding pace.

Tonight, the sky was clear, spattered with stars from horizon to horizon. G.W. stopped, midway between the barn and the house, to look up. The sight still filled him with quiet wonder, just as it had always done.

Was there life out there? Surely, in a universe that was, for all practical intents and purposes, infinite, there were other worlds, other living beings. He'd probably never know for sure, but that was all right, too, because a man ought to leave room in his heart and mind for a miracle or two.

G.W. liked a solid answer as well as anybody else, but he found the questions interesting in their own right.

Chip's sudden yip of excitement jolted him out of his philosophical mood. A car was turning in at his mailbox, headlights sweeping over the terrain. Something quickened inside G.W.

He squinted. He didn't recognize the rig, but he definitely recognized the way his heartbeat picked up speed, the way his breathing changed.

Cassidy.

For the first time since she'd left for Seattle, G.W. allowed himself to admit, at least in the privacy of his own mind, that he'd missed her. Been a little afraid she wouldn't come back.

But here she was. She brought the car to a stop, shut off the headlights and the engine, pushed open the door.

G.W. swallowed, a sweet ache filling his chest cavity. He didn't move, didn't speak. Chip, on the other hand, catapulted toward her, barking joyfully.

Cassidy laughed and bent to ruffle the dog's ears.

G.W. still didn't move or say anything. Before, he'd been too startled; now, he was just plain stuck.

Cassidy straightened, looked his way, hesitated for

a heart-stopping moment, then came toward him. She wore a long skirt that floated around her calves in the soft evening breeze, and one of those gauzy blouses, the demur kind that somehow managed to look sexy as hell.

"Hello, G.W.," she said, when she was standing a few feet in front of him. He nodded, ground out a husky "hello" in response to hers.

She smiled shyly. "I'm here to talk," she said. "Are you up for that?"

He was up for more than talk, but this wasn't the time to say so.

"Sure," he said. "Come on in."

They went into the house, G.W. leading the way, and Cassidy followed.

Moments later, they were seated at the kitchen table.

"Now that I'm here," Cassidy confessed, blushing a little, "I'm not sure I know what to say."

"The wedding's off?" G.W. asked, and then wished he hadn't. Duke had told him that, but he needed to hear it from Cassidy herself.

"Yes," she answered, meeting his gaze, and clearly surprised by the question.

"You're planning to stick around?" Another unintended question.

Awkward.

"Yes," she said, for the second time. "I'll be producing Duke's videos from now on."

"Good," G.W. said. "That's good."

Cassidy laughed then, and the spell was broken.

They both relaxed.

"I'm just wondering if we can be—friends," Cassidy ventured, serious again.

"I thought we already were," G.W. said. "Friends, I mean."

Her cheeks went pink. "You're *Duke's* friend," she replied.

G.W. sighed. "Cassidy, I'm not a complicated man. Will you please get to the point?"

"I'm a full-grown woman, G.W.," she pointed out, unnecessarily. "Not the gawky kid your best friend raised like a daughter. Admit it, that's how you see me."

Something inside G.W. spread its wings, lifted off, and soared. "I've noticed that," he said dryly. "And I think you might be surprised to know how I see you."

She arched an eyebrow. The ball was in his court.

"I think you're beautiful," he heard himself say.

"Really?"

"Yes. And you're right, we need to get to know each other as adults."

Her eyes widened. "Great," she said. "So what's the next step?"

"Dinner and a movie?"

She beamed. "Dinner and a movie," she confirmed.

"This is going to take some time," G.W. said, not entirely sure that "this" might turn out to be.

Cassidy laughed again. "I'm in no hurry," she said.

* * * * *

ABOUT THE AUTHOR

THE DAUGHTER OF a town marshal, Linda Lael Miller is a #1 *New York Times* and *USA TODAY* bestselling author of more than 100 historical and contemporary novels, most of which reflect her love of the West. Raised in Northport, Washington, the self-confessed barn goddess pursued her wanderlust, living in London and Arizona and traveling the world before returning to the state of her birth to settle down on a horse property outside Spokane. Linda traces the birth of her writing career to the day when a Northport teacher told her that the stories she was writing were good, that she just might have a future in writing. Later, when she decided to write novels, she endured her share of rejection before she sold *Fletcher's Woman* in 1983 to Pocket Books. Since then, Linda has successfully published historicals, contemporaries, paranormals, mysteries and thrillers before coming home, in a literal sense, and concentrating on novels with a Western flavor. For her devotion to her craft, the Romance Writers of America awarded her their prestigious Nora Roberts Lifetime Achievement Award in 2007. Hallmark Movie Channel is developing a television movie based on Linda's Big Sky Country novels. Dedicated to helping others, "The First Lady of the West" personally financed fifteen years of her Linda Lael Miller Scholarships for Women, which she awarded to women 25 years and older who were seeking to improve their lot in life through education. She also benefits animal rights organizations and loves all four-legged critters. More information about Linda and her novels is available at www.lindalaelmiller.com, on Facebook, and Twitter.